BOOK ONE OF THE SONS OF STEEL SAGA

Sons of Steel

Futures End

G. L. Keady

ALSO BY

G. L. Keady

SONS OF STEEL

DREAMRAIDERS

First published in Australia in 2022
by Big Island Productions

Big Island Productions
PO Box 3027, Tuross Head. 2537. NSW. Australia
www.bigislandprod.net

ISBN 978-0-909497-73-6

Edited by: Joan Grady

Cover design: Brandon Evans-Keady
Illustrations: Matthew Sze. Colourist: Nestor Redulla Jr
Printed by IngramSpark

There were footprints in the sky
gk

TABLE OF CONTENTS

PROLOGUE

Scripted on a single clay tablet in cuneiform of which two thirds is missing, the Sumerian Eridu Genesis composed in 2300 BCE predates the biblical book of Genesis. It is the tale of the creation of modern man by the god En-Ki and of the mass extinction caused by the great flood from which
Ziudsura (Noah) is saved.

DAWN OF TIME — ARRIVAL

Earth: a clearing in a tropical jungle somewhere in Africa. The sun was rising in the clear blue sky. Twelve naked male and female Homo sapiens emerged timidly from a copse into the clearing to forage for food. A female looked up sharply and pointed at something in the sky. They all huddled together fearfully watching a strange white donut-shaped ring of smoke coalesce. All had fallen silent — no birds, no rustling of leaves — the eerie stillness had spawned a gut feeling in them that something prodigious was about to happen.

In the blink of an eye it did: an enormous grey bird materialised within the ring, and then the ring dissolved. Blanketed in the shadow of the gigantic airborne beast, the natives backed trembling deeper into the cover of the forest, only the bravest of them remained fearless with his eyes fixed on the long snake-like neck of the flying monster. Then, the shadow of the strange hovering beast began to grow in proportion. A sudden loud hiss erupted from jets of vapour discharging from the giant bird's underbelly that caused the courageous gazer to flinch. The beast hung like a massive vulture at the treetops menacing in its silence. Then, another noise, a noise totally unfamiliar to the spectators: the whirring sound of a servo as a hatch opened in the bird's belly.

The dark-skinned bold observer retreated a few hurried steps when a light appeared inside the open hatch. But he couldn't take his eyes off it. Then, to his surprise a metal ladder extended from within down to the ground. He figured the gigantic bird was of the gods, the same gods that at times flashed bright lights in the sky and caused the clouds to rumble with a voice that would make the ground beneath his feet tremble.

An old Shaman with long ochre braided hair burst from the huddle of frightened natives and with his braids flicking about like snake-heads crouched down beside the brave one. Eyes wide with fear, his face decorated with raised scars, he pointed a trembling rib bone at the giant bird while squawking a warning of impending doom. But there was more to come because from within the bird, a person in a strange suit appeared and began to descend the ladder. When he reached ground, he removed his helmet and gloves, knelt down and clutched a handful of soil.

And so it came to pass that En-Ki of the Anunnaki from the planet Nibiru made first contact with primitive man.

In due course the Anunnaki established a gold mining operation utilizing a workforce of giant androids they called the Nephilim. However, it was not long before the harshness of the conditions took a toll of the Nephilim, and so a remedy was sought. En-Ki, being not only the mission commander but a genetic scientist came up with the solution to genetically engineer the primates to replace the Nephilim as the primary labour force.

And so En-Ki altered the genome of the primates and created in due course a new being in his likeness.

Upon learning of this Anu the great lord of the Anunnaki on Nibiru, was outraged. The laws he had created had been violated and so he called upon his son En-Lil, younger brother of En-Ki, to venture to Earth to obliterate the human abomination and to prosecute En-Ki for his abuse of the divine law.

As a result, a war on Earth ensued between the brothers and continued for decades until eventually, with his fighting forces diminished, En-Ki faced defeat. In the eleventh hour En-Ki called forth Ziusudra his most valued human creation and warned him that his brother En-Lil would generate a great flood to eradicate all humanity, and confided in him the means by which to survive the catastrophe with his family.

Satisfied he had set in motion a plan to save humanity, En-Ki surrendered.

En-Lil confronted his brother and they fought with swords. En-Ki was no match for his warrior brother, and was fatally wounded.

En-Lil decreed to him, "Our Lord master and father gave me the authority to sentence you. Your consciousness shall be imprisoned for eternity banished to oblivion. Your physical presence will be no longer."

Prepared to accept his fate En-Ki replied, "There will be no victor in this war En-Lil, for the time will come when you will meet your match. Destiny has been set in motion."

Showing no mercy, En-Lil fired a weapon at En-Ki, which drew the very lifeforce from him and into an orb, which he then concealed in another dimension of the metaverse for infinity.

=== ===

THIS STORY IS set in the future, in a dystopian society where the necessities of state survival are paramount, at the expense of the people and their environment. The world is split into trading blocks: the EU, the Polar Block, the Americas, the Asian Block and Oceana, the southern hemisphere block. Africa is non-aligned and is a seething cauldron of warring fiefdoms.

The arsenals of the big-league countries are now more volatile than ever, due to advanced destructive weapons capability. Terrorist attacks on civilians by sectarian extremist religious groups and socio-political fanatics have the world on a knife-edge. Society is insecure, with fears that an accident or misplaced foolish word from an over-zealous world leader could easily trigger nuclear war.

Throughout this tangled world rebellion is ubiquitous, with the common folk prepared to fight against those seeking to supress the will and voice of the people. Humanity has had enough of politics. Rebel organizations opposed to the block systems are gaining support. These rebels are not communists, nor socialists, not even capitalists. They consider themselves merely activists, champions of ideals. This is the story of one of the greatest of them.

Oceana's fascist overlords are planning to break a long-standing nuclear non-proliferation protocol by permitting an American nuclear submarine to enter Sydney Harbour. One man threatens their scheme: Black Alice.

A heavy metal singer and leader of a rebel peace movement — The Octagon — Black Alice has been labelled a dissident for having incited unrest amongst his rapidly-growing legion of supporters and fans. The top dogs of the Gestapo-like Oceana State Security Directorate want him eliminated…

CHAPTER 1
ORGANIC PANIC

A T ONE END OF a dark tunnel suspended in the air by some manner of supernatural force was a glowing orb the size of a basketball. At the other end, some fifty metres from the orb, a single glowing rotating atom appeared and then split. Within milliseconds it had become a cluster, which then coalesced into the form of a human being. A man in his early thirties had materialised. Six feet tall with a long black pony-tail reaching down to the middle of his back — a handsome, muscular man, the epitome of a rock star from the late 20th Century. The orb, now the only source of light in the strange tunnel, attracted the interest of the human who moving in a disoriented fashion, approached it.

Speaking to himself he muttered, "What is this? Where the hell am I?"

Incredulously a warm, consoling ubiquitous voice responded from the orb. "You are safe Black Alice. There is no need for concern."

The voice halted Alice's progress as it would originating from a luminous sphere.

"Who's talking?" Alice questioned boldly. "Who are you? What are you? How do you know my name?"

"I transported you here because it is your destiny."

"Yeah, right. This has gotta be some kind of sick dream. I must be tripping."

"No, you are actually in another dimension than your own. I am En-Ki, my consciousness is imprisoned within this orb."

"A Genie in a bottle huh? For sure, pull the other one," he scoffed, sceptical. "En-Ki, what sort of name is that?"

"What I say is true Black Alice."

"Hmm," Ill at ease, he edged closer. "What do you mean by my destiny?"

"To explain that I must take you back to where and how it began for you."

There was a flash of bright light within Alice's mind.

Alone at the far end of a long black table in the executive boardroom of Sydney's Oceana State Headquarters, dressed in a black uniform with silver piping that reflected his seniority, sat Ri Smith, President of Oceana. A lightning bolt emblem emblazoned on his chest pocket resembled the runic insignia of the Nazi SS. Middle-aged and overweight, of Chinese extraction, with a clean-shaven head and bushy eyebrows, he exuded self-confidence and an arrogant sense of authority. He was pondering the signing of an edict to have a dissident by the name of Black Alice dealt with by the State Security Directorate — the SSD. It had been the principal of the SSD, Senior Inspector Fanny Honor, who had brought the nonconformist activities of the celebrated heavy metal performer and leader of the Octagon peace movement to the President's attention. It would be Honor and her officer, Karzoff, who would be assigned the responsibility of eliminating Black Alice should the President decide to sign.

In need of his daily news update, the President pressed a button on the arm of his chair. A servomotor sounded and a 100-inch, 5k ultra HD TV rose from three quarters of the way along the long board table. It was the morning news that interested him, and his timing was impeccable. A middle-aged female newsreader, with a look on her face like she'd just snorted three grams of cocaine, launched into the latest news.

"Ugly scenes erupted in the New South Wales country town of Narrabri this morning when protestors interrupted a speech being made by the CEO of the coal seam gas mining giant Santa," she said. "Mr Singh was opening the controversial fracking mine in the Pilliga State Forest, when Octagon protestors wearing gas masks opened fire with a deluge of cow manure. Expecting a reaction to the reversal of the government's election promise not to grant mining rights to Santa in the Pilliga, troopers were on standby."

The footage showed Mr Singh being pelted with sloppy cow dung, and dozens of troopers in black riot gear storming into the protestors with truncheons and stingrays.

"Six protestors were hospitalised with stingray shock and another is in a critical condition after being bludgeoned with a truncheon," the newsreader continued. "There have been calls to outlaw the use of stingrays, due to the trauma caused to victims.

"On another front, in North Queensland, protestors are believed to be responsible for a fire that destroyed the offices of Adoni, the coal mining company that successfully obtained permits to commence a massive mining operation, which environmentalists claim has the potential to destroy the Great Barrier Reef.

"The Oceana State Government claims the environmental impact study proved otherwise, but when asked to produce evidence by Black Alice, leader of the Octagon, the government declined."

The President had heard enough. He pressed the button on his chair and the TV sank back into the boardroom table. It might have gone, but his troubles were hardly out of sight and out of mind. He recalled how, on numerous occasions, Black Alice had used his massive influence to rally the rank and file against him and his government. On one occasion Black Alice had displayed on stage an oversized, naked effigy of him at a huge outdoor concert — embarrassing images had been broadcast around the world. Now Honor had reported that Black Alice, in his capacity as leader of the

Octagon, was planning a massive protest march against the impending visit of a US nuclear submarine to Sydney.

Smith knew there was every chance of the protest erupting into violence, which would seriously devalue his international standing, particularly with the visiting dignitaries from the United States. It was a risk he wasn't willing to take.

He picked up a cup of freshly brewed coffee and blissfully inhaled the aroma from the column of steam, as if it contained the essence of his enemy's defeat. When he took a sip he made up his mind. He put down his cup, picked up his pen, and imperiously scratched his signature on the decree. It was a death warrant. Black Alice's fate was sealed.

It was late afternoon. Stoned on D-Lyte, a mild hallucinogen with aphrodisiac overtones, pretty 23-year-old Mowina Beetson was poised precariously on the balcony rail of her boyfriend's city apartment. As she dangled her bare feet over the edge she gazed down the ten storeys at the traffic jam in the Sydney streets below. Mowina's birthday party hadn't started yet. She'd decided to get into the mood before the guests arrived by getting out of it.

The mild breeze coming from the northeast flagged her long brown hair out behind her like a banner. The breeze was carrying with it the melodious chant of demonstrators in the street: the cause of the traffic jam.

The city was emptying of its day-job transient residents. The street protesters were causing unmitigated traffic mayhem. The signs and banners in the name of the Octagon called for revolution against the government and opposition to the impending visit of an American nuclear submarine. It was illegal to demonstrate without a permit, so the dark presence of the riot police was only to be expected. Twenty of them had arrived, clad in grey armour, bulletproof visors, helmets and shields. The grey armour made them look like evil insects, fearsomely encased in exoskeletons. They wore breathing filters on their faces, which added to their anonymity and inhuman appearance. Armed with truncheons and stingrays, they had immediately marched on the protestors and savagely mustered them together like cattle, ready to load into waiting detention vehicles. Before that could happen, the law required a senior government official to read the detainees the official riot act.

Loudhailer in hand, a pudgy Oceana government official in a drab black uniform with the lightning bolt insignia on his breast pocket climbed onto the tray-back of a riot vehicle to proclaim the act.

The wind was blowing fiercely, sending dark storm clouds scudding across the sky, but there was something else in the atmosphere, something even more sinister and foreboding.

When the official flicked the switch on his loudhailer it came to life with a deafening yowl of feedback. His high-pitched voice echoed around the watching streets.

"This is an illegal gathering!" he bellowed. "No official permit to demonstrate has been issued…"

Citizens hanging out of apartment windows and from balconies jeered the riot cops and the official. The protesters booed and chanted pro-Octagon slogans in an effort to drown him out.

Suddenly a couple of the demonstrators looked up and yelled: 'A jumper!' The other protesters looked up in awe at the twenty-storey apartment tower, just in time to catch sight of someone falling. The official caught only a momentary glimpse of Mowina Beetson before she landed on him.

The government would blame his death on the Octagon.

In a different part of the city, a long line of punters snaked along the pavement outside Frenzy: the premier concert venue in town. The line spoke volumes of the pulling power of the artist featured to perform that night — Black Alice. The line, a thousand strong, moved at a snail's pace. Each individual was wearing black, the unofficial uniform of Black Alice aficionados.

The line ascended a long staircase, leading from street level to the third-floor club. The ubiquitous threat of terrorism decreed that before anyone could go inside, they had to pass an integrated security system. A sensor carried out an ID scan and automatically debited the entry fee from the subject's crypto account. A series of three consecutive doors at the entrance to the concert room were only accessible once the subject had been cleared by the system.

Inside the dark concert room, thin blue skeins of perfumed incense drifted like gossamer through pools of descending ceiling light, stirring and swirling in vortices around the people as they filed in. A melodious drone faded up through the in-house audio system, underscoring the cacophony from the chattering crowd. The room lighting sensors triggered multi-coloured lasers to sweep the walls. Like ghostly apparitions, furniture appeared out of the darkness and fluoresced when struck by the lasers.

The swelling crowd found seats at the glowing tables scattered about the room. They appeared to be engaged in conversation, but in fact the chatter was synthesized, a component of the in-house recorded ambience. In reality they were sitting calmly in a state of stoned euphoria, each and every one of them whacked on gaseous D-Lyte, which was being administered through ducts in the walls. Drugs and alcohol were banned, and had been replaced by Zenome Controlled Environmental Sensory Stimulants produced by the Zen Corporation, a sub-contractor of the Oceana Government.

Most of the concert-goers were wearing light emotion monitor sensors known as LEMS. These reflected information the user wished to convey to others, taking background noise out of the equation. Because of their state of euphoria, however, the LEMS were displaying nothing legible. The lights were on — but there was definitely nobody home.

Once at full capacity and seated, the room was washed in a blast of white light. The auto chatter ceased. Anticipation surged. Then, like moths attracted to the light, the sea of ghostly grey faces looked in unison at a figure slinking like a panther across the stage.

Reaching the spotlight, he stopped. Legs astride he folded his bare, muscular arms and eyeballed the audience with menace. The powerful backlight cast his shadow through the room like a sweeping scythe. He had spent thousands of gruelling hours in the gym, and it showed. His head was clean-shaven at the sides, with a five-centimetre Mohawk and long black ponytail stretching down to the arch of his back. Both sides of his head were decorated with Celtic tattoos. His full-length, black sleeveless trench-coat was worn over a white renaissance sleeveless pirate shirt with jabot front, black pants and Cuban-heeled scarlet boots that elevated him to six three. He presented an intimidating figure.

As the effects of the grand entrance subsided, a loud angry voice emanated from the figure, now scowling at the audience from centre stage, and resounded throughout the room.

"In a flash of burning white light we were created. In a flash of burning white light, we will be destroyed!"

The last word was the cue for the band. They cranked up with an enormous hundred-and-twenty-decibel blast of unrestrained modern metal. The burning backlight retracted and the stage lit up to reveal the man centre stage — Black Alice, fronting his three-piece rhythm section. Arms still folded, head thrusting back and forward in time with the powerful music, he waited for his vocal cue.

Inside, Alice was pondering why, at the age of 29, he was even bothering to entertain such a pathetic, stoned mob of degenerates. He sneered at them in distaste and they loved it. They'd take all the shit he could throw at them.

He pumped himself up. His chest expanded to rival that of any bodybuilder, all but bursting from the tight confines of his shirt.

Leering at his devoted fans, his ego was feeding on them like a rapacious vampire.

Behind him, stage right, stood Ratsso the bass player. Thin and still, a red beret propped on his shock of long black hair, he coiled over his stick-like instrument like a bearded gargoyle. Stage left, in front of a massive stack of Marshall amplifiers, legs apart in the traditional heavy-metal A-pose, was lead guitarist Slut. His face was buried under long, unruly black hair that went all the way down to his butt. It didn't matter that he was faceless, only that he was locked in harmonic heaven. Slut preferred to sleep with his vintage white Fender Stratocaster every night, rather than a chick. He carried it around with him during the day, in a constant state of foreplay until he could get up in front of a crowd and make love to it.

Seated between the two guitarists, amid a mountain of sparkling chrome percussion instruments, was Blue, the drummer. He played with a fury and precision that set the backbone, heartbeat and power mood for the Black Alice metal experience.

Alice gripped the microphone with one hand and growled an introduction to the song, "This song is relevant to the fascists running the world ... it's called Organic Panic." An ever-so-slight hand signal to the band followed and he launched into a powerful vocal.

> There are a lot of ways to look at life
> It depends on you...
> There's LSD or Methamphetamine
> The trip is up to you...
> But sometimes
> There's a little voice
> Tells you what to do
> And you fight with your subconscious,
> Coz there's two views

He let the mike go and snarled, nodding in time to the powerful beat. It was obvious to the audience that he felt every word. He glared at them, knowing full well that they were mesmerised by his words and the way he moved. He held their attention in a vice-like grip. His voice was unique, his on-stage presence and charisma spellbinding. He snatched the mike and roared,

> Oh yes, your sanity's threatened
> By the world sinking around your feet
> You got to drag yourself up
> After being sucked down
> But the water's too deep
> You're only a pawn in their game
> But you try to stay free
> Someone turn on the light
> To make tomorrow bright
> For you and me!

All of the stage lighting changed to a wide projection live time-stamped feed from a drone that was hovering over the inner-city protest march happening only a few blocks from Frenzy. The audience stood captivated by the scene of riot police firing tear gas at yellow vested protestors, and what made that even more incredible was here was Black Alice describing the scene in the chorus of his song, as though he had anticipated it.

> It's all getting manic, in Organic Panic, yeah
> Yellow vest protesting, riot police arresting, yeah
> No way to disguise the tear gas in your eyes oh yeah
> No more talk of Peace, while we're
> fighting in the streets oh yeah

The projection cut and the stage lights adjusted, signalling a change in mood and tempo. The middle-eight section of the song was operatic, reminiscent of Queen's Bohemian Rhapsody. The only light was a spotlight on Alice. His face twisted into an insane scowl.

> What would happen should a god arrive?

Pin-lights spotted the other band members. They sang in unison,

> What would it matter to you?

The lights went off them, leaving Alice alone in the spot.

> We need to know it's true

The band reappeared, and replied sarcastically:

> We'd probably nail him to a cross!

Alice posed the question:

> Will the world ever be at peace?

There was a grand pause in the music. The band members replied angrily, acappella, accompanied by the audience, every one of whom knew the lyrics:

> There'll always be a war!

Alice opened his arms piously and drew out a long dramatic silent pause.

> Why be crucified upon a needlepoint?

The band and the whole room responded:

> To escape from all the trash!

The stage blacked-out. After a moment, a single spotlight lit up Alice alone. With venom in his eyes he pointed at the audience.

> You're only victims of yourselves!

The band replied from the darkness behind him:

> You're full of it!

Smirking at the audience, Alice cried:

Ha! Why then can't you quit!

He held his pose to enforce the point, while his spotlight slowly dimmed. With frightening intensity, the entire stage lit up as the band powered back into the main song.
Alice screamed into the mike.

Why can't I believe
In what I choose
Without being confused
Are we all trapped
In the propaganda crap
We read in the news
We can still make up our minds
and keep the peace
So if a God arrives
He'll see we've tried
And he'll be pleased...
But then there's a damn good chance
He'll get busted for disturbing the peace.

The projection of the protest march flashed back on blanketing the stage with images of the protestors and gas-masked riot police clashing in a caustic fog of tear gas.

It's all getting manic, in Organic Panic, yeah
Yellow vest protesting, riot police arresting, yeah
No way to disguise the tear gas in your eyes oh yeah
No more talk of Peace, while we're
fighting in the streets oh yeah...
Why don't we ever learn?
They're gonna press that button
And then we'll all burn...

Blinding lights burnt out the entire room. Alice stood as he had started, arms folded, a gargantuan silhouette. As the song wound down to the bass drum beating a slowing, dying heartbeat, Alice's God-like voice resounded in a final soliloquy.

"Death. How will it feel?"

The music erupted into a roar, emulating the apocalyptic end of the world.

Alice slipped off stage and the lights cut. The audience was left gaping, stunned by an audio-visual metaphor of death.

After a few minutes of numbing silence, a servomotor sounded and the stage began to revolve. When it locked back into place, the reverse side was set like the deck of a warship, with Blue behind an even more massive drum kit than before and flanked on both sides by huge naval cannons.

Blue began a press drum roll, which brought Alice striding back onto the stage, now wearing a naval captain's cap with a black visor, gold embroidery and a gleaming naval crest. He had a navy-blue work singlet under a black leather jacket, and a bandolier of heavy machine gun ammunition strung around the slim waist of his harlequin patterned stretch leotards. He stopped at the microphone and eyeballed his audience.

As the drum roll continued he said: "Our new record is our take on a great song from the 60s by Thunderclap Newman — Something in the Air. The words matter as much now as they did then. Dig it."

With a sly glance at Ratsso, Slut and Blue came in, playing the powerful intro to the song. Three sexy back-up singers — Meg, Stain and Voluptuous — marched onto the stage like soldiers, in time to the beat. Each of them was dressed in identical, pale blue air-force jackets and caps, teamed with black stockings. They fell into place in front of Ratsso and started dancing in unison, with tightly choreographed moves.

Alice gripped the mike stand and launched into a powerful vocal, at the same time scanning the audience for his friends, Mal Function and Prissy. His gaze landed on them, and he shot them a smile.

The stage and music gave Alice the perfect platform to exorcise his demons by howling out his rage at the government's oppressiveness.

As Slut ripped into a blistering solo, Alice signalled stage left. A ballistic missile with 'Made in USA' stencilled on its side wheeled out on stage. The audience went wild as they realized the nose cone of the missile was a giant red knob. The entire missile was a huge penis.

Alice leapt onto it, sitting astride it like a true cavalier and holding a set of reins. The rocket motor ignited and the missile began spewing flames and smoke across the stage. Offering the audience the bird, Alice pulled on the reins to lift the red knob up, giving the missile a hard-on. The audience went crazy as with a loud roar, the missile blasted up into the air, carrying Alice, fist pumping all the way, into the darkness stage right.

The band played on. Suddenly the prop cannons either side of the drummer fired a resounding boom that frightened the living crap out of everybody, including the band members left on stage.

It had been a typical Black Alice gig. The fans had known from experience to expect the unexpected. Alice's salvo at the government, and the missile metaphor had made a rebellious statement that wouldn't be missed by the totalitarian rulers.

CHAPTER 2
SOMETHING IN THE AIR

ALICE AND THE band members were backstage packing their gear to leave. Dressed in their civvies Alice was in black denim with a leather jacket. One of the back-up singers Stained Class was sitting on his lap.

Kitbag slung over his shoulder Blue stopped behind Alice and asked, "Coming for a few ales Al?"

Al looked up at Blue in the mirror that was spread across the wall. "Where you going?"

Guitar case in hand Ratsso joined Blue, "Bourbon and Beef, where else?" he chuckled.

"Our watering hole," Blue tagged.

Al gave Stained a hug and with a devilish grin sighed, "Nar, we're going home to play-up, aren't we babe?"

The thin shapely blonde nuzzled Alice's chest affectionately. "That a threat or a promise?" She purred like a cat.

He raised a cheeky eyebrow. "Both."

Blue called across the room to Slut, "You coming Slut?"

"No way man," a voice answered through a mass of black hair. "I've got half a dozen groupies waiting at the stage door for me."

Blue shot a snide glance at Ratsso. "Yeah sure man, if there's one then she's jailbait. No chick with any dignity would let a scum-bag like you within a mile of her."

Slut rose from his chair and returned serve, "Sez you who couldn't pull a chick in a brothel."

They all laughed.

"Catch you later guys," Al said keeping it light. "Good gig tonight. Loved your solo in Reck Slut."

Making his way to the door Slut stopped. "Thanks Al, I'll try and remember what I did for next time."

Blue patted the tall skinny hairy one on the back, "Fat chance of that happening Slut, it's different every time."

Alice's cellphone rang, he answered. "Yeah, speak Wilson."

At the mention of their agent's name Blue growled, "Our bloody manager Wilson Stanley, the invisible man. Can't even be bothered to rock up at one of our gigs. See ya Alice."

"Hang on Wilson." Al shot the boys a wave. "Chaa! Fellas!"

Stained climbed off Al's lap gave him a peck on cheek and whispered, "See you at the apartment love, I'll get a lift with Blue."

Al nodded, "Cool, won't be long."

Wilson's voice thundered through the speaker, "Alice, Alice, you there?"

Alice ignored him to watch Stained leave. "Yeah Wilson, listen, how come you never turn up at our gigs?"

Wilson replied facetiously, "I've got better things to do like running your business."

"That what you call it," Alice snarled, studying his face in the mirror. "So, what's up?"

"A journo named Saul Kent will meet you at the backstage door, wants an interview about the new release. It's important, it'll feature on national television and boost the song to the top of the charts. Can you handle it?"

"Yeah," said Alice, sighing inwardly. He'd tired of the man. For the past year they'd been unable to see eye to eye, largely because Wilson was pro-government, and disapproved of Alice's involvement with the Octagon. Worse than that, Alice felt he was getting too big for his boots. Although Alice had already been a star when Wilson came on board, he'd needed an experienced operator to handle the business side of things so he could focus on writing and recording. Wilson was meant to manage bookings and day-to-day business, but instead he seemed to manifest problems out of thin air that Alice had to solve, depriving him of the freedom to create. Basically, Wilson had turned out to be a dickhead.

"Excellent," the manager went on, oblivious to Alice's inner monologue. "Just shut up about the Octagon, will you? Use the interview to promote the music, not that mob of radicals."

"Keep your goddamned opinion to yourself Wilson," Alice sneered in reply. "You dig?" He hung up, aggravated by the man's attitude. Just as he was about to go out the door, his phone pinged with a text message from a number he didn't recognise. It read: 'Announce your resignation from the Octagon to Kent on national television. If you don't, the consequences will be costly.'

"Who the stuff's threatening me?" he mumbled, then to his amazement the text exploded into pixels and dissolved. He pushed open the door. Waiting for him outside amidst a raft of fans was a tall, skinny young man with short-cropped dark hair and glasses. He was dressed in a smart modern suit.

"You Kent?" asked Alice.

"Yes," said the self-confessed reporter.

"Alice! Alice!" the female fans screamed excitedly.

Kent acknowledged them by rolling his eyes. "Any chance we can do the interview inside? There's this lot and it's blowing a bloody gale out here." For emphasis, Kent blew warm air into his cupped hands.

"Depends how long it'll take and how many of you there are," Alice said.

"Just me and Sherri, my digi-cam operator. It'll take about twenty minutes."

Alice was still holding the door. Kent seemed affable enough. "Okay," he said. "Come on in." He stalked off, leading them into the backstage area. They followed him to the band room.

He led Saul into the brightly lit room, which was awash with empty beer cans, pizza boxes and general trash. Sherri followed carrying a camera bag. None of them paid any attention to the mess; they'd all been in band dressing rooms before.

Kent pulled up a chair and had Sherri position the camera so it couldn't be seen in the long wall mirror. As Alice sat down and preened himself in the mirror, Sherri clipped a lapel mike onto his leather jacket. She moved closer to him than needed, flirting, anxious to solicit a response from him.

The girl was hot. In her mid-twenties with spiked blond hair, dressed to maximum funk in a mini-skirt that left nothing for the imagination, she fluttered her long false eyelashes at Alice. He was used to it. It meant zero to him. Not getting the response she anticipated, Sherri felt spurned. That wasn't what she expected from the lead singer of metal band. Her preconceived notion that all musos were like Slut, screwing anything with a hole in it, took a serious dent. Indignantly, she turned her attention to clipping a mike on Kent. That done, wearing Alice's rejection all over her face, she went about setting up the tripod and camera.

Kent, sitting back in his chair, crossed his long legs and opened a notebook on his lap. After testing the audio levels and lighting, Sherri said: "Okay … rolling."

Kent's demeanour changed from cool to arrogant in the blink of an eye.

"I'm backstage at Sydney's Frenzy with Black Alice, singer of the heavy metal band by the same name, and leader of the Octagon peace movement. Alice, it seems your legendary status is on the rise?"

"I wouldn't know about that, Saul, I just do my thing."

"Yeah well, there's a bit more to just doing your thing in the lyrics of your songs and the issues you make public through the Octagon, isn't there?"

Alice didn't like his attitude and his face showed it, but he answered calmly: "That's up for every individual's interpretation."

"You thumb your nose at authority and the bureaucracy. Is that your rebellious nature, your upbringing, or just a convenient way to promote yourself?"

Alice shrugged. "Aren't we here to talk about my new single?" he said, dismissively.

"Yes, but surely it's all connected ... If I'm wrong, why do you present America as the enemy in your live performances? Take tonight, the phallic ballistic missile you rode off stage. Everyone could see it was marked Made in the USA."

"Look, the Oceana Government is at fault here, not America," said Alice. "They've broken the Pacific anti-nuclear treaty by giving permission for a nuclear submarine to enter Sydney Harbour."

"So how can that be of danger to anybody?" Kent said, cockily.

Alice's eyes narrowed. He leaned forward in his chair, glared down into the camera and said, sternly: "Firstly, they're defying the will of the people by breaching a long-standing treaty, endorsed by the entire population in a referendum carried out generations ago, back when we still had a democracy. Secondly, it makes us the target of enemies with nuclear capability."

"So how does organizing violent protests resolve those issues? Surely it only inflates them." The reporter was starting to get under Alice's skin. Pushing down the desire to smack him between the eyes, Alice corrected him.

"Non-violent protests," he said. "What we want is to get rid of this government and return to democracy."

"So you're talking revolution, then?"

Alice paused, a sombre look on his face, then suddenly burst into song:

> The revolution is here...
> We have got to get it together, now!

"And that was from Something in the Air," said Kent, on cue: "The hot new release by Black Alice."

He motioned for Sherri to cut the camera by slicing his finger across his throat, and then reached out his hand to Alice. "Thanks, man ... went well."

"Good-o," Alice growled, taking his hand. He wasn't too thrilled about the interview and didn't like Kent at all, but there was no point whinging about it. What was the old adage about getting press exposure? There's no such thing as bad publicity? He decided to let it go.

"Thanks for your help, Sherri," he said, smiling at the girl. "Send a copy to my manager, please. When will it go to air?"

Packing up her gear, Sherri decided to try one last come-on. Shooting him a devilish smile, she said: "There'll be something in air tonight, then repeated tomorrow. I can get a copy over to your manager before the end of the week, or if you prefer ... I could give it to you personally later on," she said lasciviously.

Alice grinned. "Give it to me, hey?" He raised an eyebrow and gave her the once over. "I like the sound of that."

"Watch her, Alice, she bites," warned Kent.

"I reckon," rasped Alice. "Like a vampire."

In the corridor at the backstage door Alice and Kent let Sherri out ahead of them. Kent stopped in the doorway and turned to Alice.

"So, what happened to the big announcement?"

Alice had had enough of his attitude and snarled, "What friggin' announcement?"

Kent shirt-fronted him angrily. "Listen, I took the interview for the exclusive. You were supposed to announce your retirement from the Octagon."

"Well you got that wrong, didn't you?"

Kent made the mistake of poking Alice in the chest with his finger while griping, "You rock mental re-treads are all alike — you're here today, gone tomorrow. Next record release you'll get nothing out of me, arsehole."

Alice had had a gut-full. He shut the door for privacy and then with lightning speed smacked Kent in the mouth with a short right jab. Kent's glasses flew off as he slammed into the wall, his nose leaking blood.

"There won't be a next time, prick!" Alice barked.

There was a flash of light.

When his vision cleared Alice was staring at the glowing orb. He was back in the strange netherworld after having relived life experiences from another perspective, it was as though he'd been watching a digital replay. A voice from the orb suddenly rattled him — reminding him of the weird situation he was in.

"Was the violence really necessary Alice?" En-Ki asked.

"Guess I could've handled it better but the guy was a prick."

"You had become the enemy of state Alice, but it was to get decidedly worse for you."

"True. How are you doing this? I'm seeing like a replay of things in my mind that I didn't even know was happening at the time."

"It will all become clear to you soon," En-Ki said, and immediately another flash of light rocked Alice transporting him once again.

CHAPTER 3
NEXUS

THE ORANGE SUN dominated the sky like a gigantic fireball. A relentless, scorching wind howled like a thousand wolves, blowing columns of red dust in angry swirls across the desert plain. It was a desolate scene of decay, a skeletal ruin — a dust bowl where no rain ever fell. It was what remained of the city of Sydney.

Overhead an atomic storm moved in: awesome black thunderheads rolled at high velocity, a mere three hundred metres above the ground. Amid the tempest of swirling nuclear energy, snake-like tongues of green lightning were expelled with fury, licking the ravaged earth. Cracks of electrostatic thunder resounded, vanquishing the sound of wolves.

Suddenly, from behind the twisted metal skeleton of a once proud building, a female figure appeared. She was on the run, clearly desperate to escape someone or something. While trying to dodge the rusted shards of corroding iron girders, she slipped and slid down a jagged slope of rubble and landed flat-out on the desert floor. Propped up on one arm, Djard checked the new cut to her already bruised and lacerated legs. Her dirty face was masked in fear. She winced in pain, and her eyes flicked nervously about, like those of a frightened cat. Stumbling back to her feet, her long, matted blonde hair trailing out behind her like a banner, she ran out onto the blistering hot desert sand, speeding over it like a startled goanna.

When she reached a low, crumbling circular wall she stopped. Trying to catch her breath, she cautiously moved away from the strange edifice — clearly it was giving her a bad vibe. Suddenly, she was distracted by a whimper from behind an outcrop of rock. She scurried over to find the source of the sound.

As she reached a shaded alcove, she found an older woman lying on the sand. Djard bent down and raised the woman's head, looking at her with caring eyes.

Both women were wearing only leather lap-laps covering their genitals. Their bodies were dark from the sun. Djard was in her early twenties, her body lean and ripe. The other woman was thirty plus, and the worse for wear.

The older woman's left thigh was scarred with the letters MT, a brand meaning Empty: barren, affected by radiation, unable to reproduce. She was a target to be hunted by hostiles.

Suddenly, the moment was broken by a loud, husky voice.

"Get MT ... Pouch mine!" it commanded.

The voice belonged to Ex, chief of the tribe of barbarians pursuing Djard. He stood confidently astride the two frightened women, stabbed his Japanese Katana sword into the ground, and, grinning triumphantly, rested his big, hairy muscular arms on the hilt. He was clothed in scavenged pieces of leather and rag, bound together with strapping. Over one shoulder was hung the rusted front mudguard of a motorbike, worn like amour. On the other shoulder was a wide strip of car tyre. His clothing, such as it was, strained to accommodate his hulking chest and shoulders. Unkempt, matted ochre hair dropped all the way down to the middle of his back, and his towering six-foot six frame and battle-scarred face gave him the awesome appearance of a warrior born to kill.

Djard jumped to her feet and shaped up defiantly to Ex, her hands clawed to scratch at his eyes. One of Ex's five men rushed past her, and raising the older woman to her knees ready to rape her. The woman groaned, but didn't have the energy to scream or resist.

Djard, unable to subdue her anger, charged Ex, thumping him hard on the chest and screaming: "No! No! Scud! Scud!" Scud was a rabies infection. The old woman had been savaged by wild dogs and infected with the contagious viral disease.

Ex savagely grabbed her hair and eyeballed her. "Scud?" he repeated, then grimaced when she nodded affirmative. His eyes wide in alarm, he snapped at his men, "Scud! ... Rub her! ... Now!"

Quickly, Karn, a smaller brute than Ex, drew a blade from his belt, scurried to the prostrate woman and, grabbing a handful of her motley greying hair, pulled her head back and slit her throat from ear to ear in one quick stroke. The woman didn't flinch. Blood gushed from the wound.

Ex violently dragged Djard to the ground and pushed her head into his crotch, signifying to all of them that she was his property. Djard struck back and sank her teeth into his thigh. Ex let out a growl and struck her with an almighty back-hander that knocked her over. But Djard was a tough girl. With a shake of her head to fight off the shooting stars that swirled around her vision, she scrambled onto her knees. Before Ex could move, a battle cry rang out unexpectedly from the distance, distracting the team of barbarians and saving Djard from further abuse.

Ex signalled his men to disperse and take up defensive positions. He scanned the hot terrain for hostiles. A stream of anxious sweat traversed his battle-scarred cheek into the thick stubble of his beard, then dripped from his hairy chin onto his filthy chest.

The desert stretched all the way to a line of low, rounded hills on the horizon. It was not without rugged beauty. The white-hot sun beat down on an expanse of predominantly ochre sand, splashed here and there with vivid streaks of grey and red rock outcrops eroded by the winds into shapes that might have been the works of some psychotic sculptor. From behind one of the outcrops Ex sighted movement. Suddenly six ferocious-looking warriors stepped out, armed to the teeth, ready for battle.

Ex looked down at Djard attempting to crawl away and took a fresh grip of her hair. He pulled her back to sit obediently by his knee, like a dog. Glaring at the leader of the opposition he yelled: "Derg ... Pouch!" He jerked his grip on Djard's hair to indicate he was referring to her. "Ex!" he growled, beating his own chest to claim possession.

Derg — for that was the leader of the rival gang's name — responded with a loud, defiant, challenging laugh.

Ex nodded at Karn, who obediently ran to his side and took over the restraining grip of Djard's hair. This battle would be over ownership.

Ex drew his sword from the ground and pointed it threateningly at Derg. Derg, a seasoned campaigner with a Samurai ponytail on the back of his tattooed, bald head, had a muscular physique just as powerful as Ex's. He grinned defiantly, displaying only a couple of teeth in the black gummy void of his mouth. Raising and whirling a long-handled axe above his head was his acceptance of Ex's challenge.

Ex growled a battle cry. At the same time Derg countered with his own cry, and with great gusto they charged at one another.

Derg powered down the rocky slope, stopping abruptly just two metres short of Ex. Dust swirled up all around them. The two big men paused, sizing each other up. Derg was shorter than Ex but more muscular, with thighs like tree trunks. He wore a rusted heavy link chain looped over his shoulder and fastened to a broad leather belt around his waist. A Katana sword was slung over his left shoulder, and he held his axe with both hands. Ex cared little that Derg was the more heavily armed. The two locked eyes in a venomous stare-down. Then, with blood-curdling cries, the two big men clashed.

In the sudden frenzy of fierce action they all but disappeared in a sea of swirling red dust. The clang of sword on axe, metal on metal, rang in the spectators' ears. Suddenly, all sound ceased, and only the dust wafted languidly around the glistening warriors. Both sides watched with interest as the dust drifted away, revealing the two men snared in a tug o' war — weapons locked together, arms trembling in a contest of sheer strength. They both released pressure at the same time and pulled back. Derg cast his axe aside and unsheathed the Katana that had been strung over his back.

Both combatants shaped up, paused, then came at each other with incredible force. The clash of steel rang out with each terrifyingly powerful blow. Derg hacked ferociously, aiming for Ex's gut, forcing Ex to defend fiercely to block the bestial slashes. Using his sword, Ex trapped a blow from Derg, and with brute strength slowly forced the locked blades so the shorter man had to raise his arms. Once Derg's arms were high enough, Ex freed his blade, turned side on, and, as Derg lunged at him, brought up a fist tightly gripping the hilt of the sword. The blow connected under Derg's chin with such force that the whiplash knocked him out cold. Derg went down for the count.

Raising his sword triumphantly, Ex was about to bring down the deathblow when he was interrupted by a charge from Derg's second in command, Gronk. Anticipating the reprisal, Ex stepped deftly aside, dodging the charging warrior and, as he passed, slashing at the backs of his legs. The flashing steel sliced through Gronk's tendons, crippling him. The tattooed warrior collapsed to his knees in the sand, crumpling into a rapidly-growing pool of his own blood.

Wasting no time, Ex slammed the hilt of his sword onto the back of Gronk's exposed neck. Standing victoriously over him, chest pumped out, he raised his sword and gloated briefly over the vanquished barbarian before slicing down with one almighty blow that cleanly severed Gronk's head. He irreverently kicked his victim's head like a soccer ball so it rolled to a stop at Djard's feet, bloody and wide-eyed. Djard winced, then winced again as Karn gave her hair a sharp yank, just to remind her he was still in charge. Djard knew Ex, as the winner of the battle, would now possess her. But as Karn raised a fist into the air and roared, heralding Ex the victor, he loosened his grip and Djard seized the opportunity to escape. Wrenching free, she took off like a frightened rabbit. But Ex was in the way. Reaching out a hand, he once again grabbed her by the hair and wrenched her in close. Struggling, kicking and squealing, she clawed at him, to no avail: as far as Ex was concerned he'd won her fair and square.

Before he could claim his prize, three more of Derg's men charged down the hill, waving their weapons. They skidded to an abrupt halt just short of Ex. Ignoring Djard, still spitting and scratching like a trapped feral cat, Ex bent down, collected the severed head and threw it at the enemy. He pointed his sword at Derg, letting them know he could easily take his head as well, then lowered it to declare the fight over. Displaying the benevolence of a great gang chief, he was giving Derg, his fellow chief, the chance to live.

Derg's men, getting the message, stood down, collected Gronk's head, and all but two of them stalked off, defeated. The remaining two — their names were Chez and Bong — attended to the reviving Derg, while Ex's men attacked the fallen Gronk's headless body, stripping it of weapons and clothing — commodities much sought after in their barbarian society.

To celebrate victory, Ex had a new plan for Djard. He dragged her across the burning sand into the middle of the strange circular wall she'd avoided earlier. Horrified, kicking up dust as she struggled with all her might, Djard knew what was coming. The now-recovered Derg and his two remaining henchmen, hearing her screams, realised there was going to be a ritual killing. Her bloodletting was a dedication to the gods, a sacrifice that would bring favour and good fortune to Ex's clan.

Holding Djard down, Ex tore a silver medallion from around her neck and held it up as a trophy for the other warriors to see. He growled loudly: "Shine!" and pushed Djard to her knees. Pulling her head back by the hair with one hand, he raised his sword in the other, ready for another beheading.

Suddenly, as though nature resented his actions, the sand beneath their feet began to give way. Derg and his men saw Ex and his captive sinking into the sand, and seized it as an opportunity to attack. Karn saw them coming, but was torn between saving Ex from the sands or fighting off Derg and his men. Before he could decide, Derg crash tackled him like a raging bull, and they both tumbled over the low wall and into the quicksand. One of Derg's men, Chez, dived forward in time to grab Derg's leg, but ended up toppling over the wall into the treacherous sand with him. Bong stopped dead, not prepared to follow the others into the swirling, sucking sands. Ex and Djard, still struggling, were sinking fast. The more the others panicked, the quicker they were drawn down. Karn and Derg were still locked in a wrestle hold. Thrashing like a drowning man, still holding Derg's leg like his life depended on it, Chez, Derg's faithful warrior, was all but gone from view.

The remaining warriors rushed to the edge of the wall, too afraid to go any closer, and watched, helplessly, as the five people caught in the whirlpool of death vanished right before their eyes. The sand filled in around Ex's hand, still holding his sword upright. Then it too slowly sank into the quicksand and disappeared. All fell still.

Through a small cracked window with torn curtains, a red neon light from the city street strobed, illuminating the interior of a tiny Kings Cross flat. Two bodies glistening with sweat rolled in a tangle of bed sheets, on a bed squeaking with the rapture of lovemaking. In the flickering sheen of the neon light pulsing in the window, two bodies appeared to be moving in slow motion. Their panting rose in tempo, their breath grew heavier and heavier, climaxing in a crescendo of groans and cries of ecstasy. Alice rolled off the slender girl, onto his back. Stain laid her head gently on his bare chest.

Wearing only his navy captain's hat from the gig, Alice scanned his drab surroundings and groaned poetically: "Before ye, this abode stands as testament to my achievements in life thus far … Frigging nothing! A lousy Kings Cross bedsit, so small ya couldn't swing a cat, a collection of rock 'n roll trophies — including me — second-hand clothes, second-hand instruments, and..." he peered down at Stain, "Second-hand..." he decided to take a new tack before he put his foot in his mouth, "... second hand-jobs!"

Despite his sneering, rebellious image, off-stage and out of the limelight, Alice was a totally different man. Warm, caring, introverted and even a little taciturn at times. He had a tendency towards philosophy and waxing lyrical about how he'd improve life for everyone if he could. A half first nations boy he'd been brought up an orphan in a foster home with nothing — no toys, lousy food, nothing but heavy-handed discipline. As for love, his 'carers' wouldn't have known how to spell it.

As soon as he was old enough he'd used music as a means to escape the horrors of his environment, and songwriting to vent his anguish. But he hadn't counted on his words striking a note with the rank and file. Nor had he reckoned on the recognition that, within only a handful of years, had changed him from a nobody to a household name. He was revered for having the guts to speak out for the underdog. Even he wasn't aware of how much his words had shaken the very fabric of the establishment. As a result, he was living on borrowed time.

Alice and Stain had been an item, off and on, for the past four years. They'd never lived together — Alice preferred independence to feed his creativity. She was a singer, and did back-up for him at his bigger gigs. Theirs had always been a casual affair. Only now was it becoming more serious to Alice. Lately he'd felt the need for a more permanent relationship, even though that might that mean giving up some of his independence. Truth be known, they knew precious little about each other. Tonight was the night, in Alice's mind, that was going to change.

Stain looked up at him and whimpered, "How was it for you, baby?"

"Amazing ... you?"

"Massive!" she replied with a naughty grin.

Alice's exterior was weather-beaten and somewhat hardened by life, but now a smile broke on his face, making him look boyish again.

"Can I ask you something Alice?"

"Sure babe, fire away."

"What was it like for you growing up?" She asked.

Alice thought about it for a moment. It wasn't an easy question to answer. It was a part of his life he hadn't confided to anyone since moving from Perth to Sydney six years ago. He'd never found it easy talking about his past, in fact his life before Sydney was a complete mystery to everyone close to him. That's what kept him aloof. He'd always preferred it that way, it supported the content of the songs he composed. But he was growing out of it, because he wanted to be closer to Stain. Their relationship was helping him to confront his inner demons.

"Okay babe," he finally said, attempting lightness even though his heart was beating hard. "Fasten your seat belt and I'll give you the drum. But I warn you in advance, it's a ride and a half."

"I can handle it baby," she said with a big smile, snuggling up close.

Alice took a deep breath. "I was born in Fremantle, just south of Perth," he began. "My folks, I'm told — I don't remember them much — were criminals. They grew dope for a living, and that meant they dealt with some shady types. My dad was an aboriginal, my mother an immigrant from Britain. Yes, that makes me half cast.

"Our house — weatherboard, peeling white paint, overgrown lawns, the whole thing —backed onto bushland. They planted the dope among the native bushes, and no one was the wiser.

"My only solid memory comes from when I was five. Dad had got a part-time gig at a local butcher shop. He got into a fight with his boss, chopped the bloke's head open with a meat clever and hung him up on a meat hook out the back. Someone found him later that day, not dead but close to it. I kind of remember my dad coming home with blood all over him, saying it was from work.

"Anyhow, I remember all this because it was my fifth birthday. It was night time, and I was just blowing out the candles on my cake when we heard a voice on a loud hailer calling for dad to come outside with his hands up. Dad jumped up from the table, mad as a cut snake, grabbed a couple of shotguns out of the pantry and handed one to mum. She was as tough as goat's knees my mum, heavy on discipline. She belted me to the floor and then went to the windows and started shooting. It went on for a while. I remember being on the floor with my fingers in my ears, blue flashing lights filling the room, glass spraying everywhere from gunfire. Eventually they ran out of ammo, I guess, and had to give themselves up.

"A policewoman held me, kindly enough I suppose, while I watched my folks bundled into a police van. My mum waved at me from the window. I never saw either of 'em again."

"You must have been heartbroken," Stain said, quietly wiping away a tear.

"Nar, they'd raised me to think it was inevitable," said Alice, quietly. "Anyhow, I was put into Clontarf Boys Town Orphanage. It was run by brothers — monks, that is. I wasn't even a Catholic. Maybe that's why I got so much abuse. It's definitely why I hate organized religion. I was only a little fella when I went in, but by the time I reached puberty I was a seriously tough nut, with a dirty big chip on my shoulder and a take-no-prisoners attitude.

"By that point the orphanage was due to close. It had been around since 1901 and nothing had changed since then, either in the joint or in the arseholes running it. God, I hated them. Escaped more times than you could count on your hands and feet. When it shut they fostered me out, and that was even worse.

"First foster home I went to, the bloke would belt me with a cane for looking at him the wrong way. I got out after a year and into the next dysfunctional home, and it went on like that til I was sixteen. That was my last foster home. I was going to school in Subiaco, finishing my school certificate — I was crap at school, hated it, by the way — but I got in a band with a bunch of schoolmates and realised I could sing.

"My foster mother at the time, Julie, encouraged it, but her husband wasn't at all woke. He used to belt her and treat me like I didn't exist, called me a white abo, a misfit. One night he came home from work drunk as a skunk and got stuck into Julie. I smacked him with a rolling pin and he was taken to hospital with a split head. I got the blame, even though Julie tried her best to stand up for me. Her husband thought I was screwing her, so he wanted me out of there."

"Were you? Screwing her?" Stain asked, tentatively.

"She was a nice lady," said Alice. "But I was just a kid. I knew the way she was being treated wasn't right. She tried to help me, so I tried to help her. That was all there was to it. Anyway, I got dragged before some sort of state government tribunal for indigenous foster kids, and they sent me up north to work on the gas fields.

"I'll never forget that first day at work. I got dropped off at the mining site, only a bunch of tin sheds, and told to go to see the foreman. He was sitting behind a makeshift desk, chain-smoking. He had a big square jaw, a big black beard and he was bald as a badger. He bellowed at me with his six-packs-a-day voice: 'Well look at what the cat dragged in, a bloody queer half cast from Perth. Heard on the grapevine you're a tough little shit — we'll see about that. Outside! Let's see what you're made of, son.'

"Christ, he was a big bludger, arms like legs, six foot four. I knew I was in trouble, scrawny little bugger that I was. We got outside and he picked up a tyre lever, threw it at my feet and said: 'Pick that up and do your best.'

"The other bloke from the office, tall skinny bugger with a face like a rat, came out and sat on a drum to watch the performance. I just stood there. No bloody way I was going to pick up that iron bar. He would've killed me. After long enough for rat face to roll and punch a durry, the big foreman rubbed his hand in my hair and said, 'Good on ya son, you'll do just fine here.' He was right. I spent two terrific years there. It knocked all the crap out of me, taught me humility. By the time I got back to Perth at eighteen, I was a different bloke."

CHAPTER 4
FIX

ALICE SETTLED BACK, getting comfy against his threadbare pillows, as he continued his story. "One thing I didn't dig during my time at the mine was the plans for fracking in other states, and setting up a huge coal mining plant with partners from India in the far north of Queensland. I knew if they ever got it going it would totally stuff the Barrier Reef."

"Wow — that's what's going on right now," said Stain, eyes wide.

"Yeah well, when I got back to Perth, I had a good bankroll. I started a band called Gypsy with a couple of mates. It was a heavy metal cover band, doing ACCA DACCA songs around the pub scene. I started writing songs about the things I hated — bad foster care, nuclear war, fracking, polluting the reef. The band didn't dig it, so I put those songs away and we stuck with doing covers. A few years later we eventually got an agent, a Malaysian Chinese bloke called Jimmy Lee. He got us a regular gig at a Perth metal venue called Blazers. A year later, a mate of Jimmy's, a promoter named Jeff Hardie, came in from Asia. After he heard us play, he had a record producer from Sydney fly over. We recorded our first album. At the same time, I showed the producer my songs. He dug them, and we used them. He also came up with a new name for the band: Black Alice. We named it for Alice Springs after an imagined nuclear attack that left the desert all blackened.

"I wrote a bunch more songs with the guitar player, Jamie, and when the album was released it did really well. I was blown away. Never thought we were any good, let alone that our songs would be appreciated. The album took off in Europe. So after six years of slogging it out in pubs, we were an overnight success, ha!

"The band split up right after making the big time, the boys didn't want to tour. I did. So I packed up my life and came to Sydney with a new identity — I'd become Black Alice."

"This is amazing," said Stain. "What happened next?"

"You sure you wanna hear all this shit love?" Alice said, suddenly self-conscious. He wasn't used to this kind of communication, this kind of bond.

"If it's about you, I want to know it all baby," said Stain. "Is that okay?"

"Just don't want to bore your tits off that's all…"

She pinched the pink nipple of her lovely left breast and said with a smirk, "Don't worry, they're not going anywhere."

He kissed her, gently. Stain was the first girl he had ever really cared for. To have her listening to his life story, and apparently with interest, was making him feel even closer to her. He realised right then that keeping his story secret all this time had done him no good. All it had done was build a wall around his emotions. He'd always believed that if he was to care, to open up — or worse, to love someone — he'd be making himself too vulnerable. The experiences of his youth had drilled into his soul the determination never to expose his feelings. He realised now he was wrong. "I'm glad I came to Sydney," he whispered. "Because I found you."

Stain's eyes where shining as she looked back at him, and all at once he realised that both of them were in the same place. But all she said was: "That's so sweet … Go on, tell me the rest."

"When I got to Sydney I had to start all over again," Alice went on. "I went and saw the bloke who'd produced the first album. He was happy to see me and told me he planned to produce a short film. I asked if there might be a gig in for me in it and he told me he'd write me into the script. A month later I was on location at the St Peter's brickpits in Sydney shooting Knightmare — a short film, basically a long-form music video — and I was the star. The song I sang in it went to number one, and that let me put a band together.

I pinched Ratsso, Blue and Slut from another band — because I had a hit record it was easy to coax 'em on board. We called the band Black Alice and we went on tour all over Australia, playing every pub, town hall, scummy club and HM disco that would take us. Pretty soon we had three quality sets of original songs. And the rest is history. Ha. We had some crazy times."

"I bet you did," said Stain, with a knowing smile. "What's your craziest story from the road?"

"Ha! That's easy ... we were booked to play at the Palace Hotel in Broken Hill, far west New South Wales. When we rocked into town we booked into the pub and went down to the bar for a drink. We probably looked to the locals like we just lobbed from another planet. It didn't help that we were dressed heavy metal — studs, leathers, tatts and weird hair — you could've heard a pin drop when we rocked in. But after a few games of pool against the best players in town, we won 'em over.

"That night, after the gig, a pretty little chick barged in backstage and hung around Slut like a bad smell. One of the roadies, Mullet, had heard the girl was under age and off limits, but Slut being Slut wasn't gunna listen. He reckoned he was onto a winner. Mullet was dirty because he'd promised the girl's brother he wouldn't let her get into any trouble. So he decided to make a moral of it...

"We were due to hit the road, the roadies had packed the truck, all we had to do was get into the van. I was packing my stuff in the hotel room, when I heard a bloke's voice, really loud, outside, saying: 'Come on baby, just take your panties off.' Then a girl's voice, saying: 'No, yuck, put that ugly thing away, I don't want to touch it!'

"I go to the window, out in the street Mullet and the other roadies are rolling round, shitting themselves laughing. They'd put a microphone under Slut's bed, with a lead running out the window, down two storeys and plugged into a bass amplifier in the back of our truck. It was broadcasting Slut's dodgy proposals to the entire population of Broken Hill. Within minutes cops arrived and he was arrested — turned out the girl was the daughter of the town Sheriff.

"Man, we thought we were sunk that time. But turns out no-one could recognise the girl's voice, so the Sheriff just told us to keep quiet and beat it out of town. We were lucky, he could have locked Slut up and thrown away the key. But he just wanted the whole thing to go away. Lucky for us. Specially Slut."

"He's a naughty boy Slut," said Stain, amused in spite of herself. "Puts it on anyone."

"Yeah, he reckons if it ain't in the back of a truck and you can't play it, you can screw it."

"That's terrible!"

"That's how he got his nickname. But he's one hell of a guitar player."

"That's true," said Stain. "Still, what a ... well, what a slut!"

Both of them laughed. Then Stain's face changes, went more serious. "Alright, tell me the rest of it," she said. "How did you end up involved with the Octagon?"

"Christ," said Alice. "That's another long story. Okay, I'll tell you!" he added, as Stain opened her mouth to encourage him.

"The election four years ago gave us an independent as Prime Minister for the first time since federation, remember? We all thought things were gonna change for the better. He changed the constitution, called himself President, dissolved parliament, made us a republic. We thought that was great, because everybody was well over the two-party system and sick to death of politics. We thought the President was a socialist. Ha. Were we wrong. He's a fascist bastard. Things went downhill fast. Remember what it was like? Mandate this mandate that..."

"I remember," said Stain. "It turned into a dictatorship. It was bad enough when he set up the Oceana trading bloc without consulting the nation. Then he went and formed that bastard SSD, bunch of freaking Neo Nazi's."

"Right," said Alice. "Anyone with a social conscience got seriously worried, right? So, I shared my point of view in interviews, packed my songs with anti-government messages, generally used my popularity to try to influence things. And that attracted the Octagon.

"Loads of musicians were joining. My pal Mal Function — you've met him — sucked me into attending a meeting. It was a set-up, because next minute I'd been voted in as the leader. Just like that. I mean, no regrets, it wasn't like they bent my arm up my back — they just asked me if I'd like to head up their campaigns and I said yes ... it's been a good thing," Alice finished. "It's connected me more closely to the people."

Stain smiled at Alice proudly, "I remember watching you on TV, before I met you," she said. "You were always amazing. The Octagon couldn't have picked a better leader."

"Thanks babe," said Alice. "Alright, I've been talking about myself for hours. I want to know more about you. What's your life been like? How did you end up here, lying next to an old metal geezer like me?"

Instead of answering, Stain rolled out of bed, picked up her handbag and sashayed over to the tiny en-suite bathroom, swinging her naked bottom in a tantalising tease.

Alice grinned, watching her firm round butt flashing with red neon and glistening with sweat. She blew him a cheeky kiss and said: "We've got all night, babe. Just let me freshen up a little, I'll be right back." Half closing the door behind her, she started singing a sexy version of her back-up line from Something in the Air:

"We have got to get it together, now!"

"I'm on the news tonight at eleven," Alice called out to her.

"Well, we wouldn't wanna miss that, would we?"

Alice could make out her reflection in the mirrored bathroom door. She was standing on her tiptoes over the sink, douching. "All those little Alices being washed down the drain," he yelled. "You're a mass murderer!"

She turned threw the washer she'd been using at him, slapping him right in the face. "You're the one who condemned them to death!" she joked.

Peeling the washer off his mush he returned serve, "You're right you know, that pretty well sums up mankind. A prick sends in the troops, some pussy wipes 'em all out. Sex is a metaphor for life, we're always at war with the great unknown."

"You're so profound," said Stain, rolling her eyes with a giggle. Her toe delicately nudged the bathroom door closed for a little more privacy.

Outside, although it was still dark, the early-hours morning air was tainted with the sound of police sirens, traffic noise and the general hum of the city machine. Alice sat back in bed, thinking about the world beyond his room. His eyes were filled with intelligence and wit, and a new warmth that contradicted his usual rough-and-ready, don't-care demeanour. He reached beside the bed and picked up an old, well-worn acoustic guitar, balanced it on his lap and picked a few out-of-tune notes. He started tuning, when a slight noise from the bathroom caught his ear.

"What's happening, treasure around whom my universe rotates?" he crooned, glancing up at the bathroom door. It had creaked open just enough for him to see Stain's reflection. This time he had to squint, trying to refocus his eyes, unsure of what he was seeing.

Her naked back to him, Stain had a rubber tourniquet flexed round her arm, then clamped in her teeth. Her other hand, crooked to her elbow, was just about to insert a needle into a bulging vein. As she started to press the plunger of the syringe, her head rolled back, a look of ecstasy in her eyes.

Alice leapt from the bed, and ran like a man possessed to the bathroom, smashing the guitar into pieces against the door on the way.

Stain swung around sharply towards him, eyes and mouth wide with fright. "No!" screamed Alice, smacking the syringe out of her hand. "No!"

Too late. The syringe, now empty, hit the floor and Stain dropped like a rag doll. Alice caught her, panicking. This was the last thing he'd expected from her. But he could help her, he'd help her quit, get clean, get healthy. They'd have plenty of time together, he could help her change.

Suddenly he noticed the ruby lips he had been kissing all night were turning blue. Stain's eyes were glazed, she was staring listlessly at the wall. Reality struck — she had overdosed, she was dying. The noise of the city pounded in his ears, celebrating its claim, another victim for the night. He had to save her. He had to. Lying her gently on the floor, he placed his folded hands over her chest and started CPR, pleading all the while: "Stain! Stain! Stain!"

CHAPTER 5
FALLING

SOME HOURS LATER, duded up in his best snakeskin jacket over a torn blue singlet, skinny fit black jeans, Alice cruised past the many homeless camped outside the Oceana Citizen's Hospital. Even at 3 AM there was plenty of activity in the smoky street. A night market with stalls selling everything from dead cats, rats and dogs, skinned and hanging, to weapons. It was a popular location for vendors due to the proximity of the hospital. It was hellish, rundown, filthy and unhygienic — a contradiction to the antiseptic hospital.

The majority of the vendors were wearing face-masks, some with respirators.

Alice pushed through the plethora of people past a vendor who tried to sell him a hit of oxygen. Some recognized him and called out. He acknowledged them with a sharp wave of a hand. He entered ER

Triage was like a battlefield: there were injured and sick people scattered about. The badly injured, unable to walk, were on gurneys jammed in the corridors. The sound of suffering and frustration was pervasive to Alice. He fell in line at triage,

There were only three nurses on duty, one of them recognised Alice and waved him over.

Rocked by all the distress Alice asked, "Is it always like this?"

The young nurse cracked a smile. "Worse than normal being Saturday night. You're Black Alice, aren't you?"

Al nodded, "You guys do one helluver job."

"Who are you looking for?" she said, flicking the screen of her digital notepad.

A little embarrassed for jumping the queue he said self-consciously, "Um, my girl, Stained Class. She would've been admitted an hour or so ago for an overdose. Hey, I've got to ask, the paramedics wouldn't let me ride with her in the ambo, why was that? I couldn't get..."

The nurse looked up from typing on the notepad, "Oh, protocol. Too much domestic violence."

Al didn't get it. "Yeah? How's that?"

"The meds get attacked, spat on ... you name it ... it can get pretty ugly out there..." Suddenly her expression changed to sorrowful. "Um, I'm sorry. Stained Class passed away from her injuries."

Alice was totally rocked and muttered in disbelief, "No, no that can't be right. Check again please. She, she was okay when they took her..."

There was no point in re-examination, the result was conclusive. With as much sensitivity as she could muster she said warmly, "I'm so sorry."

Traumatised Alice turned away and then drifted zombie-like along the corridor towards the exit oblivious to the acknowledgements of fans. Suddenly, it all got too much for him, he stumbled, propping himself against the glass entrance door to prevent collapsing. The corridor, the people were shimmering and distorting — vivid images of Stain on the bathroom floor were flashing in his mind; a confusing montage of reflections — the paramedics affirming she was okay — flopping onto the bed with relief as Stain was being stretchered out — watching her being loaded into the rear of the ambulance, the colour back in her lips — the colour back in her lips!

Something weird had come over him. He glared at the people in ER watching him: their mouths were moving but he couldn't hear what they were saying only a high-pitched whistle. He looked at his hands. He was holding nine-millimetre Glock. He straightened up, took aim and opened fire at the people in the corridor. They were going down like flies, blood spattered painting the walls red.

He wavered, unbalanced. The entire corridor seemed to be shimmering like a mirage. The bloody tiled walls ballooned surreally, closing in. Overcome with dread he stood still in a ghostly void of gun smoke. Suddenly, the smoke was gone and the sound returned to normal. His arms were still outstretched in a firing position. There was no gun in his hands.

The floor and the ceiling distorted in perspective like a Salvador Dali painting. There was a thinning of the veil between dimensions. He grasped his forehead, trying desperately to steady himself. He backed up hard against the wall, unable to process what he'd been told by the burse. She shouldn't be dead ... the colour was back ... she was alive when the paramedics took her, I know, I revived her ... the colour was... He was losing it. Overcome by shock, his eyes glazed over and he mouthed the word no, no, no over and over, as if stuck in a groove. It was like a bad acid trip, and he was in a fight for self-control. Disturbing images invaded in his mind. He was fighting a terrifying half human, half machine android monster. Then, out of darkness materialised a frightening zombie, her hands clawed, her face a horrible snarling rictus of the living dead. Were these just random images or were they portents of horrors to come?

Then, suddenly overwhelmed by grief, he gave in to it. The mirage dissolved and his fuzzy mind cleared. But everything had changed. He was in a dark place he'd never been before. A veil of dust-covered cobwebs stretched in front of him, through which a strange pair of chrome horns protruded. Then, as if reverberating out of a PA stack behind the cobwebs and all around him, a chilling, demonic voice growled: "The Shine!"

In a flash of white light Alice's mind cleared for him to realise he was sitting cross-legged on the floor in the netherworld tunnel. En-Ki's voice startled him.

"That was a shock."

Staring blankly at the glowing orb, Alice muttered numbly, "I still don't think I've recovered, even now I can't reconcile her senseless death. All that stuff with Ex and Djard, incredible ... I had no idea."

"Let us see where that led you."

Ribbons of light descended from cracks in the massively high ceiling into a vast chasm above a pool of water. Five bodies plunged the thirty-metre drop inside a ray of light and splashed into the subterranean lake. The fall would have normally have killed them, but the water was deep enough to cushion their impact.

Djard rose first to the surface of the icy black water, gasping for air and panic-stricken. Ex surfaced beside her, blinded by the water in his eyes and disoriented. Djard seized the moment, and ripped her talisman from around his neck.

Ex yelled, enraged: "Shine!" But his anger changed to shock when Derg, Karn and Chez shot up out of the water around him.

Karn leapt onto Derg's back and continued the wrestling death-match they had started on the surface. Chez, a big round-faced hulk with a mop of curly brown hair and arms covered in tattoos, was gasping for air, having swallowed more than his fair share of the inky water.

Standing waist deep at the edge of the pool, Ex bellowed loudly at Derg and Karn, "No!" They stopped fighting.

In the dim light, Djard sighted the shore and took off for it. When Ex realised she was getting away, he started after her. Derg and Karn followed, and Chez, after shaking the water out of his ears, went after them.

Being smaller, with less water resistance, Djard reached the shore well ahead of Ex. Once on solid ground she shot off, in a big hurry to escape her pursuers and find an exit.

Ex wasn't about to be outdone by the girl. Besides, he wanted his Shine back. When he reached the shore he stood still, signalled with his hand for the others to freeze, and listened intently. He could hear her footsteps on the rocks to his right, and immediately set off after them.

Djard came to the base of a long metal ladder that reached up to what could be an exit. Unsure whether to take it or not, her mind was made up for her by the sound of Ex's running feet clumping over the rocky ground and closing in. Climbing the ladder, holding the Shine in her teeth by its leather thong, she made it to the top and looked down at Ex and the others. She tried to push the ladder down, but found it was fixed solidly to the craggy cliff face. Ex started up after her. Djard took flight.

She entered another cavern, darker than the previous one. She couldn't see any water, but there were two metal rails stretching along the tunnel floor as far as she could see. The others were nearing the top of the ladder, so she pelted along the tunnel, following the metal rails. Running as fast as she could, she looked back over her shoulder at Ex, tripped on a large piece of timber and fell heavily. As the Shine struck the metal rail it sparked, as though charged with some sort of magical power.

Ex arrived, and ripped the Shine out of her grasp in a flash. He growled, "Shine mine!"

Djard decided not to care about the medallion. Scrambling to her feet, she shot along the parallel tracks at speed, branching off the metal tracks into a long tunnel with a low ceiling. She stopped at the end, trying to regain her breath. To her dismay, she heard the others coming; she'd hoped she'd lost them by ducking off the tracks. She spotted a dark alcove and, thinking they mightn't follow her in there, slipped inside. A dark, dusty staircase led up. It meant passing through masses of cobwebs that chilled her to the bone. It was dusty, dry, old. The dust welling up with each step made her cough.

At last, Djard came to a landing and entered a large room. Standing in the darkness, she could make out the outlines of gargantuan machines, covered in cobwebs and dust, that looked to her like rusted monsters waiting to come to life. She flinched when she noticed two huge men in a dark corner of the room. But when she looked closer, she could see the bodies of the men were covered in cobwebs. They were faced-off, fists raised, ready to fight. Realizing they weren't alive, she reached out and tentatively touched a sharp chrome spike attached to one of the boxing gloves they each wore. She moved on in awe, like a kid in a museum, wondering what amazing discovery would come next.

Thin, dust-filled streams of light were shining down through broken skylights way up in the ceiling. There were long chains dangling from a gantry, from which water was cascading, forming puddles on the floor. The splashes echoed around the dark chamber. A sudden crunch of broken glass under foot alerted Djard that Ex and the others had arrived. Hiding in the darkness, she watched Ex move in, holding his sword, ready to strike. Karn prowled cat-like a metre behind, a dagger in his hand. Chez followed close behind, equally watchful, the heavy linked chain over his shoulder tinkling with every step. Derg came last, guarding the rear, sword held at the ready. Now demoted to captives, he and Chez were ranked lower than Ex and his warrior. Lore demanded them to be subservient to their conqueror, and that naturally grated on Derg's ego. He was also dirty that he'd left his axe at the bottom of the subterranean lake.

As Ex closed in on Djard, she hissed at him like an agitated cat. It spooked him and he snarled at her, with his sword raised threateningly. She knew he wasn't afraid of her. As she started to move away, Ex caught sight of the boxers with the spiked gloves, staring at him out of the darkness. In a reflex action he raised his sword. The others, behind him, took guard.

With Ex and the others occupied by the statues, Djard took the opportunity to slip into the darkness.

Ex looked them over. They resembled footballers in Grid Iron regalia, but with a major difference: the helmet was spiked, the gloves were spiked, and their uniforms were tight-fitting armour rather than sports apparel.

Ex looked up at a corroding sign just over the heads of the statues. The ten-pointed star logo looked interesting, but the words meant nothing. The sign read:

TECHNOLOGY EXHIBIT
PROTOTYPE RF SERIES CYBORG RUGBY FOOTBALLERS
RADIATED PELLET POWERED
COURTESY OF ZEN CORPORATION

Chez wanted a closer look. Moving around Ex for a better view, he shoved aside a dangling cable, which swung towards the androids. When the cable struck the android's chest, it let out a loud crack and gave off a massive blue flash and a shower of sparks. There was still power in this labyrinth. Ex, startled, jumped backwards. In his haste to retreat, Chez bumped into Karn. Derg had his back to them, and when Karn staggered back and bumped into him he swung around, ready to strike.

A red light flickered on inside the mask of the android.

Ex had moved on, looking for Djard, but as Chez turned his back on the android it forearmed him on the back of the head and knocked him down. Ex stopped in his tracks, and swung around in time to see the seven-foot android taking a step towards him. With one almighty swipe of his sword he decapitated it. All four warriors made room to get clear of the big monster, as it stumbled round like a headless drunk, sparks flying from the fusing electronics in its neck. It staggered into the other android and they both crashed to the ground.

Ex strode confidently over to the headless monster, twitching on the floor with intermittent sparks coming from its neck. He raised his sword. "Ex!" he yelled, declaring himself the victor.

Karn offered Chez a hand up from the floor.

They moved on to pursue Djard, more cautiously than before. They had no idea where they were or what other hazards awaited them.

Alice was still in the same position facing the orb. "Yeah, that's all well and good magically playing a movie in my head, but if you're just a consciousness in a bottle, where the hell are you from? Are you some kind of alien?"

"That will be revealed to you soon enough Alice."

Alice was becoming tired of hearing the same excuse. "Yeah, so you keep saying," he grumbled. "How do I get out of—"

En-Ki cut him off. "Risk taking does not seem to trouble you?"

Alice clambered to his feet. "Yeah well, I live by the personal maxim living is harder than dying. Now answer my question, how do I get out of here?"

"Back to you then," the voice from the orb said totally ignoring Alice's request. "After Stain's funeral you finally emerged from self-imposed exile. You had been given notice to attend an interview at Oceana State Security Directorate, but you were in no hurry to get to it…"

A week had passed since Stain's death. In that time Alice had withdrawn from life, music, The Octagon … he couldn't summon his former devotion to any cause. Something in the Air was number one in the charts and had been adopted as an anthem by the activists wracking the city with protests, each more violent than its predecessor. As a consequence, Alice had been branded public enemy number one by the Oceana secret police and ordered to attend an interview. Even without his sorely-missed leadership, The Octagon was preparing for revolution. The arrival of the American nuclear submarine, the focus of the protests, was imminent. It was time for action.

On his way to the interview Alice took to the streets, seeking answers to questions he didn't even know how to ask. A part of him had died with Stain. He was unable to reconcile the fact of her death after he'd got her breathing. When the paramedics had arrived, they'd confirmed she was stabilised and out of danger. The shock he'd received at the Citizens' Hospital had left him a troubled man. The tragic loss of Stain had spawned a new feeling in Alice, a callous, aggrieved, revengeful feeling. His naturally humble nature had all but faded away. He had opened himself up to Stain, to love, and everything he'd feared would happen because of that had come to fruition. Whatever he loved he would lose. He felt cursed. As a consequence, his stage persona had taken over his offstage psyche ... he was a tough guy with an almighty cross to bear. He was no detective, but his objective now was to determine who killed Stain, why, and then avenge her murder.

CHAPTER 6
BOURBON & BIFF

T HE WOOLLOOMOOLOO WHARF is one of the oldest parts of Sydney Harbour. Behind the warehouses and piers is a maze of narrow streets, alleyways, dilapidated buildings and 19th Century terrace houses. It was a place where the press gangs of the 19th century forcibly recruited unsuspecting drunks into the Royal Navy or onto cargo ships, if the whores, pickpockets or muggers hadn't got to them first. These days it was a place of small bars, a bordello or two and plenty of drug dealers ... still a paradise for thieves and cutthroats, and always a sanctuary for men on the run from the law, themselves or anything else. No one asked questions of you here. The dark energy of the place attracted Alice. Here, he could be in touch with the real essence of the struggle of life.

As Alice moved deeper into the old town, street vendors offered everything from jewellery to fresh meat pies. Girls offered only variations on one standard thing, repeatedly approaching him. Beggars pleaded for alms, an old witch offered to tell his fortune. None of them recognized him. In a full-length back trench coat over a white shirt and black pants, wearing a black Fedora and scarlet boots, Alice mixed with the street folk in relative anonymity.

He was thinking about how he didn't want to forget Stain, just the fact that she was dead, when he heard a familiar voice.

"Hey Al!"

He looked up at the balcony of the old terrace house he was passing and saw it was packed with Goths. Then he recognized the face of his bass guitarist.

"Hey Ratsso. What's happening?"

"Just having a few cones with friends. Come on up buddy, it's good to see ya."

"Nar, not in the mood for slumming it."

"Come on mate, it'll do you good. They're cool people. Goths, and mostly musos. Its Lou-gash's birthday."

Alice thought about it for a second, then relented and entered the house.

The smell of dope in the living room was overwhelming. The room was dimly lit by a colourful revolving laser ball, Pink Floyd's Wish You Were Here was playing on the entertainment console. Half a dozen same-sex couples were slow dancing to it.

Ratsso came rumbling down the staircase and embraced Alice on the landing.

"Good to see ya finally surfaced man. How are ya?" He held Alice at arms-length and studied his craggy face. He hesitated to mention Stain's death.

"Running like a well-oiled engine," Alice quipped, bitterly.

"Hey, how about all them riots?" Ratsso said, trying to think of a subject that might interest his friend. "Boy, the Octagon have missed you. Been getting pretty ugly without you at the helm."

He placed a consoling arm around Alice's shoulders and led him to the staircase. "Come on buddy, meet a couple of nice folk and chill for a bit. Me and the band have missed you big time." He led Alice up the stairs.

"The song is doing well, eh?"

"Got no idea. Don't give a shit."

Ratsso tried: "Did you hear about the government planning to bust biker gangs out west for having fallout shelters and shit?"

"Nup, haven't heard anything. Why would that make 'em a threat?"

"Oh, they reckon they're planning a rebellion. They've got the guns and ammo, ha! Pardon the pun."

"Lock up the street and houses." Alice shot back another line from their current hit, but there was no life in it. "They're paranoid."

There was nothing else for it. Ratsso realized he'd have to broach the subject.

"Horrible what happened to Stain, mate," he said, carefully.

"Yeah...," said Alice, sadly. "Still can't cop it."

"What do you mean mate, didn't she OD?"

"No way, she was okay when the medics took her. She bloody died in hospital."

Ratsso stopped three quarters of the way up the staircase, turned and eyeballed Alice intently. "You thinkin' foul play?"

"Reckon," said Alice, gravely, "couldn't have died from the fix."

They'd reached the top landing, and found loads more people.

"No one's wearing masks."

"Yeah, no one gives a crap."

A dude in a serious Goth outfit handed Alice a joint. He took a long toke and passed it on. The grass lightened up his mood a modicum.

At first the party seemed Goth hedonistic to Alice. Voices were overloud, competing with the music, and faces were over-animated. It was the way of the world, so much more amplified than before. The room was big and purple with a bar at the back. All the way around it grooved the bloodshot-eyed, stoned throng.

A young girl was up on a coffee table, most of her clothes gone, shaking herself to solitary ecstasy in a fuzz of jiggling boobs and gyrating hips. Her hands moved over her body, stroking and caressing, partly in invitation but mostly in self-obsession.

Ratsso dragged Alice away from her and the vociferous crowd out into the relative calm of the balcony to introduce his friends.

"Caught up with Mal yet?" said Ratsso on the way.

"Nar, might drop in on the Units gig tonight."

"Oh, that's right, they're playing the Jungle Bar, Blue's on kit. Hey, saw Beano the other day, he reckons he's got a new lyric for you for a hit song."

"Bloody Beano ... he could write a lyric to a dripping tap. You work on it with him, it'll take me a while to get back into the groove of composing ... too much bitterness for now."

The effects of the joint were kicking in and Alice felt he was fitting in with the scene a lot better.

Ratsso stopped next to two girls with wild hair, dressed in short black Tutus and black leather jackets. One of them was wearing Demonia Goth boots while the other wore black tights and black high-heeled pumps.

"Al, this is Lucinda and Vega," Ratsso said.

Alice grunted disinterestedly and then gazed off into oblivion.

"Bored?"

The voice was girlish. Alice turned to find it belonged to Vega, the one in the black tights and pumps. He tried to push aside his feelings, treated her to a half-hearted but still wolfish grin.

"Not so much bored as stoned, smoked brain flat spin," he said, lyrically.

"You don't look out of it," she purred quizzically and took a sip of her drink. "I'm a bit high myself."

"Yeah? What can you see from up there?"

She let a frown slowly gather around her eyes that then spread to the rest of her pretty face. "Speaking of high, did you hear about that chick last week who fell off a balcony in town, landed on an Oceana official and killed him?"

"Er ... Nar," Al said, following her eye line over the balcony to the street below.

"Ten frickin' storeys ... a long way down," she added, morbidly.

Lucinda piped up, "Try twenty storeys honey. I was there, it was seriously gross."

Alice winced. "Must've made a mess. Someone shove her?"

"Nup, they say she just toppled over." Vega giggled and playfully nudged him with her elbow. "I've got a friend who works at Oceana HQ. Reckons they blame the killing on the Octagon ... said she done it on purpose."

"We thought she fell but they reckon she jumped," Lucinda added.

"What? That's a bit far-fetched," Alice growled. "Like, how could it be murder? She'd have to be a good aim to drop twenty floors and land directly on a bloke. That's just a fresh serve of Oceana propaganda spin."

"News said she was a ... a suicide attacker!" Vega added, with a grimace.

Lucinda shook her head, "No way, she was probably out of it, looking at us and toppled over."

Al reacted. "The Octagon's a non-violent peace movement. They can't be blamed. It's a stitch-up."

Ratsso butted in. "It was the same protest we took a live drone feed from for the Frenzy gig, remember Al?"

Al nodded. "Yeah, how could I forget that night." It was the night Stain died.

"Anyhow, you can ask my friend 'bout it, he'll be here soon. Hey! Now I recognize you ... you're Black Alice, aren't ya?" Vega said, a surprised expression crossing on her cute face.

Alice half-raised his hands in surrender and grinned. "Guilty as charged," he said

"Take a sip of this, Black Alice." She offered him her pink drink. "It's laced with Bliss."

Alice took a sip. He'd tried Bliss before: it was a serious turn-on.

He handed her back the glass and she drained it.

Lou-gash joined them.

"Hey, happy birthday Lou," Alice said to the tall, outlandishly dressed woman.

"Thank you darlink," she replied in a deep throaty Italian accented voice. "Golly Alice, I haven't seen you for ages. We were school buddies back in Perth, you know," she told the others.

"Yeah, I remember you winning the pissing up the wall competition in the boy's brasco at lunch time," joked Alice. "No-one could beat Lou."

They all laughed.

"That was when I had a cock, darling," said Lou-gash. "But oh, how my life changed since I had that little piece of skin removed." She chuckled devilishly, ending with a contented smile.

"Not so little, but good for you mate," praised Alice. "Anyhow, I'm out of here, I've got an appointment with Oceana Security."

Ratsso couldn't believe what he'd heard. "You're kiddin' me mate? What would you want to meet those creeps for?"

Al put a hand gently on Ratsso's shoulder to placate him, "Some rave about wanting to make a hologram of me."

Ratsso shook his head, "Nar mate," he said emphatically, "give it the slip, can't trust 'em. Not with all this shit going on. Mate, they're blaming the Octagon for killing that official, that's you mate, you're the Octagon. Besides, you gotta meet us on the ferry at midnight tonight, remember?"

Al had made up his mind. "It's cool Ratsso, I can look after myself."

Vega gazed sadly at Alice and said like she knew something the others didn't, "Your life will change tonight Alice, nothing will ever be the same again for you. I feel it."

Her warning sent chill ran through Alice's nervous system but his covered the reaction by giving her a gentle peck on the cheek. "That happens with me baby. Hey Lou, Lucinda dudes, later."

Vega gazed at him sadly. "Bye Al. Be safe."

"See you later tonight — on the ferry," Ratsso said despondently.

"Chaa!" said Alice, and with a sharp wave of his hand he vanished into the crowd.

As he made his way out of the house he was feeling much better about himself. He stood out front and looked back up at the balcony. Vega was staring down at him with a sad look on her sweet face. He shot her a wave. He didn't know if he was feeling better because of the dope or the Bliss, but it didn't matter. What did matter was that he couldn't ignore the feeling in his gut that there was something in the story Vega had told him, the story about the girl falling off the balcony, and it being blamed on the Octagon by the Oceana government.

Wheels were turning in Alice's brain. Somehow, Vega's story about the jumping girl and the circumstances of Stain's death, seemed linked. He couldn't put his finger on how. He turned up his collar and trudged off into the blustery night. While walking his mind was cast back to his last night with Stain.

After getting the text message and interview with Kent, he'd met her for a midnight snack at the Bourbon and Beefsteak Bar in Kings Cross. He was always hungry after a gig, and that was his favourite watering hole. He remembered sitting in the near-empty restaurant, and noticing a dude in the corner eyeing him off. It was hard to tell if he was malevolent or not, because Alice was often recognised, sometimes by fans, and sometimes by detractors. But this dude seemed quite different.

He'd nudged Stain, who was sipping on a bloody Mary. "Hey Stain, don't look now, but there's a dude in the corner pegging us. You know him or something? Coz he's looking at me like I'm wearing something of his."

Stain had taken a sneak peek and turned sharply back at Alice with a frightened expression. "Oh hell, it's Drago! We need to get out of here!" she said, panicking.

"Hey, hey, I'm not finished eating, and I'm not about to let some old boyfriend put me off my grub ... just settle down."

Stain leaned forward and with teeth gritted whispered harshly, so Drago couldn't hear. "He's not an old boyfriend! the guy's a serial killer or something. He stalked me a bunch of times so I had him arrested. When they busted him, he got done for other stuff, drugs probably. I had to go to court. He shouted he'd square with me. They put him away for two years. Must've just got out. I've been dreading the day."

Alice could tell the dude had genuinely freaked her out. He glanced over to size him up. He was a big, broad-shouldered mother, short-cropped black hair, a big square jaw, full-sleeve tatts on both arms, and a mean, take-no-prisoners scowl in dark, soulless eyes. He had 'iron bar challenge' written all over him.

Alice let out a sigh, patted his lips with a napkin and then slowly stood up.

Stain grabbed his arm, "Where are you going hun?"

"Back in a flash," he said.

"No Alice please," she pleaded.

It was on deaf ears, Alice cruised over to Drago, pulled up a chair at his table and sat down opposite him. Taking a toothpick from the jar on the table he put it between his teeth and said, "You're freaking out my babe, and that's giving me indigestion."

The big man drilled Alice with an ice-cold stare, "So?"

"Have you got a problem?"

Without blinking Drago growled, "You. Fuck off."

"I was having a New York Cut Steak, what about you?" Alice said casually.

"What the stuff has that got to do with anything?" he snarled.

"Well, feel this?"

Drago felt something and looked down under the table at a steak knife Alice had precariously pressing against his crotch.

"I got a steak knife ... you got a spoon ... now what does that tell you about what we ordered?" Alice snarled.

He was taking a huge risk that Drago wasn't armed but figured it would be unlikely, seeing he was fresh out of the big house and probably on parole.

"You're Black Alice aren't ya?"

"You got that much right."

Ignoring the knife, quick as a lightning flash, Drago grabbed the hand holding the knife and squeezed. The knife dropped from Alice's grip. Drago continued to squeeze. The strength of his grip was crushing.

In a move Drago hadn't expected, Alice let go a powerful left cross that hit him flush on the chin. The big man slumped forward onto the table, his face plunging into his bowl of lobster bisque soup.

Alice stood up, massaging his right hand and flexing his fingers. It was another trick he'd learned from the foreman in the West Australian mines – use something to distract your opponent, then make a haymaker a moral. It had certainly worked, but he wasn't about to hang around for Drago to regain consciousness.

He gave the man a wave and snarled: "Chaa!"

CHAPTER 7

NARKS

I T WAS PLAYING on Alice's mind that the text and the incident in the bar were somehow connected to Stain's death. Thoughts wheeled in his head. Is Drago working for the SSD? They're known for cajoling prisoners to do their dirty work for them — sometimes even issuing a day pass out of jail to hit someone, before returning to the big house. Being in prison was the alibi — it was called the perfect crime. Did Drago send that text? Or had it been a case of getting square, as Stain had suggested? If that was right, had Drago killed Stain in hospital?

Someone had, he was sure of that, and in reality, the killing had to have been another warning, just like text had indicated.

Stain's death had caused him to question his involvement in the Octagon. It had shattered his principles, made him more wary of the world around him. He couldn't see himself performing with the band for a while. Any songs he tried to compose would be full of regret and remorse for the loss of Stain, and that shouldn't happen. Her death was his to mourn, nobody else's. But he was determined to find her killer, that was for certain.

There was definitely something in the air. He could feel it, and he had a hunch he was about to come face to face with it whether he liked it or not.

Becoming restless, Alice was slowly circling the orb in the netherworld tunnel. "That's all very interesting," he growled. "But I still don't get the point of this?"

"Humans who like giving advice rarely take it themselves. Have you noticed that?"

Alice stopped, "So now you're a philosopher. You trying to tell me something?"

"It does seem obvious that nothing but trouble was going to result from your visit to SSD. Have you ever considered how that might have affected others?"

"There's always some collateral damage," Alice said dismissively.

"That is quite true but it pays to know who is fighting for you."

"Not the first time I've been told that. I'm always at war with the great unknown."

"Might well be, but also perhaps your celebrity has you lose sense sometimes of the identity of your real allies."

Doctor Hope made her way into the lobby of Oceana Headquarters like a woman on a mission. An attractive 30-year-old, she was turned out in a crisp white lab coat with the black and chrome Oceana insignia embroidered on the right breast pocket, and wearing horn-rimmed glasses. Her long blonde hair was held in place by two black chopsticks.

She stopped at an elevator door and pressed the call button. The doors opened, she stepped inside and selected the top floor.

Hope had joined the Oceana Scientific Research Department (OSRD) on the express invitation of her brother Secta, the senior scientist and department head. Secta, six years older than she, recognised her potential in chemistry and physics research, and snapped her up as soon as she graduated with a doctorate in applied physics from Sydney University. It didn't take much to convince the

President, to whom Secta reported directly, that she was a chip off the old block.

Hope had her reservations about joining and it took quite a determined pitch from Secta to convince her to come aboard. She eventually bought in because Secta explained the job wasn't subject to the politics or the totalitarianism of which the government and its dictator president were being accused. However, over time, she had started to wonder. With a strong moral compass and social conscience, Hope was doubting herself for believing in her brother's determined pitch, especially now that the government was on the brink of permitting a nuclear submarine to enter Sydney Harbour, in complete defiance of the long-standing treaty. Such a careless act was likely to undermine the fragile trust she had in her employer, a trust that was really only there because of her brother.

To Hope's way of thinking, the field of scientific research in which she and Secta were working would improve the world, not threaten it. With these new revelations, she was beginning to believe she had more in common with the nuclear non-proliferation policies of the Octagon, who were in total opposition to the government she worked for. She was developing a deep respect for morals and initiatives of Black Alice, leader of the Octagon. Hope had been around idealists long enough to know that the peace movement was not safe from schism and ideological infighting. They had split into equal-sized groups. On one side there were the fundamentalists, who believed everything should be done at once, and that living standards of the whole country should be equal. They wanted technology reduced and religion abolished. The less extreme pragmatists wanted a middle-class society driven by technological change but not consumed by it. Alice seemed to her to fit in with the latter faction. Hope was biased towards the pragmatist view, but neither faction aligned enough with her sentiments to garner her complete support. Both options were, however, better than the tyranny of the current government.

Hope had been ordered to attend an interview with the SSD. She had no time for the secret police and was offended by the order. It was a part of working for the government that she found abhorrent. She considered the hard-core scientific research she and her brother were undertaking to be infinitely more vital for the wellbeing of the world than the disruptive banality of bureaucracy, and the machinations of the secret police. ~~~

Senior Inspector Fanny Honor took the rolled-up banknote from her officer, Agent Karzoff, and proceeded to snort a long rail of cocaine from the boardroom table. Karzoff had already done a line and was busy pinching his partially numb nose between his fingers. Both were dressed in the black, red-piped uniform of the Oceana secret police.

A tall attractive woman in her late thirties, Honor wore her black hair up, tied with a thin sash of crimson ribbon that matched the piping on her uniform. Her three-quarter length, tight-fitting black skirt was split conservatively up to a little past the knee.

Karzoff, on the other hand, was in his early fifties and sported short-cropped, artificially coloured bright red hair. Both were of East European extraction. Honor was Polish and had come to Oceana as a child, while Karzoff had migrated from the former East Germany when he was 20, after graduating from the STASI training school.

They were waiting to conduct an interview. Honor was removing the last remnant of blow from her nostrils with her long, chrome-painted pinkie fingernail, when a flash of white entered the room. Doctor Hope strode in and took a seat at the table.

The lighting in the executive boardroom on the top floor of Oceana SSD Headquarters was subdued. The tense atmosphere could have been cut with a knife. Hope wasn't happy about being there.

Standing at the head of the table like an overgrown raven, Honor was engrossed in a report and didn't look up to acknowledge Hope's entrance. Honor's jealousy of the younger, smarter and infinitely more attractive woman opposite caused her Eastern European accent to become even more conspicuous. "Doktor Hope, Agent Karzoff and I haff read your report and ve totally disagree wiz your doltish attitude to zer problem at hand."

With daggers in her eyes, Hope glared over her glasses at Honor and snarled: "You have the attitude problem Honor. Black Alice, the man in question, is a peace activist. He—"

Honor cut her off. "I don't care for your scientific opinion," she sneered.

"What would you know of a scientific opinion?" snapped Hope. "Come to think of it, what would you know about anything?"

"Ve cannot legislate for feelings, Doktor," Honor countered, facetiously. With a flash of her dark eyes, she signalled Karzoff to add his sentiments.

He chose a more passive approach. "Doctor Hope," he started with his slight Teutonic accent. "We all have a job to do, and it is not up to us to question our orders. You see, the man is a rebel ... and rebels must be eliminated. No single person is bigger than the Oceana government — and that goes for you too!" He suddenly realized he was pounding his fists on the table and froze as thunder resounded outside, providing punctuation to his action. Karzoff was easily overcome by excitement; it brought out the neo-Nazi in him.

The rapidly-developing storm brewing outside had announced itself with intermittent flashes of lightning, followed by rolling thunder. Hope knew that the time disparity between lightning and thunder in seconds roughly equated to how far away the storm was: for every five second interval the storm would be one mile away. She'd automatically calculated that this one was about four miles away. She removed her glasses and spoke emphatically. "Really? Well consider yourself informed: no-one is about to use our experiment on a human subject. No-one."

Honor fractionally curled the left of a perfect upper lip in the start of a carefully-constructed sneer. She learned forward and placed a document on the table in front of Hope. "Vell, zat is vere you are wrong, Hope," she hissed. "Doktor Secta has given his permission. So, how does zat affect your moral compass, huh?" Confident she had the scientist exactly where she wanted her, she fired Karzoff a smug smirk.

Hope read the document. Shocked by its contents, she angrily screwed it into a ball and hurled it at Honor. "I can't believe he'd sell out to you vultures!"

Honor bristled, and snapped back: "Any rebel is a threat to Oceana security!"

"You and your disciples of death are the only threat to security I can see around here," said Hope.

"You'd better be careful, doktor," snarled Honor. "Or you might meet zer same fate as Black Alice."

"Cut the nonsense, Hope," said Karzoff, sharply, cutting Honor off before she admitted something she shouldn't. "You are here either to pledge your loyalty to the project, or to hand in your resignation."

Hope rose abruptly from her chair and strongly but calmly said: "Then I'll continue my work elsewhere."

Honor sat down and leaned back in her chair pleased with herself. She added, nonchalantly: "Good ... no great loss."

Hope eyeballed the pair and snarled: "I don't envy the person with the job of picking up the pieces of the world after you cokeheads have finished with it." She spun on her heel and stormed out of the room.

"How fucking dramatic," Honor purred at Karzoff, content with the outcome. "Best we prepare, our visitor will be here soon."

The sound of a chanting crowd filtered in from outside. Honor got up from the table and strode over to one of the oval windows. She peered down to the street, forty floors below.

"Ah, vhat a night Karzoff. Look at zose idiots down zere ... another rally zat vill undoubtedly result in a riot." She had heard the voices of anti-nuclear protestors, chanting while marching: 'One two three four we don't want no nuclear war, five six seven eight, we don't want to radiate!'

Karzoff joined her at the window and looked down at the seething crowd. "They're probably on their way to the rally against the American nuclear submarine. It arrives in the harbour tonight?"

"Oh, zey zink zey are bigger than us, but look how small zey are," sneered Honor. "And I vill bring zem to an end." She turned sharply from the window and added: "Zat rat race down there... vot vould zey know? All zey do is protest! Zey vould protest against anyzing, as long as it vas anti-establishment. Zat is precisely vy ve haff orders to put a stop to zer likes of zis rock rebel, zis leader of zose morons, zis Black Alice. Oceana, now zat it has been joined by South Africa, cannot remain nuclear-free. It needs security, and must be armed. So, ve have our orders to break them."

She left Karzoff standing at the window, staring down in disbelief. "South Africa? ... That's news to me." Honor flopped into a swivel chair behind Karzoff and swung around to stare blankly at the back of his balding head. "It vill be announced in zer media tomorrow."

Still staring at the sea of moving people and lights below, Karzoff mumbled to himself: "That's sure to incite a riot ... Maybe even ... revolution!"

Alice could only agree with En-Ki. "Now I get your point. But hey, I know Hope is my ally."

"There is more, but first to continue with your passage to the interview."

Fed up Alice said, "If you must."

CHAPTER 8
JUNGLE BAR

HOPE EXITED THE main entrance of Oceana Towers with its Gothic spires, flying buttresses and sandstone staircase flanked by gruesomely-fanged and clawed gargoyles. She was enraged by the inquisition to which agents Honor and Karzoff had subjected her. Questions remained in her mind about why her brother had signed the edict without discussing it with her, and what Honor had been about to say concerning Black Alice. What could possibly be such a big deal that it forced Karzoff, her junior, to cut her off so abruptly?

Lightning cracked and thunder rumbled, confirming a storm was upon her, literally as well as figuratively. In a hurry to catch the streetlights in time to cross, she was stopped by a pre-recorded voice loudly broadcasting the warning: Acid rain! Acid rain! Acid rain!

She glanced up through a gap in the skyscrapers at the ominous clouds swirling in the night sky. Heeding the warning, she withdrew a credit card-sized device from her inside coat pocket and punched in a code. A glowing force field surrounded her, protecting her from the acid rain. She knew the rain would only last a few minutes, but she still needed to protect herself against the corrosive crystalline sulphuric acid.

It fell as hail from the heavily polluted clouds, leaving thin columns of smoke rising from sizzling scorch-marks on the pavement.

G. L. Keady

The increasing ambient temperatures from carbon omissions had accelerated the impact of climate change, and triggered the massive atmospheric increase in sulphur dioxide and nitrogen oxide gases, which react with water molecules to form acids. Even though the scientific community had warned Oceana to reduce emissions or suffer the consequences, the caution had been mostly ignored. As a result, acid rain had become a serious health issue.

The crossing light blinked red at Hope and monotonously repeated: Don't walk – Seek Cover. The device had her protected, so she ignored the warning and stepped onto the crossing, only to be immediately stopped in her tracks by the loud screech of skidding tyres. The sound snapped her out of her torpor, and she saw a Harley Davidson skidding to a halt, with its bulky rider battling to avoid hitting her. It stopped only a metre away. She looked up at the big, hairy, tattooed and muscular biker, totally embarrassed, and smiled apologetically.

He glared menacingly at her over his wrap-around sunglasses. The smoke rising from his leather jacket and headgear from the burning acid rain made him look demonic.

"I'm sorry mister … I … I … wasn't thinking," she pleaded.

His formidable bearded face softened as he realised she had been spooked by the incident.

A car stopped behind the biker, and the driver impatiently sat on his horn. A broad smirk of distaste broke across the biker's battle-scarred face, and he flipped the driver the bird. That irritated the man even more, and he stayed sitting on the horn, to the irritation of both Hope and the biker.

Finally the driver angrily swerved his car out to draw up beside the bike. Without even looking at him, the biker unsheathed a blade from his belt, and stabbed it into the front fender of the car.

The driver lowered his window and yelled angrily: "Hey, who the hell do you think you are, punk?"

The biker simply revved his engine, drowning out the irate driver, saluted Hope, and rode off.

She watched him ride away, relieved that there were still decent people left in what she felt was an unforgiving world. She hurried across the road, leaving the irritated driver yelling abuse after her.

Having avoided the acid rain Alice was strolling the empty city street activating his cell phone for the first time in over a week, when a loud roar distracted him. He looked up at the Harley Heritage Softail speeding past and grinned. He could relate to the biker's freedom. How he would love to drop everything, jump on a Harley and ride off into the sunset.

"All right!" he exclaimed, under his breath.

The pedestrian light he'd stopped at had turned green, so he stepped off the kerb. After a few steps, he looked up sharply — there was an EV silently hurtling towards him. He stood his ground in the middle of the road and, like a bullfighter dodging a marauding bull, calmly stepped aside to let the car pass. Dirty on the careless driver, he yelled at the top of his voice: "Arsehole!" His heart was pumping to the max, his blood pressure was skyrocketing — he felt another red mist coming on. Everything around him wavered. An ugly, high-pitched whistle started in his ears. He took deep breaths and shut his eyes, trying to regain equilibrium. Suddenly the tinnitus stopped and his balance returned. He opened his eyes and was shocked to find he had adopted a 'Dirty Harry' stance, holding a .44 Magnum revolver in both hands, aimed at the car that had almost hit him. He fired off four shots, and each bullet found its target. The car exploded into flames and, with a screech of smoking tyres, broadsided to a halt. The driver's side door flew open and the driver dived out onto the road. Alice took aim. His target was only fifteen metres away. Boom — he fired. The recoil threw his extended arms upward.

The driver's head exploded with a spray of blood and brain matter. He collapsed onto the road, dead as a doornail. Alice was bumped from behind, and flinched. It was a protestor in a hurry to catch up with the rally. The knock snapped Alice out of his reverie. There was no .44 Magnum in his grip, only an extended index finger and a raised thumb, like a kid playing cowboys and Indians. There was no car on fire or blown-away driver in a pool of blood. It had been another hallucination, like the one he'd experienced at the hospital the night of Stain's death. He wondered if he was losing his mind, then recalled the words of one of his songs: Organic Panic. He continued his journey, singing the words quietly to himself.

> "Your sanity's threatened by a world
> That's sinking around your feet
> You got to drag yourself up
> After being sucked down
> But the water's too deep
> You're only a pawn in a game
> But you try to stay free
> Someone turn on the light
> To make tomorrow bright
> For you and me"

The one toke of dope he'd had at the party had all but worn off, as had the Bliss. Suddenly he became aware of a presence nearby and took a furtive glance over his shoulder. A dude had stopped a short distance from him and was gazing innocently up at a small patch of sky wedged between the surrounding dark shadowy skyscrapers. He was being tailed again.

"That cop looks more like a cop than a cop does," Alice snarled to himself, and continued walking. When he rounded a corner, a hobo stepped out from a dark alcove, holding out a dirty hand and saying: "Give us ten dollars for a sandwich mate?"

"Depends what's in it!" Alice laughed, but flipped the old boy a ten dollar coin.

Continuing along the otherwise empty street, he saw a holographic news readout displayed on the awning of a nearby building, which read: Illegal demonstration against US nuke sub expected. Citizens advised to stay clear. Government issues arrest warning to demonstrators. Alice snarled at the news.

He was outside his destination — not Oceana SSD Headquarters, but the Octagon Jungle Bar. Just as he was about to enter, his cell phone rang. He checked the ID before answering. It was his manager, Wilson Stanley.

"Yeah Wilson, what do you want?" said Alice, derisively.

"Alice, I haven't heard from you since Stain..."

Alice cut him off unceremoniously: "Yeah, yeah, yeah, I'm alright, so?"

About thirty metres behind, Alice caught a glance of the guy tailing him. He watched him quickly slip into an alcove between two buildings, stupidly assuming he was out of sight.

"I just got a call from Oceana SSD," Wilson said. "They're nervous you won't make it to your appointment with Senior Inspector Honor."

"Stuff 'em, and stuff you too, what are you, their patsy or something?" Alice was growling into the phone. "Last time I heard from you it was to tell me to shut my mouth about the Octagon."

"But Alice ... I..."

"Now you shut your mouth ... Imagine you telling me, the mug who pays your wages, to shut my mouth," Alice thundered.

"Alice, they threatened me!" Wilson said nervously.

"They threatened you? Well, let me tell you, dude, someone threatened me that night too. I got a text telling me, just like you did, to stop fronting for the Octagon. Seems a bit coincidental, two people in the one night — and then what happens? Stain dies!"

"She died from an overdose of smack, Alice, you know that."

"No way, pal. She was murdered."

"You're crazy," wavered Stanley. "The government wouldn't have anything to do with something that!"

"Am I? Am I? Then why were you threatened? Why was I threatened? Why am I being summoned to a meeting with bloody Nazi agents? You tell me!"

"Because the President doesn't want to risk international embarrassment by massive protests against the Yank submarine, so he's set the dogs on you," cried the manager's voice. "There are riots starting everywhere Alice, suicide bombers, they think you're behind it all!"

"Yeah, and just how do you know that?"

"Because as far as the government is concerned you're public enemy number one and they don't know how to deal with you!"

"Speaks volumes about your loyalty ... Alright, cop this: numero uno here says stuff them!"

"Don't be stupid Alice. Look, just drop the ferry protest tonight, it's just not worth it, take my advice. There's no use bucking the system, the government is bigger than you. You've got a hit record ... you want to jeopardise your career?"

"There's only one answer to that ... stuff you too!"

"Alice, this isn't like you ... you're not yourself, you've got PTSD or something. I'm giving you what you pay me for, career advice."

"Yeah, well not any more you ain't. Goodbye, Wilson."

"Alice, it's a warning you can't ignore ... you..."

"Good bye!" screamed Alice, terminating the call. He was over taking crap from people who thought they knew better than him. Never again was he going to be railroaded by anyone, and that included his manager, the President of Oceana and this Senior Inspector Honor.

As Alice stalked like an angry lion into the mall corridor leading to the club, his phone rang again. The ID showed his manager ringing back. Spotting a bin, he went over to it, flipped open his phone, pulled out the sim and tossed the phone in the bin. It was an act of defiance, symbolizing his desire to break free from his previous existence and start anew. He was on a mission to clean up his life and rid it of wankers. Wilson was a wimp as well as a wanker, so he was the first to go.

Feeling relieved, Alice made his way to a door marked 'Jungle Bar'. Plastered on the wall beside it was a poster of the featured band that night: Units. He turned his head sharply and caught his tail ducking out of sight at the club entrance. It was a fairly amateurish attempt to shadow him. He gave the secret knock. After a moment the door opened to reveal a bouncer built like a brick shit-house. Big Joe immediately recognised Alice, stepped aside and ushered him into the club.

"Thanks Joe. Packed house, eh?"

"Yeah, they'll all be on the ferry protest later tonight," said Joe, gruffly.

CHAPTER 9
FIGHTING FOR YOU

T HE JUNGLE BAR was more crowded than Alice had expected. Most of the punters had been at the street rally. For others, it was a regular watering hole. Another reason for the crowd was unemployment: it was at its highest level ever, and an additional cause of public angst and civil unrest. Most of the punters there were on the dole.

The bar could have been designed by the creators of Tarzan, working with a lesser budget but a greater sense of vulgar absurdity. Alice derived a childish delight in its tasteless layering of cargo-cult bamboo and plastic tropical foliage, the simulated hides of exotic animals, and the garishly coloured, concealed mood lighting. Overhead wheeled wooden fans with brass fittings, and digital flaming torches burned in half a dozen braziers along the bar, from which of course no alcohol was allowed to be served. A cultish mishmash of African carvings, Easter Island heads, first nation Australian wooden carved statues and Polynesian Tiki gods stared down from the walls, and there was such an abundance of palms and exotic plants it would have qualified as a small rainforest. At the far end of the room was a stage with four, fold-back speakers at the front, flanked by a small front-of-house PA. Even though it was by definition an ersatz jungle, for members of the Octagon Peace Movement, it was sanctuary.

Studying the room from the entrance Alice suffered a twinge of something akin to stage fright. What am I doing here, and why? He wasn't feeling quite right, not himself, giddy. He hoped it wasn't one of those strange turns he'd been having: a trippy hallucination, LSD flash or whatever the stuff it was. But then his self-control reasserted itself as he remembered he was here to see his mates.

Bustling through the crowd he was recognized with plenty of pats on the back. All around him, amid the African tribal music and the general chatter, he could hear cries of: that's Alice! ... Hey Alice! There was no doubting his popularity. He acknowledged them with a nod and a grunt.

As Alice approached the backstage entrance curtain, the zebra painted backdrop on the stage rippled, and to Alice's surprise a naked dancer appeared. She had been camouflaged by zebra body paint, and was now dancing to a wild African rhythm juggled by the DJ. When the crowd failed to react to her it confirmed to Alice that the youth of the day were too spoilt to appreciate her talent.

Mumbling condemningly: "Wouldn't know if your arses were on fire. What a bloody waste of talent," Alice went through the curtain backstage where he found the members of Units. They were sitting on speaker cabinets and instrument cases, preparing to go on stage.

Alice entered and roared: "Hey, Units! Happening!"

The leader of the band and Alice's best mate, Mal Function, went quickly to Alice with his big muscular arms opened wide. "Hey, the main man. Hangin? We've missed you, Al." They enacted the Octagon loyalty greeting, chanting "Oct-a-gon!" in unison with mirrored body movements that ended with three hip pumps ... all good fun.

Wearing only a G-string, Mal was halfway through putting on his stage make-up. A tall, handsome guy with short-cropped blonde hair, it was obvious from his tattooed physique he wasn't the sort of bloke to take crap from anyone. He was lean, fit and built like a kickboxer. Alice slapped him affectionately on the back.

"Function, you turd," he joked. "All's well, all's well. Looks like your muscles have atrophied, need a top-up on the 'roids mate?" Alice nodded to the other two band members. "Red, Blue."

Blue doubled as the drummer for Alice's band, while Red was the bass player of the Units. He was dressed in red coveralls.

"Still takin' ugly pills Red, I see," Alice went on. "Well, I'm on my way to see the law!"

Red and Blue immediately jumped up and comically stretched their hands up against the wall posing for a pat down. Function's mood, on the other hand, changed to deadly serious. He fronted Alice. "The law?" he asked. "You're crazy man. They'll buttbang yer."

Alice chuckled. "Alright, alright, I know. So you're asking: 'what's Alice doing mixin' with the long arm?' Well, this little black duck doesn't even know what the mongrels want."

Before anyone could get another word in, the stage manager's head appeared around the curtain and called out, "G'day Alice ... Mal, guys? Units, you're on!" The head withdrew. Red and Blue filed past Alice on their way to the stage. "Bup bup, Alice", said Red, in his native indigenous Australian tongue. "Bup bup, Red," Alice replied, as he took a cigarette from a pack and lit up. Mal turned, ready to hit the stage, and snatched the cigarette out of Alice's mouth. He took a drag then stamped it out on the floor.

"Hey!" Alice grumbled in protest.

"I thought you'd quit?"

"I was just keeping in practice in case I start up again."

Both laughed.

"Mate, I'm sorry about Stain. Must've been terrible, think she'd know better than to OD," Mal said.

"Mate, it wasn't the smack that got her ... She was killed in hospital."

Mal's jaw dropped in surprise. "What makes you think that, man?"

"She was fine when the medics picked her up from my gaff. But before then, after the gig that night, I got an anonymous threat that something bad would happen if I didn't pull out of the Octagon."

Mal's face paled. He sat on the edge of a speaker cabinet, running his fingers through his short hair, mind blown. "Hell, mate..." he breathed. "Who do you reckon ... Wait, Oceana SSD. Mate, how the stuff can you walk into their trap knowing this?"

"The only way I can find out if they murdered her is to front them," replied Alice, softly, adding: "I need to put it to bed."

"You're a braver man than I," said Mal, emphatically. "We get the truth we seek mate, but hey, these pricks have a dud reputation. What makes you think it's not a set-up to take you out?"

"I don't see how I can get answers any other way mate," said Alice. "If I can prove these bastards did her in, I'll use it in every way I can to bring them down."

Mal saw the evil look in his friend's eye. He'd known Alice long enough to understand when he meant business. But he also knew what Alice was up against, and didn't like the odds.

"There's gotta be a better way mate," he implored.

"There isn't," said Alice. "I've thought it through. I've gotta front them, that's it. End of story."

Mal grinned, "Mate, a bit of diplomacy would go a long way. I hope it's not the end of the story..." Mal paused and eyeballed Alice worriedly. "I'm not convinced."

"You worry too much," Alice said, with a deprecating chuckle. "You'd make a good president Mal."

"Yeah right, that'd be the day. I can see it now Mal Function for president. Ha! It'd be different if he could be voted out mate, but he changed the law so that can't happen. Look, you're a famous dude, a rockstar, with influence, you can't risk it Al ... Mate, I don't buy this making a hologram of your crap talked about in the press."

The sound of Blue testing his drums on stage got Mal back on his feet.

"Stay for the gig Al, stuff the heat."

"Nar mate, I'm going to meet the arm... Gotta put it to bed. If I don't come back, send flowers. Look mate, you're on. Time to get up on stage and sing ... if you can call it that."

"Ahhhhh!" Mal screeched an off-key operatic note, appreciating the jibe.

"I'll catch you later." Alice gave him an affectionate slap on the shoulder.

Mal stopped at the curtain, turned and walked slowly back to Alice, a concerned look on his face. "Seriously Al, be careful," he said. "I don't like you mixing it with the law. You know what they're saying about that girl who landed on the official and killed him. They're blaming us. They know we don't have a permit for the protest tonight, and if they threatened you before, if they had anything to do with what happened to Stain, there's no telling what they might do when they get their clutches on you."

Alice took hold of his arm and ushered him towards the curtain. "We don't need a permit for a bloody harbour cruise, right? Don't worry about me mate." He stared his friend in the eyes. "I'll be okay. Trust me."

Mal smiled. "I trust you buddy, just don't trust them ... count yer fingers after you shake hands with 'em, won't ya?" With a grave expression he added: "All jokes aside ... be bloody careful mate."

They paused for a moment with eyes locked, as though it might be the last time they'd ever meet. Then Alice broke the solemn moment. He whipped the 8-ball out of his pocket and tossed it up. Before he could catch it, Mal snapped it out of the air. He disappeared through the curtain with the 8-ball, leaving Alice blinking in surprise. Suddenly, Mal's head reappeared through the curtain. "Hey Al," he yelled, and threw the 8-ball. "See you on the ferry tonight!"

Alice caught the ball, staring at it like it was about to explode. His hand began to tremble. A vision of a cobwebbed haze came over his mind, and he could only vaguely hear Mal's voice on the other side of the curtain, singing: "Tonight, tonight, we're ferrying tonight..."

His mind swirled in a kaleidoscope of mental images. The entire room suddenly distorted into something surreal, otherworldly. Stain was standing naked, covered in mud, holding her hands out to him, beckoning.

"Stain … What? You telling me you were murdered?" he muttered, trance-like. Then his mental screen flipped to the begging hobo, the ten-dollar coin revolving in the air … and then, once again his thoughts were projected into somewhere else entirely. A deathly silent darkness — a tinnitus-like whistle getting louder, and louder — then from out of the pitch black appeared a screaming horrific horned demon with bat wings and claws. Then silence and a shift to a dully-lit room. Protruding from a grey wall of cobwebs at its rear were chrome horns, gleaming among a swirl of dust and smoke. That deep demonic voice he'd heard at the hospital, resounding inside his head, saying: "The Shine!"

A loud chord from the Units onstage snapped him back to reality. He took a deep breath, wondering when, or if, these horrendous hallucinations would end. He was the kind of bloke that only felt comfortable in total control of himself. Nevertheless, he had to ignore it and get on with what he had to do. He went to the backstage door, pulled down the brim of his Fedora, drew his coat closed and turned up the collar, ready to take on the cold night air. Pushing open the door, he was almost blown over by a strong gust of icy wind. With his head down, he powered his way against the wind into the dark alley. As he headed along the footpath to the main street, he could hear the thump of Red's bass guitar, and Mal's voice singing Fighting for You. It was one of his songs, and it made him smile. Mal was singing it for him to hear, the lyrics relevant to the conversation they'd just had.

The music faded in his wake into the sound of his own lonely footsteps echoing off the cold high-rise buildings walling the narrow laneway. He stopped at a street corner under a streetlamp, slipped a cigarette between his lips and lit up. With his profile shadowed by the brim of his hat, the light from the match illuminated his face. Holding the flame short of the cigarette he concentrated on the faint sound of approaching footsteps. They suddenly stopped. It was his tail. Alice smirked knowingly and took a deep drag on the cigarette, inhaled, coughed and looked down at the butt with distaste. He flicked it angrily away. He'd quit some time back, but kept a packet in his pocket just in case: it was a hard habit to kick.

He continued to walk, listening to his tail's footsteps in time with his. Just to stir him up, he skipped once to break rhythm, then walked on. The two sets of footsteps were out of sync, and he heard his tail skip to get in time. In a cynical laugh, a puff of steam fired from Alice's nostrils like dragon's breath. He came out of the alley and looked around. To him, that night, the city was strangely beautiful. The darkness successfully concealed the corruption, the crime and the misery that lurked behind the sparkling lights.

CHAPTER 10
MR SYSTEM

T HREE CITY BLOCKS from Alice, Doctor Hope's footsteps were echoing off the tiled tunnel leading to the Domain moving footway. She was headed for one of the underground entrances to subterranean Oceana Level 7. There were secret entrances to Oceana facilities all over the city. This one was specific to the underground laboratories.

She passed a sign on the wall warning:

BEWARE OF MUGGERS

She stepped onto the moving footway that mechanically transported her past the graffiti-covered walls. Suddenly, she was aware of the sound of someone approaching her from behind. A sixth sense told her to throw out an arm, and as she did, it flattened an oncoming mugger. He crashed, a tangled mess of roller skates and limbs, onto the wide barrier between the two moving footways. Moving as fast as her legs could carry her, Hope frantically raced along the footway to escape her attacker.

The mugger hauled himself to his feet, pulled a knife from his belt, gripped it between his teeth and skated off in pursuit of his prey.

Hope leapt from the end of the footway at a blistering pace, because the travelator had almost doubled her speed. She bounced off a wall, regained her balance and raced into a dimly-lit tunnel at panic speed, finally arriving, out of breath, in an old, nondescript dusty foyer. She stopped at the grille of an antique elevator and pressed the call button incessantly, glancing back over her shoulder for any sign of her assailant.

"Come on! Come on!" she growled, impatiently at the elevator.

The ominous rumbling of the approaching skates was building to a crescendo. The mugger skated up behind her, screeched to a halt, whipped the knife from between his teeth and held it up threateningly. Resigned to taking him out, Hope swivelled to face him. Neither said a word.

Wearing coveralls and with a brown nylon stocking stretched over his head, the mugger's face appeared contorted, making him even more intimidating. The dim light from the moving footway glinted off the finely-honed blade in his hand. But Hope was no slouch — she'd had years of close combat training.

Holding her breath, Hope waited for the mugger to make the first move. He lunged forward with the knife. She deftly transferred her weight and, moving with lightning speed, grabbed the weapon arm and savagely kicked him in the groin. With a firm grip on his arm she transferred her weight again, turning him to face away from her and using her other hand to grip the back of his head and hammer him face-first, hard, into the tiled wall. The force of the blow knocked him out, and the knife dropped from his limp hand. She released her grip and he slid down the wall, leaving a trail of blood from his shattered nose.

A loud clunk announced the arrival of the elevator. Hope spun on her heel and raced for it, pulled open the grille, stepped inside and slammed it shut. She pulled a coded card from her top pocket and slid it into the slot on the security module. The elevator was ancient, but its operating mechanism had been modernised. She inserted her index finger into the module for fingerprint recognition. A green light flashed, and a screen indicated she had been approved access to the 7th floor sub-basement. She withdrew her card from the device and was just taking a deep breath when she was shocked by a loud bang — the mugger had recovered and grabbed the grille, and was now glaring at her with a hideous expression on his blood-drenched, stockinged face.

The elevator jerked and began its descent. She turned her back on the mugger, breathing heavily and with her hand over her pounding heart. Her own tired reflection looked back at her from a small, tarnished mirror mounted just above the control module. "What a day!" she sighed.

The Bridge Street entrance to Oceana SSD headquarters opened onto a tastefully old-world, marble-walled atrium. Three elevators had architraves and doors of shining brass, above which old-school floor indicators resembled brass clocks. Waiting by the elevator doors, five men dressed in identical Government-issue black suits stood in line, a pair flanking each of the first two elevators, and a single man beside the third.

Alice cruised into the atrium. He knew he was running late but didn't give a shit. He glared with contempt at the men lined up, knowing damned well they were agents. They remained steadfast, facing the elevator doors, ignoring him. The agent who had been following him arrived and fell into line opposite the single agent at the third elevator.

Nonchalantly, Alice shot him a knowing glare, unimpressed by the pretentious Oceana lobby and the poorly-disguised agents. All six of them looked up in unison at the floor indicator, wondering which of the three elevators would be first to arrive. Then, like clockwork, they turned their heads and faced Alice, each with a repugnant stare.

Alice leered at them like they were a gaggle of objectionable monsters. They all appeared to have the same face. The surreal nature of what he was seeing struck him. Once again, he felt that illusory veil overcoming his senses, he was losing self-control. He reached to his inside coat pocket and withdrew a collapsible MAC-10 machine pistol, unfolded it like a trained mercenary, palmed the magazine into place, and sprayed the agents with bullets. The roar of the automatic weapon echoed in the narrow confines of the marbled lobby. Each agent was catapulted violently backwards by the impact of the high-velocity bullets. Blood spattered on the elevator doors and the white marble walls. Smoke from the carbine swirled in the lobby, and the floor had become a scarlet river of blood, the dying victims contorted on it in silent agony as the resounding thunder of the blasts died away. Alice stood amidst the haze with the formidable black carbine rested on his shoulder, smoke drifting from its barrel. He glared at his victims and grinned: killing them had been a total turn-on.

A loud ding snapped him out of his violent fantasy. The elevator door opened, revealing a mahogany-panelled interior with polished brass fittings. Alice stepped inside, followed by the men he'd mentally killed.

Hope entered a long, dimly-lit, grey-walled corridor and walked past a sign that read:

LEVEL 7 - LABS 6-12 - SECURITY ZONE RED

She had walked this corridor countless times since joining Oceana HQ, but she couldn't help thinking this time would be the last. The truth was that she had no regrets about resigning her post. She had lost faith in her employers, and her sympathies now lay with the Octagon. In her opinion, the integrity of the government had been compromised, with power being granted to idiots the likes of Honor and Karzoff.

She continued along the corridor until she came to Lab 7, and inserted her ID card into the security module at the side of the metal door. A servomotor sounded as it slid open and she entered.

Lurking in a far dark corner of the well-equipped lab, the ominous figure of a man dressed in a long black lab coat was perched on a stool. He was holding a test tube up to the light and studying its contents. He put it down and stood up.

Doctor Secta was a really weird dude. Eccentric, with his head razor-cut into a widow's peak and a long black ponytail from the crown of his head to the middle of his back. Androgynous looking, six feet four and skinny, he had a sharp wit and a matching tongue. Secta was sarcastic, narcissistic and known for his devilish sense of humour, but despite those traits the genius of the man couldn't be denied. He was revered by the international scientific community for his brilliance, and considered a national treasure by the President of Oceana. His pioneering inventions, like Nanobot blood sweepers and mastoid communications implants, had brought in billions in foreign revenue. He was a world leader in cybergenetics and holographic particle matter transfer. He was also a valued member of the Transhumanism movement, which was aiming to transform the human condition by developing sophisticated technologies to enhance human intellect and physiology.

Secta had published a scientific paper on transhumanism while at university. His hypotheses was that the rapid progress of communication technology meant one day everyone would have a brainwave receiver in their ear, with which they could receive and convey their thoughts. His recent invention of the mastoid communication implant was seen as a revolutionary step towards this vision. He had also recently developed an android guard, built using living human tissue. It was still at an experimental stage, but took the advancement of artificial intelligence to another level. Secta believed implicitly in the future vision of a new intelligent species, into which humanity will ultimately evolve.

"Hope! I've done it, I can create a race of beings!" he exclaimed as his sister entered the room. "The serum is stabilized — think of it Hope, my own race … I've done it Hope … I mean we've done it, of course…"

Hope was livid. "You've sold out, Secta!" she yelled. "Don't try to deny it dear brother, that bitch Honor filled me in."

"I don't know what you're talking about," Secta said, coolly. "And it doesn't matter, Hope. I've already injected myself with longevity serum. I'm going to live forever."

Hope's anger boiled over. "I really don't care, Secta," she snarled. "You might live forever, but it will be without me…"

Perturbed by her attack, he paused, then tried another tack. "Don't be like that, little sister," he said, calmingly. "You know how important our work is. With the serum stabilized, we've achieved our goal … Look," he added, holding out his hand. "No trembling … I injected it over an hour ago, and there have been no side-effects. Forget the politics — we're scientists, and this is a cutting-edge result."

Secta was right in one thing: the results were significant. Together, they had been working on a formula to prolong cell life, a switch to alter DNA. Instead of cells dying, they revitalised. It had the potential to extend human life by hundreds of years, allowing subjects, in theory, to continue their important works for the betterment of mankind. Secta believes that their work should take precedence over the matter that had incensed Hope, but that wasn't how she was seeing it.

Infuriated, she snarled: "Enough of your sanctimonious crap, Secta! You and I both know I'm not talking about the serum. I'm talking about what you're trying to avoid … Black Alice!"

"Oh, him," said Secta, dismissively. "Look, just think of him as another experiment, Hope. You're being far too sensitive. You know there's no place for empathy in science."

"I can't think of him as a lab rat," snapped Hope. "I have my principles. As scientists, especially as scientists, we shouldn't lose our moral compass. You've committed to doing just that. Anyhow," she spat, "You'll be working without me. I've resigned from the project, and I'm joining the Octagon peace movement."

"What?" he yelled, in disbelief. "How can you leave now, after all I've have done for you?" He grabbed Hope's arm. "I need you to monitor me," he pleaded. "The serum…"

Hope tugged her arm angrily out of his grip, and strode defiantly to the door, where she stopped. For a moment, Secta hoped she was having second thoughts. But she turned sharply to face him, and with daggers in her eyes said: "Maybe you'll be your own victim. I hope you and your new race will be happy in your own private hell!" She stormed out of the lab.

"Octagon peace movement, damned undisciplined rabble of tree huggers…" growled Secta. "You'll pay for this Hope. Mark my words little sister. Mark. My. Words."

The Oceana SSD boardroom receptionist's headgear was attached by a series of fibre optic leads to a voca-phone internal intercom system. This routed calls via the mastoid implant communications intranet to all government employees who had been granted security clearance and linked to the network. Secta had developed the system, which was still in its infancy and experimental. The implant in the mastoid bone behind the ear was the size of a grain of rice, and allowed the system to connect directly to implanted peoples' brains. It melded with the nervous system in a similar way to an AI bionic limb control unit, or cochlear hearing implant. With a combined GPS and data signal facilitated by a government satellite, it was intended ultimately to replace telephones and other communications devices, not only for government workers but also, eventually, for the entire population of the world.

Alice cruised out of the elevator and up to the receptionist, coming to a halt by sitting playfully on the edge of her desk.

"Yes sir, can I help you?" she said, shocked.

"I have an appointment with Inspector Honor," he said.

She blushed and stammered into the head mike of the voca-phone. "Senior Inspector H-Honor to reception, please."

She was aware that the rock idol Black Alice was scheduled for an appointment, but the reality of having him sitting on the edge of her desk was overwhelming.

Alice turned to see the spectre of Honor standing like a vulture at the base of a staircase, which led to a mezzanine floor not serviced by the elevator.

"Senior Inspector Fanny Honor," Honor snarled, looking down her own nose at him. "Please follow me."

Alice had anticipated her neo-Nazi attitude loathing for him and everything he stood for.

It was a brave move walking into the fascist, corrupt den of the SSD, totally ignorant of why he had been summoned. But he was hell-bent on determining whether they had murdered Stain. To that end, he was prepared to take the risk. Truth be known, Alice sometimes felt that his fame as a public figure would protect him against the likes of the SSD, that he was, almost, invincible. Perhaps naively, he was convinced they wouldn't dare harm him.

Honor marched pompously up the wooden staircase to the top floor. Alice slid off the desk and followed.

He tailed Honor into a long, rectangular room at the top of the staircase. It had a low ceiling and dappled grey walls with a horizontal red insignia line all the way round the room, punctuated on the two long walls by a line of tall oval windows. In the centre of the room a long black boardroom table was surrounded by chairs. Seated at one of them was Karzoff with his blaze of short red hair, grinning at Alice like a groupie.

Honor stopped at the head of the table and barked like a school headmistress: "Take a seat, Mr Alice."

When Alice hesitated, Karzoff echoed her, though more courteously: "Yes, please take a seat Alice."

Alice, not one for taking orders of any kind, grunted. He took the 8-ball out of his pocket and bounced it up and down in his hand.

CHAPTER 11
TIME FLUX

HONOR COULD FEEL the tension in the air. She sat down and crossed her legs in an effort to appear relaxed. They had orders to use whatever means at their disposal to eliminate Alice, but because of his high public profile, it was crucial for them to do it in a manner that appeared to be an accident.

The objective was to con Alice into participating in a test to generate a lifelike hologram of him. The deception was designed to demonstrate to the public the government's willingness to bridge the gap between the people and the bureaucracy. The head of the Oceana department of science, Dr Secta, with his sister, Dr Hope, had invented the holographic process. Though it was still very much experimental, Secta had agreed to use the procedure to eliminate Alice, after being pressured by his superiors. It would look like an unfortunate accident and accepted as such, because such things sometimes happen. It was up to Honor and Karzoff to somehow convince Alice to participate in the process.

Alice found both of them repugnant. In his book, they were the kind who wielded power without being able to enforce it. In his mind's eye, he visualized them as a pair of mouths on sticks. He pulled out the chair at the far end of the table, figuring he'd keep as much distance between them as possible, and sat down.

"Zo, Black Alice, you are a man of peace, leader of zer Octagon Movement, organiser of zer rallies against visiting vessels, as vell as being a rock star," said Honor, with cynicism in her tone. "A profiteering prophet, perhaps?"

Alice didn't like her or her ridiculous accent, and made it obvious with a scornful chuckle. "I haven't got time for you to rehearse your comedy routine, Honor," he sneered. "I've got serious things to attend to." Her reaction was unanticipatedly shocking: she virtually exploded into a rage.

"Vot do you mean, you haven't got time?" she roared.

Alice, scowling at her with a single eyebrow raised, rasped: "Settle down, lady ... I'm not into violence."

That only fired her up more. She sprang to her feet and prowled over to him, stopping behind his chair and leaning in closely to whisper threateningly into his ear.

"Vell, mister, let me tell you, inside every solitary human are zer seeds of violence ... and you, sir," she eyeballed him, "are no exception!"

Alice stared back at her, "Yeah, yeah, yeah," he sighed. "But it's how you release that violence that counts." He stood up, still eyeballing her. "See this?" he growled, pointing at his head.

Confused, she peered at him through narrowed eyes, "Yes, vot of it?" Karzoff chimed in with: "A head, yes..."

"So vot?" Honor snarled dismissively.

Alice simply smirked. "A head. Not a warhead. I'm not as dangerous as that fucking sub sitting in our harbour with five million innocent people living around it. You dig?"

Karzoff chuckled. That didn't impress Honor. She scowled at him. Vexed by Alice's intransigence and refusal to be intimidated, she prowled the room, trying to subdue her temper.

"It seems your nihilistic comrades, such as Mowina Beetson, do not subscribe to your non-violent ideology," Karzoff offered in the meantime.

"I don't know any Mowina Beetson," said Alice brusquely. "Look, the idea is to scare people into their wits not out of them. By breaking the treaty, and that is what you've done, you'll start a revolution.

Believe me. I don't sit on my fat arse in an ivory tower pushing a pen around and making shit rules ... I actually exist among the citizens of this country, so I know what they're thinking."

"Vot a load of leftist, activist rubbish!" Honor spat. Sensing she was losing it, Karzoff intervened. In a calm tone, he said: "Mr Alice, there is no need for hostility. You were asked here so we could introduce you to a wonderful opportunity."

"I wasn't asked, buddy, I was ordered," Alice growled. "But go on."

Honor, sensing that Karzoff's more diplomatic approach was making ground, took her seat and kept quiet.

"We want to offer you a unique opportunity, the first of its kind," Karzoff continued. "We want to make a hologram of you." Alice's mouth dropped open, but Karzoff pressed on: "We believe it is time to build a bridge between the government and the people. A public figure like you could be that bridge. Of course, you cannot be everywhere at once. So the hologram would be used to help deliver mutually-agreed messaging to citizens across the country.

"We have new technology, invented by a world-renowned expert in the field, and our senior scientist, Dr Secta—"

Alice had heard enough and cut him off abruptly. "No thanks," he said, sardonically, folding his arms defiantly.

"At least give me a chance to explain," continued Karzoff, soothingly. "A hologram will also help you and your industry. With world economics in such bad shape, rock bands cannot tour anymore. But the hologram could do it for you, at very little cost. We are offering you a wonderful opportunity, entirely for free. Think of it, you will be the first, the trailblazer, the pioneer..."

Karzoff and Honor were confident that Alice would buy into their story. They knew he was passionate about communicating with the people. Plus, they thought, his over-inflated ego would love the idea of being the first artist in the world to tour holographically.

Instead, Alice smirked. "It's — er — somewhat out of character for you to offer me this kind of opportunity, considering my status as public enemy number one," he said. "Tell you what. Answer a question for me and I'll consider it."

Karzoff glanced at Honor for affirmation, got it. He continued, confident he was making progress. "Okay, ask your question," he said.

"Do either of you know a bloke called Drago?" Alice asked, slowly.

Karzoff and Honor exchanged a glance. Honor frowned, a signal to Karzoff not to divulge anything.

"Never heard of him. Why?" Karzoff replied.

"Because I reckon he had orders from you to murder my girlfriend."

"What, that is ridiculous! And quite an accusation! I ... I..." Karzoff stuttered to a halt.

"Zat is totally unvarranted," Honor put in. "It is not our policy to order assassinations. You cannot blame zer government for her death ... It vas an overdose."

"No it wasn't!" said Alice, too angry for the moment to wonder how Honor knew anything about the circumstances of Stain's death. "She was absolutely fine when the medics came for her. I should know, I revived her!"

"So you say. But zer medical report states othervise," said Honor, smugly.

Alice had a short fuse when it came to dealing with authority. It blew now.

"I can't cop anything that comes out of your gob Honor," he exploded. "You're so full of shit!"

"Ach, get on with zis, Karzoff," said Honor, through tight lips. "I have no time for zese limp-wristed melodramatics!" Karzoff drummed his fingers on the table, thinking, and said calmly: "Look Alice, we cannot answer your question any better than we have. We would like to help you, but we cannot. So, we can only ask you — will you participate in the test?"

The air was thick with tension. Alice had to contemplate his next move with great care. He wasn't satisfied with the answer he'd got. He left his chair and stalked over to Honor, leaning close and growling in her ear, as she'd done to him.

"You'll have to discuss this with my manager," he hissed. "He handles all my gigs. I'll tell him to give you a ring tomorrow."

It was a blow. Karzoff's attempt at diplomacy had clearly failed. Honor had no choice but to change tack.

"Sit!" she ordered, angrily.

Ignoring her rising rage, Alice continued to casually speak his mind. "Ah, politics and power ... you people are nothing but egotistical scam merchants. You were nothing in ordinary society, but now, with your fascist power, you're just career bloody narcissists. Yes, you have a say in the daily lives of the people, but you ritually abuse that privilege. The world needs to get rid of the likes of you. You're nothing but faceless wimps who send others to do your evil bidding."

"Hence zer reason you are here!" Honor returned, with interest.

Alice ignored her. Bending down to Karzoff's ear, he spoke too loudly, causing the little man to flinch. "Karzoff! I bet you're the sort of bloke that picks his undies out of his bum while he's talking to ya, huh?"

Karzoff stammered: "I – I - I do not know ... Look, look, all we need is a few minutes of your time for a simple demonstration of the hologram process..."

"I don't give a rat's arse for your simple demonstration, Karzoff!" Alice roared.

"You vere varned before and paid no attention, and look vot resulted!" Honor snarled.

Alice spun to face her. "Are you talking about that threatening text? Huh? Are you? You do know Drago don't you? Who gave the order? Who gave it?" He yelled viciously, his face turning scarlet with anger.

The explosion of emotion caused the room to shimmer. The walls began to bulge, he felt like he was about to be swallowed by them. He collapsed into the chair at the end of the table, a faraway, glazed look in his eyes, and muttered: "The Shine!"

Karzoff sat up taller in his chair. "The what?" he asked. "What did he say?"

Puzzled by Alice's strange antics, Honor climbed slowly out of her chair and cautiously made her way to him, wondering if he'd lost it completely.

"I think he said fine … yes, I am sure of it … he said fine," she said, slyly. "He is agreeing to ze hologram procedure…"

To Alice, her coarse voice was far in the distance, reverberating like an echo in a vast canyon. Again, he'd slipped into the room where those same cobwebbed chromed horns were protruding from what, this time, looked like the shape of a naked female laid out on an altar. "The Shine!" he groaned again, gazing into space, in a clear stupor.

Honor and Karzoff crept nearer. Karzoff put his monocle up to his eye and looked closely at him. "What the hell is he on?" he said. "Is he having some sort of fit?" asked Honor. "Is he out of his face, or off his tree, or votever people say? No matter, we can use zis. Ve have him where ve vant him. Quick, get on viz it."

A short time later Honor, Black Alice and Karzoff were in a dimly-lit underground corridor. Alice was still groggy and confused. The hallucinations were beginning to take a toll on him. At this point, he had no choice but to go along with them to the lab of Dr Secta. Somewhere in his addled mind, he was hoping that it would somehow buy him time to recover, so he could learn more about their complicity in Stain's death.

There were many entrances to the labyrinth of subterranean Oceana facilities under Sydney. Each entry point had individual security clearance and preference, with Honor and Karzoff having the highest. They were also privileged to the most direct access. They stopped at a sign on the wall, which read:

LEVEL 7, LABS 6-12, SECURITY ZONE RED

"What's this?" Alice managed to mumble. "Seven floors underground, some kind of secret fallout shelter?" But before he could get an answer he was distracted by the mechanical clunking of approaching heavy footsteps.

A massive seven-foot android confronted them. Its skin was fashioned from silver metallic fabric. It was built like a robotic version of Mr Universe, with huge muscular arms and strong athletic legs. But that's where the human elements ended. A big square head had no human facial features at all, just one big, round, electronic red eye, which constantly swept from side to side with metronomic precision.

Honor tried to ease the still-recovering Alice. They'd managed to get him this far, and didn't want him to freak out.

"It is an android," she said, calmly. She turned, faced it and ordered: "Honor clearance 2-4-D. It is one of Secta's prototypes," she added, to Alice.

The android spoke in a deep metallic monotone voice: "Did-not-compute-clearance-code."

It was clear her Eastern European accent had affected its comprehension.

Karzoff stepped up to the plate. "She said clearance code 2-4-D!"

"Did-not-compute-ten-seconds-and-evasive-action-will-be-taken," the android warned.

Alice figured this could go on all night. He pushed Karzoff out of the way and tried.

"They said 2-4-D, you dig, idiot?"

"2-4-D ... you-may-pass," the android confirmed, and backed against the wall, parking itself in an alcove.

Pleased with himself despite his groggy state, Alice cheekily said: "Anything else, dudes?"

Pissed that Alice had shown her up, Honor spun on her heel and strode off down the corridor. She called back caustically: "Follow me, rock star."

Alice followed her, Karzoff trailing behind.

Honor stopped at the door of Lab 7, swiped a metal card in the security module, then inserted her finger into the print recognition slot.

"Oh, yes," came a sexy female voice, offering comical clearance to the facility.

Honor stood back, a slightly embarrassed look on her sullen face. "Vun of Doctor Secta's little pranks ... only he would have programmed something zo distasteful."

A servomotor sounded and the door glided open. Alice watched Honor enter, paying particular attention to her shapely posterior. "Oh, yes," he sighed, mimicking the security voice. Karzoff chuckled, appreciating the gag.

Alice and Karzoff joined Honor in the otherwise unoccupied lab. Honor stopped by a strange-looking chair, which reminded Alice of what his dentist used when he was a kid. He used to call it the torture chair. The chair had restraints on the arms and footrest, and above the headrest was a transparent spherical dome resembling a bizarre fishbowl, with cables and sensors embedded in it. He gave it a wide berth.

The room was filled with a bewildering array of scientific gadgetry, which didn't trouble Alice, it reminded him of the recording studio. But what did make him feel uncomfortable were his hosts.

"Take a seat please, Alice," said Honor, offhandedly gesturing at the dentist's chair.

Alice shook his head. There was no way she was going to coax him into that thing.

He ambled over to a bench and perched on the edge.

Honor stared at Karzoff. "A word Karzoff, please," she said.

He joined her and they turned their backs on Alice.

Through gritted teeth she ordered him: "You can leave now."

Karzoff was taken aback. "Yes, but I thought..." he began.

She cut him off impatiently. "Go now, I vill handle zis. Zat is an order, Karzoff. And send in Secta."

She had seniority. Karzoff made his way dispiritedly to the door, but stopped and turned slowly to face Alice with a macabre scowl on his weather-beaten dial.

"See you later, Alice," he sneered.

To Alice, the statement carried all the innuendo of a terminal goodbye. Matching the man sneer for sneer, he replied: "Yeah Karzoff, later."

As the door closed behind Karzoff, Alice decided he'd had enough. He stood, ready to leave even if he had to fight on his increasingly less wobbly legs.

"Honor, I'm over this," he said. "I've got a ferry to catch. I'm out of here."

Honor calmly turned her back on him, and slyly unfastened the clip on a black leather wristband, which released a small metal sphere into the palm of her hand. As Alice got up, Honor pirouetted and flung the metal sphere at him. As it flew through the air a sharp, clawed prong emerged from it just before it lodged in his neck. At such a close proximity, Alice had been an easy target.

Alice squawked and reached to pull it out, but before his hand could get to it Honor turned a dial on the wristband, sending a high-voltage charge through Alice's nervous system. It was like a Taser, only much more intense. His nervous system was paralysed — his knees buckled and his body began to convulse uncontrollably. He only just managed to hold himself upright by grabbing the edge of the bench.

Honor edged towards him, holding the arm with the controller extended, while adjusting the attenuator dial to keep Alice immobilized but still standing. By increasing and decreasing the intensity of the shock, she was able to manoeuvre him from the bench to the chair, into which he slumped when she turned off the juice.

"Good boy," she said, patronizingly. "Yes Alice, a Stingray. You see, Mr Peace Monger, Mr Male Ego, who is charge now?" She moved closer and said, in a softer voice: "I do not really vant to hurt you Alice. Honestly. Relax … I haf nozzing against you personally. In fact, I qvite enjoy your primitive music."

Even though he was conscious and listening, Alice's rationality had been shattered. His mind was a meld of confusion, saliva was dribbling from his mouth onto his chest. Honor knew this, and it permitted her to safely lower the Stingray controller. Taking a handkerchief from her pocket, she dabbed at the blood trickling from the wound in his neck. Then, as though a switch was flicked in her brain, she lifted her skirt above the knee, flung her leg over him, and squatted on his lap.

"You haff to understand I am only doing my job. Zer president is anxious about a possible revolution. Viz suicide attackers and biker gangs siding viz terrorist organizations and building underground fortresses impervious to nuclear attack and dissidents like you rallying zer rank and file to oppose government policy…Who is not viz us is against us, and I can … help you … now…"

Her lips were close to his, so close he could smell her red lipstick.

"Vot do you say, Alice?"

"Go to hell," Alice groaned.

She stepped back and turned the control on her wrist, causing Alice to thrust upwards, arching his back, stiffening every muscle in his body. He growled in pain.

She twisted the dial again. This time it was too much. The massive charge induced a seizure. Shaking uncontrollably, saliva dribbling from the corner of his mouth, his lips had turned blue from lack of oxygen. His eyes rolled back in the sockets, his eyelids fluttering as though stuck in a loop. For Alice, everything went black.

CHAPTER 12
RECK

HONOR'S HEINOUS BEHAVIOUR was suddenly curtailed by the arrival of Doctor Secta. He breezed into the room, glaring at her in distaste.

"Finished with your interrogation, Honor?" he asked. "He's had a seizure," he added, checking Alice. "If you don't know how to use one of those things correctly, I suggest you read the manual. In fact, why don't you just go away and do that right now?"

"Yeah, get rid of the bitch, will you?" Alice rasped. He was exhausted. The Stingray had almost burnt out his nervous system, and totally sapped what remained of his strength. He was conscious, but only just. Despite a deep mistrust of the man, he was relieved by Secta's arrival.

"So. This is the specimen I've been hearing so much about," said Secta, holding out his hand to Honor for the Stingray controller. Acting like a spoiled brat, Honor reluctantly handed it over.

"Specimen?" Alice growled. "I'm not a urine sample, dude!"

It was obvious that Secta had little time for Honor, and she knew it. She scowled at Alice, and marched briskly towards the door. As she reached it, the door opened and Hope barged in.

She took one look at Alice in the chair, then at Secta holding the Stingray controller. "You can't do this, Secta!" she bellowed.

Honor leapt, grabbing Hope around the throat from behind. "I vill get her out of here!" she shouted, sourly. Hope struggled against her grip, but to no avail.

"Let go of me, bitch!" she growled, but it was no contest. Even her combat skills were of no value up against secret police-trained Honor.

Secta aimed the Stingray controller at Alice and said, sternly: "You've made your own bed Hope. One more step and I'll destroy his nervous system…"

"How can you Secta!" Hope roared, fighting Honor's tightening her grip around her throat.

"Don't get beat up by that bag of shit on my account, lady," Alice rasped. "These freaks are off their faces."

The two women continued to tussle as Honor dragged Hope towards the door. As it finally closed behind them, Secta chuckled and casually ambled over to the computer on the workbench.

"Honor is a worry isn't she?" he asked. "As for Hope — well, there is no hope for you, old son."

Alice squirmed at Secta's attempt at a joke. "Yeah, yeah, hilarious," he groaned. "What are you, a frustrated game show compere? Get this mongrel thing out of my neck!"

Secta walked over. "A game show compere?" he said, with a smirk. "That's not such a bad idea … want to manage me?"

Alice couldn't find the humour in the moment. He fumbled in his pocket for the 8-ball, meaning to throw it at Secta. Raising it, he growled: "Get this thing out of my neck, or I'll…"

Secta held up the Stingray dial on the wristlet he still held in his hand. "I wouldn't if I were you, old son."

Not wanting any Stingray treatment, Alice capitulated. "You bastards want to kill me for getting in the way of your stupid politics, don't you?" he said.

"No Alice, you've got it all wrong. I'm not your executioner," Secta replied.

"Then what the stuff am I doing here?"

"You're here because, Alice, I'm an inventor. And you are my experiment."

"Yeah sure," said Alice, desperately stalling for time. "Like what have you invented?"

"Oh, a myriad of innovative items, Alice. Programmable wallpaper—"

"Yeah, just what the world needs," Alice interrupted. "I bet you're also the idiot that made that android out there."

"Yes," said Secta, calmly. "Cyber-genetics, Alice. Oh, and of course, holographic particle matter transfer. Which you, my friend, are about to experience. Brilliant stuff, if I might say so myself."

"Then just cut the trash and get on with it," said Alice. "There's hardly any need for all the bloody theatrics."

Secta turned a dial on the fishbowl-like apparatus above Alice's head. It made a whirring sound as it lowered into place just above his eyes, covering most of his head.

"Don't be concerned," said Secta, attempting to sound soothing. "It's only a demolecularizer. I'll use it to take a digital print of your atomic structure." The lie was obvious.

Alice looked up at the glass bowl. "Sure," he said, his voice muffled by the glass. "What the hell's really going on?"

Secta could see Alice was almost ready to leap out of the chair. He flicked a switch on the side, and two metal clasp restraints immediately sprang from the arms, fastening around Alice's wrists. Another set sprang from the footrest, clamping around Alice's shins. He was well and truly trapped.

Struggling to free himself, he yelled at Secta: "Come on man, for Christ's sake! You don't need to do this! Let me out of this contraption!"

"Settle down Alice, relax," said Secta. "You're only a rock singer, you see … You can't be permitted to be bigger than the government. I've been charged with the responsibility of cutting you down to size."

Alice growled, tugging at the restraints.

"Look, it's all part of the hologram process, just relax," said Secta, moving to the other side of the chair. "Now, I'm going to remove the Stinger. It will hurt a bit."

He clicked a button on the side of the sphere, which retracted the sharp little claws gripping deeply into Alice's flesh. With a sharp pull, Secta removed it from his neck. Blood trickled from the wound. Secta took a tissue from his pocket and dabbed at it.

"There you go," he said, sounding like a doctor giving a kid a Covid shot. "That wasn't so bad, was it?"

The wound hurt, but the withdrawal of the Stingray was a relief. Alice watched, warily, as Secta returned to the bench and collected a large syringe, filled with a luminous green liquid. He casually approached Alice. "Now for a little jab," he said.

"A what?" Alice reacted. "Hey...!"

Secta jabbed the needle into the hole left by the Stingray, and drove it deeper into the wound. Alice writhed in pain as the radioactive fluid flowed into his jugular vein.

"I'm going ... to kill you ... Secta ... I promise!" Alice growled, through gritted teeth.

"Now, Alice..."

Alice's palms were sweating, and parts of his body were lobbying in favour of panic. He closed his eyes, thinking he was facing his demise. Millions of years of animal survival instincts screamed that something unnatural was happening to his entire body. His nerves jangled, his stomach churned, and his subconscious screamed for a rock to hide under, while one thought went through his mind, over and over again ... his life was in the hands of a maniac.

"Well Alice this is it," said Secta, cheerfully. "You're going to be immortal ... well, the hologram of you is ... Unfortunately, your physical being will be vaporised. But your spirit will live on, the hologram will replace you. Well at least I think it will.

"Your fans will be sad to hear about the accident that took your life, but at least they'll be able to see you as a holographic display at the new Powerhouse Museum. I think it'll be a hit, don't you?"

With a macabre chuckle, Secta returned to his computer and slipped on a pair of goggles. Spidery fluorescent green veins appeared on the backs of Alice's hands, then spread up his arms, disappearing under his shirt. They re-emerged on his neck and began to cover his face.

Alice's mind was swimming. His heart was pounding ten to the dozen, he had to fight with every breath to avoid passing out. An ice-cold patina of sweat broke all over his body. This has to be death, this bastard is killing me … killing me … The words resounded in his mind like a sort of psychogenic loop. A montage of memory snaps flicked past like a slide show... playing with the band, Stain smiling, a coin flipping over in the air. Mal repeating, over and over: You're crazy man, they'll buttbang yer.

Secta moved quickly around the chair and grasped a lever protruding from a panel of digital instruments on the wall. He pulled the lever, triggering a flurry of glowing electronic impulses and sparks in the bowl over Alice's head.

Alice started to shake uncontrollably, as though being electrocuted. His body began to glow. He stared disbelievingly at his hands, and his mouth opened in a silent scream. He felt no pain, only fear — not so much fear of dying, as fear of the unknown. He'd never been religious, but for a fleeting moment he hoped he'd been wrong and that there was a god, because if there was, he was about to make his acquaintance.

The pandemonium from the individual instruments and the arcing of electronics under stress reached an almighty, pulsating crescendo, and Alice's entire body began to shift in and out of focus. The world around him exploded into a vast array of colourful atoms. Tiny, revolving stars appeared in their millions, seemingly alive and moving with purpose. He was shooting through them at speed — and yet, he could look down and see himself in the strange chair, sliding in and out of focus like a blinking fluorescent light. A yellow-violet haze engulfed him … He felt free.

Alice had physically transformed into nothing more than a rotating ball of colourful molecular particles that were sucked up into the bowl, leaving nothing behind. No leather coat, no scarlet boots, no Alice ... just an empty chair and the 8-ball, which rolled onto the floor.

The lights on the digital instruments blinked off. The electronic cacophony ceased. A deathly silence filled the laboratory. Secta's demolecularizer had done its job: the world was rid of Black Alice.

Pleased with himself and the successful execution of his 'experiment', Secta noticed the 8-ball on the floor. He stooped and picked it up, pocketing it cheerfully as he walked happily out of the lab.

"So that's how it happened," Alice said, his interest piqued. "I remember none of that."

"Now comes the interesting part in which I played a small but significant role," En-Ki admitted.

Djard's flight had brought her to another dusty, cobwebbed room. She knew Ex and his gang weren't far behind, but was intrigued by what she saw in the gloom. In the centre of the room stood a round, rusted metal pedestal, chest-height from the floor and a metre in diameter. The sound of approaching footsteps reminded her that her pursuers were close. There was no time to run. She stepped into the shadows to hide.

Ex entered and walked slowly over to the pedestal, followed cautiously by Derg, Karn and Chez. Ex gingerly prodded the metal platform with the tip of his sword. While Ex was preoccupied with the pedestal, Djard gently eased further away. She bumped into a metal pylon and a huge cobweb suspended from it. The sensation sent a shiver though her as she wondered where the spider big enough to make such a huge web would be hiding. Then she noticed a panel attached to the pylon, with pretty red and green buttons. They intrigued her. She felt drawn to them. She brushed the cobwebs off the panel, and pressed the green button. Instantly a deafening, thunderous roar resounded throughout the room.

Ex leapt back from the pedestal in shock as a bright red laser shot from high up in the ceiling and struck its centre with a loud crack. Powerful heavy metal music rang out from huge speakers suspended from the gantry. The percussive vibration from the drums caused the dust of ages to billow from the huge speaker cones and rain down on the whole party.

Ex was spinning in a circle with his sword held out, totally overwhelmed by the whole shebang. Derg, Karn and Chez didn't seem to know which direction to defend. But Djard couldn't take her eyes off the red laser beam, because she could see something manifesting on the pedestal inside it. Bravely, she moved closer to see what it was.

Thinking it some kind of strange magic, Ex was also attracted to the pedestal. None of them had seen anything like it before. Then, right before their eyes, a digital marvel coalesced: a life-sized human skeleton materialized, followed by the musculature wrapped around it. Gradually, skin and clothing covered the body — a white dress shirt, black trousers, red boots, a long black trench coat. Then a head, a face, a long ponytail. Finally, the creature sprang to life and burst into song. As the apparition performed, it faded in and out of focus. Djard, Ex, Derg, Karn and Chez had no idea that the image was a hologram of Black Alice. But they could all see that it didn't perceive their presence.

The music was powerful, a Black Alice original with lyrics about the world going wrong and the threat of war: Reck. The Alice hologram sang:

> I say something's going on
> And I'm sick and tired of

G. L. Keady

> The world going wrong
> I say if we leave it any longer
> Then the boots of war
> Will tread us under
> That's a little on the sci-fi
> But I might be right
> Who can say?

The meaning was completely lost on the audience. But they were nevertheless in awe of the incredible performance they were witnessing.

> Fear grows, rock 'n roll
> Tells all and points the way
> You know the yellow brick road
> Well, the overpass was built to stay
> That's a little on the sci-fi
> But I might be right
> Who can say?

Feeling that it posed no threat to her, Djard moved in for a closer look at the hologram. Reaching out, she tried to touch it, but retracted her hand quickly when it passed right through the image. That didn't impress Ex. He felt threatened, and raised his sword in defence.

> Let's get our act together
> Why must we fight
> In the name of peace?
> War we can do without
> Come on, let's scream
> And shout it out.
> You know love grows
> When the tree of peace
> Is left growing free

> And it's time
> To let the world know
> If we want to keep living
> Then let's plant the seeds
> That's a little on the sci-fi
> But I might be right
> Who can say?

As the song reached its climax, with the chorus chanting like a protest march: 'One two three four we don't want nuclear war, five six seven eight, we don't want to radiate', Alice's movements became more and more animated. Moved by the emotion of the music, Djard mirrored them. Then Alice seemed to look directly into Ex's eyes. Ex grasped the hilt of his sword with both hands and, with an almighty swing, struck out at the hologram. The blade passed straight through, and Ex very nearly swung himself off his feet. The tempered steel blade cutting through the particle field caused the hologram to erupt into a wall of blue swirling energy. The music suddenly ceased.

CHAPTER 13
NECROPOLIS

THE DEMATERIALIZED HOLOGRAM swirled in rotating molecules of sparking energy, noisy and arcing with a manic fury. Djard, Ex and the others shielded their eyes from the intense luminescent commotion on the pedestal. Djard feared it might explode. In the radiant light, akin to the blazing power of a welding arc, Djard could make out the interior of the room for the first time. She spotted what appeared to be an exit, and bolted for it like a gazelle. Anxious to escape whatever was happening on the pedestal, Ex and the others followed.

Up on the pedestal, within the atomic chaos, something stranger than fiction was going on. The singing hologram image had lost its opacity. Its outside edge was glowing, and within it the physical form of Alice had morphed into a three-dimensional being, transmuted by the blow of Ex's sword. As the glow and atomic chaos subsided, Alice's image began to breathe, gulping for air like a person recovering from drowning. His coughing echoed through the cavernous room, causing Derg, still on the run, to glance back over his shoulder at the spectre stepping down from the pedestal. Alice had returned from the dead, his spirit restored, his body reconstituted into a physical form.

Djard raced down a narrow tunnel leading to another corridor. It was brighter than the room she'd come from. She stopped to catch her breath, and as the others were about to catch up with her, a voice came from behind them: "Hey, wait!" The warriors froze, and turned to face the approaching footsteps. They were stunned when Black Alice appeared magically out of the darkness … it was as though they were seeing a ghost.

Shaken, holding his head in confusion, Alice glared at his saviours. "What the hell is going on here?" he snarled. "Where the stuff am I? A fancy dress party? I've got a ferry to catch…" He fronted Ex and demanded: "Who in the blazers are you?"

Ex answered with a right hook, designed to take Alice's head clean off his shoulders. Fortunately for Alice he was able to dodge the full force of the blow, and the punch only grazed his chin. Djard let out a giggle at the miss. Derg, Karn and Chez snickered amongst themselves too, figuring Ex was about to make mincemeat of Alice.

Full of confidence, Ex lined up for a haymaker, but Alice saw it coming. Banking on it being a big roundhouse right, he took one step to the side as Ex let it go, raised a solid block with his left forearm, and counterpunched with a powerful straight right that connected right on the button and sat Ex on his butt.

Karn, Derg and Chez growled. Though he was outnumbered, Alice knew he'd just won them over. He stood over Ex and offered him a hand up. Ex wiped a dribble of blood from his nose, then took Alice's hand to get back to his feet. They eyed each other for a moment in mutual respect. The tension disappeared from the air, and was replaced by smiles all round.

"So, who are you then?" Alice asked.

Ex stared blankly, not appearing to understand. Alice turned to Djard. He looked her over, impressed by her shapely, near-naked figure, barely concealed by her scanty clothing.

"What's the story babe?" he asked. "Can you speak?"

As he reached out to touch her, he noticed something behind her on the wall. He moved past her and wiped the sign free of what appeared to be years of built-up dust and grime. Suddenly, he recognized it.

"Level 7?" he muttered to himself. Amazed, he frantically wiped more grime away. "Labs 6-12, Security Zone Red!" He turned sharply to Ex. "This is the underground fallout shelter I was in ... What's happened here? Why's everything changed? I must be tripping or something..." He prowled the room in a state of confusion. "Nar, this has to be some sort of brain drain, a mind game," he decided. "Secta! Where are you, you arsehole?" he yelled.

It seemed only minutes ago he had been sitting in a weird chair with a contraption over his head, and Secta had injected him with something. He fronted Ex again, desperate for answers.

"Where are you from mate? Do you live down here? What year is it?"

Djard, getting the drift of Alice's questions, tried to explain. "We fall from up there," she said, pointing at the ceiling. "You help?"

The others nodded, agreeing with her.

Relief broke on Alice's face. "So you can talk! Great!" he said. Suddenly what Djard had said rang home. "Wait, you fell from up there?" he questioned, pointing at the ceiling with a frown. "What's that supposed to mean, 'up there'?"

Instead of answering, Djard grabbed Alice's finger and pointed it to herself. "Me Djard," she said, then pointed it at Ex. "Him Ex." Ex crossed his arms in front of him.

Alice grinned. "All right, now we're getting somewhere. And who are you?" he said, pointing at Karn.

"Karn," said the skinny, longhaired, tattooed man, slapping his chest.

Alice pointed to the next dude in line.

"Me Derg," snarled the big, formidable bald man, his head decorated in tattoos.

Finally, Alice fronted Chez and asked: "And you?"

A smile, minus a few front teeth, broke on the big man's round face. "Chez. Me Chez," he said.

"Hey Chez," said Alice, holding out his hand to shake. Chez stared at it, took it and squeezed. Alice regretted the move. Chez had a vice-like grip. Sensing his fingers were about to be crushed, Alice grabbed Chez's hand and extracted them. Shaking his own aching hand, he grinned and said: "Ow! That's one hell of a grip!"

Chez laughed. That got a giggle out of the others.

"Okay," said Alice, studying Ex. Six feet five, with long matted hair and wearing a sheathed katana across his back, Alice questioned why he'd picked a fight with the man before. He could easily have been whacked with the sword. Then he thought what's the guy doing with a sword, anyway?

Before he could mention it, Ex grabbed the medallion around his neck and, shaking it at Alice with one hand and pointing at the ceiling with the other, growled: "Shine!"

He was declaring his chieftainship as wearer of the amulet, and that he needed to return to his people on the surface. The word 'shine' rang in Alice's memory like an alarm.

"Wait, did you say shine?" he said.

But Ex wasn't about to hang around. He waved an arm for the others to follow, and then stomped off along the corridor.

Alice called after him: "Wait. Ex, listen…" But the others walked off after Ex, leaving Alice mumbling to himself, feeling decidedly unhinged by the entire experience.

"A chick in a chamois bikini and a bloody great ape with a sword on his back," he said to himself, shaking his head. "Hey, wait! I wanna talk to you!"

A flash of light inside Alice's mind and he was back at the orb in the netherworld. He began pacing the floor deep in thought. "Can't say I remember much of that." He stopped and studied his surroundings a look of confusion on his face. "Maybe I'm dead and gone to heaven…"

The voice from the orb resounded, "You do not go to heaven Alice, you become it."

"That's seriously profound. Sometimes I think I've just got too many lyrics swimming around in my brain. Look, it's time you answered a question or two of mine. How the hell did you get in that thing? What do you look like?"

"Your destiny is to free me from this prison."

"There's that word destiny again but why me?"

"I am responsible for the person you will soon become, but before I tell you more, you need to understand how everything is linked, and how your destiny has been written."

Alice moved a little closer the orb and his form in the radiance caused long distorted shadows on the walls. "What do you mean my destiny has been written? You say it like I've got no say in it."

"Oh, you can always alter your destiny Alice. What I refer to is the wheels that were set in motion the moment Dr Secta injected you with the formula he and Dr Hope had pioneered."

"Pardon my ignorance, I'm just a singer in a rock 'n roll band ... but how do you come into the equation?"

"You should not underestimate yourself Alice, you have a major role to play in saving humanity from mass extinction. The blood of a hero courses through your veins."

That appealed to Alice's vanity. "Hmmm, okay. Go on."

A sudden flash of light...

Alice was back watching the barbarians disappearing into the darkness of the corridor. He chased after them to a staircase at the end of the corridor where he found them trying to decide whether to go up or down.

"We should go up, towards where you came from," said Alice, pointing. "If I'm right, we're seven floors underground."

By the foggy looks on their faces he realised there was no use talking to them in long sentences. "We go up," he said, again motioning with his hand. They got the idea, so he led them through the cobwebs and up the staircase. It was difficult to see in the dark confines of the stairwell, but after two flights of stairs he came to a landing with the entrance to an elevator. Djard tried to open the door, but it seemed to be jammed. Ex had a go, but couldn't budge it, and called Chez to use his brute strength. Chez fired off a piece of cake grin and gripped the door, but even he couldn't wrench it open.

Alice stepped up to the plate. This was his big chance to show off the results of years of pumping iron. He removed his coat and handed it to Djard to hold. He flexed up and gripped the door. With a massive tug, he wrenched it open, smiling at their impressed faces. Lucky for Alice, they hadn't noticed him releasing the safety catch before his strong man performance. It was a ruse to win their esteem — and it had worked.

There was no elevator behind the door. Alice leaned into the shaft and looked up and down. Below, it descended into a dark abyss. Above, he could see the base of the elevator three floors up. It was no use. They'd have to continue up the stairs. He waved a hand and shook his head to get the message across, and the group got it. Djard handed him back his coat. Putting it on, Alice started up the staircase. They only made it to the next landing before Alice stopped. They could go no further: the ceiling had collapsed.

"Go back," Alice called, motioning with his hand.

Back at the elevator landing, Alice reached inside the lift well, took hold of the cable, swung out and then hauled himself up. Ex and the others leaned in to watch him ascend.

Legs kicking about in the air, grunting with effort, Alice made it to level four, just under the base of the elevator, and swung across to the door. Holding the cable, with his feet on the narrow ledge, he unlatched the grille, opened it and stepped out onto the level four landing.

The others waited anxiously for him to show his face again. A long moment passed, that had them thinking Alice might have left them for dead, when suddenly he popped back into the shaft and called out his voice echoing: "Come up!"

One by one they scaled the cable to the fourth floor.

There they faced their next obstacle. The staircase was jammed — a massive hunk of concrete that was impossible to bypass. They had no alternative but to search level four for another route to the surface.

It was beginning to look more and more to Alice that there had been some sort of catastrophe that had devastated the Oceana building. But even that couldn't explain the presence of his new, practically mute barbarian friends. He needed to see more of the city to piece it all together. Or, even better, to find someone to explain it to him.

Like the other corridors they'd negotiated, this one was dark, dusty and heavily cobwebbed. Alice found a broom-handle on the ground and used it to knock away the webs. He hadn't yet seen the spiders responsible for them, but the broom-handle provided at least a little security in case they made an appearance.

They rounded a corner. The air was still, putrid and heavy. Sound was muted. The walls were smooth, and the floor even. This tunnel was higher and wider than the previous one, but the thick foul air made them all gasp for breath. Leading the way, Alice used the broom handle to brush through the thick, stringy cobwebs that hung like long tentacles and stuck with some to his arms and face.

The webs were becoming thicker and thicker, spread across the width and height of the tunnel. In some places they were as thick as cord. Alice stopped. It was getting darker, and he feared that whatever had produced these horrifying, massive webs could be lurking nearby. He hated spiders.

Ex wanted to push past Alice and continue along the tunnel. Trusting his gut instinct, Alice threw out an arm and stopped him. "Wait!" he hissed. "Something's wrong — look!"

He pointed ahead, to where the giant web had formed a tight tunnel, the centre of which looked like a black hole — a big black hole — big enough for something the size of a small car. Ex nodded in agreement, and slowly drew his katana from its scabbard. As he did so, the sword struck a thick cord, and the motion sent a vibration into the hole. A vibration that aroused the resident of the giant web.

Long, spindly, black, hairy legs started to emerge. Alice and Ex recoiled with shock: if the legs were anything to go by, the spider they had roused was the size of an adult feral pig.

Ex steadied himself, sword held at the ready. Alice looked forlornly at the broom handle, thinking a spider that big would use it as a toothpick.

Djard backed away, frightened, while Karn, Chez and Derg took up positions to back up Alice and Ex.

The web started to vibrate more fiercely as the legs crept forward, bringing the bulk of the monster behind them. Its head was awesome — four steely black eyes in a straight line and, below them and gnashing hungrily, two terrifying, razor-sharp mandibles. When the bulk of the enormous arachnid's body appeared, Alice recognised the red stripe across its bulbous torso. It was gigantic black widow — a redback — and that meant this wasn't just any old mutated giant spider with gnashing teeth. This hair-raising, monstrous brute was also venomous. And what made it even worse, if it could get worse, was that there was no going back. To get past the colossal thing, they would have to kill it.

Even in the midst of his terror, Alice asked himself: "How the stuff did that thing get so big?" It was a question that, for the moment, remained unanswered.

Ex shuffled towards the spider, with his sword held, ready to strike.

Alice knew he needed to make the spider rear up to allow Ex to stab. Standing beside Ex, he took aim and threw the broomstick like a spear. It hit the spider in the mandible and, as Alice planned, caused it to rear its front legs. Ex lunged forward, plunging his sword into its gargantuan underbelly.

Letting out an ear-piercing shriek, the spider pounced forward and grabbed Ex with its forelegs. Ex was struggling to extract his sword from its gut. Alice watched in horror, knowing the spider was about to deliver its fatal, venomous bite.

Suddenly, Derg pushed past. He fronted the gigantic creature fearlessly, hacking wildly at its legs with his sword. He severed two, causing the spider to release Ex. As it did so, Ex extracted his sword. Seeing that his enemy was back-pedalling, he made an almighty lunge and thrust his blade into its mouth, driving it with all his might up into the gruesome head. The redback collapsed. Dead. Ex tugged his blade free and raised it triumphantly in the air. Derg slapped him admiringly on the shoulder. They were victors over an awesome adversary.

"Yeah! We did bloody it!" Alice yelled, excitedly.

Ex sheathed his blade and patted Alice on the back of the head as he repeated: "Bloody did it!"

Chuckling, Alice glanced at Djard and the other two, who were also celebrating. But at the same time, he couldn't help but wonder how many more mutant monsters were lurking in the dark tunnels ahead of them.

Alice looked back at the dead spider, and the web moving — a light breeze was coming from beyond it. Figuring that was an indication of a link to the upper levels, he signalled for the others to follow him, and squeezed past the giant body. Ex took the lead and hacked them a way through the huge web. They were thankful to find the other side was spider-web free.

Alice was staring at the orb with a horrified expression. "That was insane," he mumbled. "I might have arachnophobia but mate, that thing was ridiculous."

"While you were busy battling the spider one of your greatest allies was suffering from the chicanery of the Oceana government."

A lightning bolt flashed in Alice's mind.

Hope was packing personal items in boxes. All that remained in her lab was old chemical samples, archives and some out-of-date research books. Hope was ignoring Honor, who was hovering, vulture-like, just inside the door, making sure she was going to leave.

"Vell, zat about finishes Black Alice's reign," said the SSD officer, matter-of-factly.

With tears tracking down her pale cheeks, Hope ignored her. She loaded the last few items into a cardboard box.

"Enjoy zer rally," Honor sneered. "It will probably be—"

Hope cut her off. "Just shut up, Honor! You've got your way. Now get out of mine!"

Ignoring her outburst, Honor continued arrogantly: "As I vos saying: it vill probably be zer last rally ... Perhaps it vill be more like a funeral procession zan a peace march!" She cackled at her own feeble joke.

Ignoring her heartless jibe, Hope glared at her with contempt.

"Get out!" she snapped.

Honor smirked, turned and left, only to be replaced seconds later by Secta, throwing the 8-ball and catching it in unconscious imitation of his victim. He seemed perplexed by all the packed boxes. "So you were serious," he said, his eyes narrowing. "Well, little sister, this time you've gone too far."

"Get out of here, you insensitive bastard," snarled Hope.

Nonchalantly continuing to pitch the 8-ball up and snatch it from the air, Secta sneered: "A bastard, eh? Well, that makes you one too ... You know, I think you should just stay in here for a while, and think. I'll let you out when I'm convinced you've come to your senses."

With that, he smashed the 8-ball hard against the power board by the door. It controlled the room. The panel sparked and fused. Sects ducked out of the door as the lights went out and the room went into emergency lockdown. Hope was left trapped in darkness.

"No, Secta please!" she pleaded. "Let me out, don't do this to me! You know I'm afraid of the dark … Let me out! Please!"

Secta stood in the corridor with his back to the door. "No use complaining, Hopeless," he sneered. "You can just stay in there until I think you're ready to come out. Now — shut up."

He walked away to the sound of her frantic pounding on the door and increasingly hysterical pleas. Entering the corridor to his own lab, still throwing the 8-ball up and catching it, he found Honor blocking his way. She had overheard his merciless torment of his sister — and it had turned her on.

"You have hidden talents, Secta," she purred, seductively. Her advances, however, turned him off, he had no time for Honor or any of the SSD. "Look Honor, I'm only part of this setup because it suits me," he snapped. "I have a need for an unlimited supply of funds. I have no need for an unlimited supply of your bullshit."

Honor gripped his arm, pressing herself against him, pleading with him to appreciate her. "Leave Hope in there to rot," she said. "We … I mean, you and I … I admire your dash…"

Secta pushed her out of the way. "Don't even think it Honor," he snapped. "I'd rather make it with a corpse."

Honor pulled away, sourly. Spotting a cockroach on the floor, she vented her anger by crushing it under her boot. Purring lubriciously, she fired back: "Don't knock it till you've tried it, dear Doktor…"

The new corridor joined a wider walkway, which Alice recognised as a link to one of Sydney's many underground shopping malls. It was nowhere near as dark, which was a relief.

The trail of devastation continued. All the shops looked as though they'd been blasted and shaken by an earthquake. But what made it more intriguing for Alice was, judging by the decay of the shop facades and interiors, whatever had happened had been a long time ago. Suddenly, Karn grabbed Alice's shoulder and stopped him. He pointed at a set of human footprints in the dusty floor. They were not alone.

Ex quickly had them in defence mode. They proceeded like commandos, prepared for an ambush, a trap or a snare, eventually coming to a barricade. Alice stopped and studied it. "This was built on purpose," he said, inspecting the jagged metallic wall blocking their way. "We'll have to move it." He turned and faced Ex. "There's no point going back, we must..." he motioned with his arm, "Move all this crap to get through."

Ex frowned and parroted: "Crap?" Then he got it, repeating: "Move crap!" He waved an arm at his men, and they got stuck into the pieces of twisted metal, wooden beams and bricks to open a passage. It took a while, as it was better constructed than they had first thought, but eventually they managed to clear a gap wide enough to squeeze through.

The other side of barricade seemed like a totally different world. Alice wondered whether it had been designed to keep something out, or to keep something in. Karn was quick to point out more footprints on the dusty floor. Following them, they came to a huge, metal fire door, locked from the other side.

"This place is more secure than bloody Fort Knox," Alice complained, frustrated.

"Bluh-dee Fort Knox," Ex repeated to Derg, Chez and Karn. They nodded in approval.

Djard walked up to the door and pointed at a lever near the top.

"Maybe," Alice said, and tried to reach it, but couldn't stretch far enough. Chez came over and gave him a leg up. Alice gripped the lever and dangled from it.

"Nar, can't budge it," he said through clenched teeth and then dropped back down. Then he noticed the chain draped over Chez's shoulder. He pointed at it, then at the lever — Chez got the idea. Ex got down on his hands and knees so Chez could stand on his back. Reaching up, Chez looped the chain over the lever and hopped down. He and Derg took hold of one end of the chain, Ex and Alice took the other. After three loud grunts from Ex, they pulled together with all their might. After much groaning and heaving, the lever slid down and the door began to crack open.

When they managed to shove the big door open, they were amazed by what was on the other side. They were standing on the edge of a precipice. Thirty metres below was a jungle, lush and green, with a grey mist hanging in the trees. But that wasn't all. The entire area was encased inside a massive cavern. Streams of light cascaded through holes in a ceiling at least sixty metres above them. To Alice it looked like a lost world lit in an ambient, yellowish glow. He recognised it as having been a park — strewn around the edges and sticking out of the sheer rock walls were chunks of motorcars, buses and trucks. At the centre, rising thirty metres from the dense undergrowth, stood a pink granite building with a ziggurat stepped roof, reminiscent of an ancient Central American Mayan Temple.

"I can't believe this," Alice groaned, totally thunderstruck. "That's the Hyde Park Anzac Memorial. We're in the middle of Sydney. But what it's all doing underground in some sort of enormous cave?" He slumped onto the ground, head in his hands.

Djard placed a comforting hand on his shoulder, and crouched beside him, "Alice fear?" she asked, gently.

He looked up at her, "Nar, not frightened," he said. "Just ... just freaked out, I guess."

None of it was making sense. How could an entire city park end up underground?

Djard looked up at the concerned faces of the others and said: "Alice freaked out."

Ex nodded. "Hmm, freaked out."

The others copied him, also nodding. "Freaked out."

If he didn't feel so seriously confused, Alice would have found their antics amusing. But there was nothing funny about the devastation he could see. Gathering himself together and taking in the view of the park below, he suddenly realised that, apart from the

Anzac Memorial, there were no other buildings to be seen. It was as though the park had collapsed hundreds of metres from the surface and been sealed over. He noticed the main roads that had bordered the rectangular park were missing, as though a giant knife had cut along them. No matter how hard he tried, he just couldn't fathom it.

The others were beginning to look restless. It was time to move on. "We go there," he said, pointing at the Memorial.

The next problem was how to get down the thirty or so metres to the park. An excellent tracker, Karn noticed a barely visible trail zig-zagging down the cliff face. They all followed him. After an hour of heavy going, especially for Alice, slipping and sliding with his Cuban heeled boots on the loose surface, they made it to the cavern floor, right at the edge of the park.

Moving on, the vegetation posed a fresh problem. It was so thick they found it difficult to find a way through. Ex and Derg had to use their swords like machetes. After a while, they came to a clearing and stopped. With no more hacking and struggling, Alice noticed something wrong. There was a total absence of sound. No birds, no insects ... nothing. It was eerie.

Karn, digging at the ground with his dagger, distracted Alice. When he went over to see what had attracted the barbarian's attention, he found Karn had unearthed a skeletal hand. As he dug further, he uncovered more of a body, a human body. But this wasn't an old, bleached skeleton. This was fresh, and recently buried. They could tell from the remains that it was the body of a young woman.

CHAPTER 14
DEN OF INIQUITY

EX SHOUTED "NO!" and backed off. The others followed suit, afraid of something that eluded Alice.

"What is it?" he asked. Djard put her hand up to her mouth, shaping her fingers to represent teeth and growling like a vicious dog.

"An animal? You're saying an animal did this? And then buried her?" said Alice, making digging motions with his hands. When he looked more closely at the remains, he could see what the others had known instinctively: the body showed bite marks. The victim had been partially eaten.

Djard nodded.

The others had taken guard again, scouring the thick jungle for signs of predators. They were on edge. After the oversized spider, they could be up against anything.

Chez, sniffing the air, grunted. That set the others off, all of them sniffing like dogs. Alice tried too, but couldn't smell anything. Djard, looking a little panicked, pointed at the bushes. "It comes! It comes!" Alice couldn't see anything, but he heard the faint sound of twigs breaking underfoot.

Karn pointed to where the sound was coming from. Ex nodded sharply at him, and signalled the rest of the group to follow him into the bush, on a trail he'd detected leading away from whatever it was that was closing in. In some places the foliage was so thick and matted with curling vines that they had no hope of penetrating it, and were forced to find a way round. It was during one of these detours that Karn abruptly stopped and put a finger to his lips: he'd heard something following them.

Ex motioned for them to hide. They darted off every which way, and concealed themselves as best they could. Then they held their collective breaths.

Alice had knelt down behind a large zamia palm. He was just wondering what the hell it was doing growing in Sydney, nearly four thousand kilometres from where it should be, when something sharp jabbed him from behind. He looked over his shoulder and, to his surprise, found a topless female warrior, her mostly-naked body decorated in tribal war paint and tattoos. She was standing over him with a very sharp spear pointed at his throat. Alice slowly rose to his feet, hands raised in surrender.

"Whoa! I'm unarmed—" he cut himself off. "No use talking to her Alice," he chastised himself. "She probably won't understand."

The muscular young woman had striking features: high, firm breasts, brown hair woven into a long plait all the way down to the middle of her back, a six pack to die for and trim, muscular legs with striking tattoos on each thigh. Both arms were cut like a gymnast's. She was wearing only a dark brown, animal hide loincloth, sandals with leg strapping and a leather garter, decorated with feathers and coloured beads, around her bicep and the wrist of the other arm. A string of wooden beads adorned her gracious neck, and a flash of ochre across her eyes gave her a fearsome appearance. Her skin was pale from lack of sunlight, but that didn't stop her from looking incredibly fit, healthy and above all, awesome.

"Keep your hands raised and turn around," she ordered, in a slightly British accent.

Alice was relieved she could speak. "Hey! My name's Alice, Black Alice, and I—"

"Shut up!" she snapped, cutting him off.

As he obediently turned, she jabbed him in the rump with the spear.

"Ouch! Take it easy!" he complained. "That thing's sharp!"

Slowly, other women emerged from their hiding places in the bush, each with a spear at her back. Djard hissed at her captor like a feral cat.

With no other option, they were led along a trail. The women were in no hurry. It seemed the predator Alice's group had feared was stalking them didn't bother these Amazon-like warriors.

Every time Alice tried to talk it resulted in a sharp jab in the rear end. He was busting for an explanation of who they were, where they were, what had happened to Sydney, but preferred to avoid the prods. After an hour and a half of silent trekking, they arrived at the Anzac Memorial. Alice looked up at it. From here he could see the ravages of some mighty catastrophe the building's façade was blackened, as though it had been licked by a dragon's tongue. A web of cracks, some as thick as a finger, ran through the pink granite blocks, suggesting that the entire building had been violently shaken. He remembered there was supposed to be a pool of reflection at the front of the memorial, but it had been gobbled up by overgrowing vegetation.

As they climbed the marble staircase to enter the building, Alice looked up at the fascia of the eastern wall. The bas-relief bronze panels that had illustrated the campaigns of the Great War were missing. He figured they'd been stripped and melted down to produce weapons or something similar.

They entered the building. Here too, the bronze memorial statues had been stripped away and replaced with primitive weaponry and a huge collection of car and bike parts, some of them quite large. There was the front end of a taxi, a section of fire engine and a large chunk of tram. But it wasn't just strewn about randomly. It was on show, held in some reverence, like a museum display.

Ex and his friends had been stripped of their weapons, and they were all made to sit on the floor with their hands behind their backs.

Alice felt he was being punished, like a naughty schoolboy, and was desperate to talk with someone.

The six Amazons who had brought them here were dressed similarly, although they had different body proportions, tattoos, hair and ornamentation. But all were young, topless, attractive and obviously extremely fit. Chez was grinning like a Cheshire cat at the biggest girl, who was well endowed in the breast department. She seemed to be enjoying his admiration.

Alice figured by her actions that the Amazon who had captured him was the leader. She left the others, passed through a curtain draped across an alcove at the far end of the room, and disappeared deeper inside the building. Although it had originally been built as a memorial, it seemed to Alice that it had been repurposed as a temple. While they waited for the lead Amazon to return, Alice tried to communicate with the rest, as they stoically kept their spears trained on their captives.

"Is she your leader?" he asked the big girl standing over Chez.

"No, she is Kinks," she said, flicking her head in the direction Alice's captor had gone.

"Kinks? Well … she really got me. Ha!" Alice chuckled at a joke only he got.

A short girl with her spear on Ex snarled: "Shhh!"

Alice chose not to provoke them, and kept quiet. After a few minutes the curtain opened and Kinks led out a woman dressed like a Queen.

The guards prodded the captives with their spears to encourage them to rise in the presence of their monarch.

Kinks walked up a small staircase and drew open another curtain, this time on the left at the far end of the room. She left the curtain open to reveal a small mezzanine containing a throne fashioned from a big, old, leather lounge chair.

The shapely barefooted Queen, whom Alice guessed was in her late twenties, gracefully floated up the marble staircase to the throne room. When she reached the landing at the top, she turned and faced them. Her elegance was embellished by a ray of light from the skylight above the throne, giving her a regal radiance. Her long, flimsy, white chiffon vestment was transparent in the beam, showing off a shapely, naked body beneath.

The boys exchanged looks of keen interest. Djard simply rolled her eyes.

The Queen stepped up to the throne, turned and elegantly sat upon it. Kinks moved to her right hand and stood firm, her arms folded: the Queen's legate.

Kinks nodded to the short girl guarding Ex, who immediately raced outside. After a moment a bell chimed and she returned, followed by a dozen more near-naked female warriors. They all stopped just inside the entrance and waited.

Kinks took a step forward and proclaimed to those assembled: "Praise Zule, Queen of the Vixen!"

Her subjects clapped once and, as the sound echoed off the marble walls, chanted: "Praise the Queen!"

The Queen pointed at Ex and asked, sternly: "Who are you?"

Alice answered for him. "His name is Ex. Unfortunately, he's still learning to speak. I will have to speak for my friends here."

"And you are?"

"I'm Black Alice," he answered, cordially. "Most people call me Alice, or just Al."

"And from where do you come, Black Alice?" the Queen asked.

"Well, they come from up there," he pointed. "The surface. I come from somewhere else."

"I can see they come from the Deadlands. We have heard of such savages there. But you are different."

"There is a lot to explain Queen Zule, and a lot I would like to know too."

She stood. All her subjects immediately bowed their heads. She mumbled something privately to Kinks, then glided down the stairs to vanish behind the curtain.

"Vixen scat!" Kinks decreed, and the temple emptied, with the exception of the prisoners and their guards.

What Alice learned? They called themselves the Vixen, and Kinks was Zule's second-in-command. It seemed they only numbered twenty, and that none were over the age of thirty. There weren't any children to be seen, and certainly no males. It seemed Vixen society was a matriarchy.

Kinks approached Alice "Follow me," she said.

Alice followed her through the curtain and into a long, narrow passageway. She stopped at a venetian blind at the end, and pulled a cord to raise it. They entered a small chamber decked out like a study. Zule was seated on a large sofa with a threadbare cover that had definitely seen better days. She had changed into black ripped jeans and a tattered Pink Floyd T-shirt, which looked cool with her long, blonde, plaited hair. Her bare feet were up on the lounge. She motioned for Alice to sit in the armchair opposite, and he obeyed. Kinks left them alone.

Zule was more elegant than the others. No tattoos, fine features and extremely sexy, with an ultra-intelligent look in her cobalt-blue eyes.

Alice glanced around the room. It was adorned with scavenged items from a bygone era: hubcaps, a steering wheel, the front end of a Harley. Two of the walls had floor-to-ceiling bookshelves, filled to capacity with old paperbacks. Another wall with a similar-sized floor-to-ceiling rack was loaded with CDs and vinyl albums. In the centre of the room, an old round table was surrounded by eight chairs, and on the table was an audio turntable with leads running to a stereo amplifier. From there, cables led to a set of large speaker boxes. There was an exercise bike in excellent condition in a corner, and beside it half a dozen dumbbells of weights up to twenty kilos. Alice was impressed.

"Good to see exercise equipment," he said warmly.

"Are you not hot in that coat?" Zule enquired.

"I am actually, you mind?"

She shook her head, so he stood and peeled it off. She admired his build.

"Looks like you get your share of exercise as well," she said.

"When I get the chance."

"So tell me Black Alice—"

"Just Alice, or Al, please."

"Alice, then. Explain how you found us?"

"I'll do that. But first can you tell me what year this is, how you got here, how Sydney got like this and where you get the power to run that?" he said, pointing at the turntable.

She thought about it for a moment, then seemed to decide she would answer his questions first.

"I have no idea what year this is," she said. "I grew up here, as we all did. Our founding fathers and mothers are dead. As far as we know there were sixteen of them. They produced children — nine girls and seven boys — and they in turn produced us. Originally there were twenty-five girls and five boys. For us, Sydney has always been like this. As for your last question, we don't have any power. The exercise bike drives a small generator and storage cells that in turn power a few simple items, like the turntable. It's how we learned to speak — from records. Reading was a little more difficult."

"Where did all this come from?" Alice asked.

"Over the years, warriors have returned from hunting parties with things they have found, and here they all are." She waved a hand around.

"How many of you did you say there are?"

"Originally? Twenty-five girls and five boys. We are all nearly the same age."

"No old people, no children..."

"No men," she finished for him.

"So where are the five boys?"

"Dead."

"This is incredible. How do you survive?"

"There is food and water in the forest, though we have to compete for it," she said, cautiously.

A flash of light.

Alice was grasping his chin staring at the glowing orb. "On the question of you coming into the equation…"

En-Ki's voice resounded in the close confines, "I intervened to allow you to materialize after Ex hit your holographic image with his sword. It was the only way to free you."

"Free me? How did that work?"

"Similar to the way I brought you here. But the most important issue is your preparedness, recounting what has happened."

Alice started to pace the floor, still pondering, trying to make sense of his predicament.

"So, you're educating me for some specific purpose?"

There was a pause. It stopped Alice from pacing. He lowered his hand from his chin turned and studied the orb instinctively knowing that En-Ki was carefully considering how to answer his question.

"Yes Alice, to save my children: humanity. We shall continue."

Once again, a lightning bolt flashed in Alice's mind.

Alice was staring at Zule waiting for the dazzle from the strange flash in his mind's eye to subside. As he got his head together it came to him he was having trouble making sense of the Vixen's existence. He figured Sydney must have suffered some sort of major catastrophe, an earthquake perhaps, that had resulted in the devastation he'd encountered. But that didn't explain where the Vixens had come from. The founding fathers and mothers must have been survivors of the cataclysm, which would appear to have been a long time ago. Two generations, in fact — which made it even more difficult to reconcile the time that had passed since Secta had injected him. It wasn't as though all this ruination happened only yesterday, when, as far as he knew, he'd been injected.

"Now tell me your story," Zule said. Her voice was just a little raspy, and sexy as hell.

It took Alice the best part of an hour to try to explain. Being turned into a hologram. Being freed by a bunch of barbarians. Discovering this world, which didn't match his own. When he'd finished, Zule wasn't looking nearly as surprised as he had expected.

"What you say does not surprise me," she said, calmly. "We have come to accept the impossible here. It is, however, amazing that by some great luck or fortune Djard accidentally flicked the switch that set off your hologram. And that the sword of Ex somehow caused you to become real again."

"I know," said Alice. "I can't explain it myself. But I do wonder where the power for the hologram projector came from."

"There are so many questions that need answers, Alice," said Zule, softly. "But let me say this: it is good to have a man to speak with. I only vaguely remember last speaking to our father when I was twelve."

"What happened to him?" asked Alice. "And to the boys ... the men?"

"After the founding couples had reproduced, beasts began to come out the forest, foraging for food," answered Zule, her voice quiet and sad. "Some of them were Roogas. The men, all of them, fought the Roogas, right down to our fathers and our young brothers. The Roogas killed them all. Since then, we have killed many of them in return. So many that there is now only one left."

"Tell me more about this thing, this Rooga," said Alice.

"It is a carnivorous creature. It lives in the forest. Like I said, it has eaten five of our Vixen, as its race before it ate our brothers and most of our parents and grandparents."

Alice didn't like the sound of that at all. "Jesus!" he exclaimed. "We found a body in the woods, before you captured us. A freshly-eaten body."

"That was Jessie," said Zule, matter-of-factly. The Rooga took her six darks ago."

"Darks?"

"When there is no daylight."

"Night time?"

"Yes, but dark is a better description."

"Is there no other food in the forest this Rooga could hunt?"

"Plenty. We don't know the names, but there is enough to go round. It is only when the Rooga catches one of us off guard that he feasts on our kind."

"I see," said Alice, thoughtfully.

They talked on, Alice still desperately trying to pick up anything from the conversation that might tell him why Sydney was like it was. He came up dry.

Eventually, Zule showed him out. "I will see you at the feast before dark," she said. "Kinks will take you to a place where you can wash and prepare."

Kinks, waiting in the hallway, led Alice back outside.

The streams of light from the canopy had gone. Alice figured they only occurred when the sun was directly overhead. It was dim now, like twilight, and he understood what Zule meant by calling night 'the dark'. With no artificial light, it would be pitch black once the sun had set.

"Where did you get the name Kinks?" he asked, casually.

"From the band," she said. "We have a few of their albums — Well Respected Kinks, Lola versus Powerman and the Money-Go-Round, part one, and Face to Face."

"Are any of the others named after bands?"

"Everyone except Zule."

"What does Zule mean?"

"I think it came from a character in a computer game."

"What about your tribe? Why are you called the Vixen?"

"They were a female heavy metal band from the 20th century"

"Cool," said Alice. "I know of them. This Rooga," he went on. "You ever seen one?"

"Yes, plenty of times." She stopped and pointed to a nasty scar on her hip. "We fought once. He tried to rape me."

Alice was finding it difficult to keep his eyes off her lovely pointed breasts. Unperturbed by his amorous glances, she carried on along the side of the Temple.

"So, your scar ... was that from a weapon?" Alice asked.

"No, from its teeth. It first rapes its prey, then eats it alive."

"Christ," thought Alice, rocked almost as much by her unexpected swearing as her story.

"Lately, it's been waiting in ambush for us," Kinks went on. "It's only a matter of time before it kills again."

"So ... is it human then?" Alice asked. "You said it tried to rape you. Does it fancy humans?"

"It is part human I think, but mostly animal. It's huge, strong, grotesque. And it has an enormous cock."

"Uh ... good to know, I guess."

Alice was having difficulty imagining what kind of creature the Rooga was. But after the gargantuan redback, he figured anything was possible. One thing he was sure of — sooner or later, he was going to find out.

Finally, Alice and Kinks came to a pond, where the others were immersed in water up to their necks. Judging by the mist floating above the water, Alice guessed the pool was warm, probably geothermal. He also figured the canopy over the park operated like a greenhouse, which would explain the tropical vegetation.

"Get in with them," said Kinks. "It is very warm. It bubbles up from the earth below."

Kinks feasted her eyes as he stripped off his clothes.

"Nice," she said, admiringly.

Alice, grinning, slipped into the pond and sat with the others. "Nice," said Derg, repeating Kinks. Chez sniggered. Alice laughed too. They were certainly picking up language quickly, even if it was only the naughty bits.

"Ah!" Alice sighed with pleasure, sinking into the bubbling hot water. "Feels happening."

Ex parroted, "Happening."

Kinks called out: "When you are finished, come to the temple for the feast. It will be ready in an hour." She turned and walked back the way they'd come.

I was like taking a hot bath. Alice could smell sulphur, which confirmed that the source was volcanic. He was sitting between Djard and Ex. He looked slyly at Djard's small, firm, naked breasts. She caught him pegging, and folded her arms modestly over them.

Ex was cleaning the medallion hanging around his neck.

"What is that?" Alice asked.

"The Shine is the key," answered Djard.

"Key to what?"

"We not know what key for," she said. "But chief has always The Shine."

That suggested The Shine was handed down among chiefs, and confirmed that Ex must be one. Which meant perhaps he shouldn't screw Djard — he certainly fancied her, but then he also fancied Zule and Kinks. He pondered, briefly, their sexual preferences, considering there were no men — they could very well be a tribe of lesbians. Djard, on other hand, definitely seemed to want him. But then, he didn't want to antagonise Ex, who, as chief, obviously considered Djard his property. It was a poser, alright, he thought, grinning to himself. He'd have to think it over. A lot.

CHAPTER 15
EXTINCTION CHRONICLES

BY THE TIME they had finished bathing in the wonderfully warm water, it was near dark. Alice enjoyed Djard's taut, naked body as she got out of the pond. She was ripped, and would compete admirably with any of the Vixens — apart, maybe, from Kinks and Zule.

They dressed, and headed back to the temple. It had been lit with oil lamps, and a long table had been set up for dining. It looked like the interior of a medieval palace. There were no chairs, but stacks of plates and cutlery. On closer inspection, Alice realized that the plates were hubcaps, beautifully cleaned.

"Where do you get the oil for the lamps?" he asked Kinks, who had appeared alongside him.

"It's sump oil," she said. "There are places where vehicles are buried, mostly along the borders. We think that once there were roads."

"That makes sense," Alice agreed.

Zule appeared from behind the curtain, and instantly arrested Alice's attention. She was dressed differently again. With her hair up, she was wearing a chrome-studded bra under a ragged, sleeveless denim jacket with a blood-red scarf threaded through the right epaulet, dangling to her knee. On her nethers, she wore a studded string bikini bottom, complemented by a pair of black, stiletto-heeled knee-high boots. Slung around her thin waist was a thick black leather belt. Zule was decked out heavy metal. A full-on vixen indeed.

"Hey Zule, happening!" Alice complimented.

She shot him back a curt smile.

Ex mirrored Alice: "Happening!" And was rewarded with a stiff elbow in the ribs from Djard.

It was the first sign of jealousy Alice had noticed from her.

"Where did you get the treads?" asked Alice.

"Hand-me-downs. From my grandmother," she replied, with a saucy smile.

"She must've been one helluva gal."

A line of Vixens entered, each carrying pairs of hubcaps, one covering the other. They placed them on the table. Chez lifted one, sniffed the contents, then snatched a bone from it and started gnawing. Kinks slapped his hand. "Naughty, Chez!"

It was too late, he had already almost finished it. He grinned, chewing, and repeated: "Chez naughty."

"Let's eat!" commanded Zule, with a clap of her hands.

Two girls entered, carrying woks. They were wearing white men's boxer shorts, and their topless bodies were painted green to the neck. A third girl handed Zule a sceptre with a Harley Davidson flying eagle badge at the end. Zule waved it over the food and, looking skywards, pronounced: "We thank the Star Lord for what we are about to receive."

The other girls, with the exception of Djard, looked up and murmured: "The Star Lord."

Ex and the others were bemused. Alice simply waited for the ritual to end, then turned to Zule. "Why the ceremony?" he asked. "What's the dish?"

"We bless this dish because it is a delicacy," she said. "It is rare for us to catch the creature we cooked."

"What creature was that?" Alice asked, reservedly eyeing the large dish being offered to him.

"Snake," said Zule.

"Snake, aye? Happening," he said, scraping a good size chunk off the wok and onto his hubcap. It was immersed in a rich gravy, which he scooped on top.

"Tell me," Alice asked Zule. "Who is the Star Lord?"

"Oh, because we can't see the stars, we can only imagine what they, together with the moon and the sun, look like," she replied. "So for as long as I can remember, we have offered thanks for our food and safety to the Star Lord."

"That's trippy," said Alice, smiling. "I wrote and recorded a song called Star Lord on one of my albums."

Zule looked shocked. "Are you a performer?" she asked.

"Yes," said Alice. "A heavy metal singer and composer."

"Would you sing us your song? Star Lord?" asked Zule.

Alice hesitated. Thinking she needed to persuade him, Zule stood up and tapped her sceptre on the table for attention.

"Listen, everyone!" she shouted. "Alice is a singer. If we ask him nicely, he might sing us his song: Star Lord."

A murmur of excitement went around the room. Kinks started a chant, quickly grabbed by the rest of the Vixen. In unison, the women yelled: "We want Alice! We want Alice!"

Ex and the others thought it was fun, and joined in. Chez took the opportunity to grab another bone while everyone was distracted. For the first time since losing Stain, Alice wanted to take the opportunity to sing. Rising to his feet, he raised a hand to stop the chant, then launched into an unaccompanied rendition of Star Lord.

Star Lord
Your footprints in the sky
Take me
Let's fly through space and time
Far away to a distant galaxy
Star Lord
You and me

Your world is a strange place

With no one to guide you
Though you're only human
Why does greed divide you
But I have the power
I'm born of the force
I'm the Star Lord
I can fly

I can take you away to the stars
We can fly through the universe
And in the darkness of space
I can show you a place
You will be lost for words

I, I can offer peace of mind
I'm the Star Lord
Come we'll fly
I'm the Star Lord
Come we'll fly.

He sat back down. The audience, awestruck by his powerful, soulful voice, sat in silence for a moment. Zule began the applause. It was something the barbarians weren't familiar with, but apparently found enjoyable once they got going. The room thundered.

When it had died down, Zule turned to Alice. "Thank you," she said. "That was really something. No-one has ever sung for us before. The words told a story of the people of your time. I would love to see the footprints in the sky," she added, wistfully.

"Maybe one day you will, Zule," said Alice, softly. "Let me tell you, it is wonderful experience."

"Was it seeing them that caused you to write the song?"

"Yes. Once, at midnight, I was sitting on a high hill called Glastonbury Tor. That's in England, another country from this. It's an incredibly mystical place. I looked up at the stars. The clouds covering the full moon and the sky began to part, to let the stars and moon shine through. They looked to me like footprints left by ripple soles. And that's when the song came to me."

"What an experience that must have been," said Zule. "I hope, one day, I get to experience it too."

When they had finished feasting, Zule ordered a final delicacy. One of the green-painted girls brought a hubcap filled with broth. On a signal from Zule, she offered a sip to Alice. It was obviously an honour bestowed upon him by Zule. The smell and taste were surprisingly familiar, and Alice started to grin. The broth was offered to Zule, then to each of the guests before being passed around the Vixens.

Alice whispered in Zule's ear: "We call this magic mushrooms."

Zule leaned close to him and whispered back, "We call this … magic mushrooms."

Unsure if she was just repeating what he said or actually understood, Alice leaned even closer and said, slowly: "I said, we call this soup … magic … mushrooms..."

Zule bent forward until they almost touched noses. She locked eyes with him and answered, equally slowly: "I … know."

Sitting on the floor, Alice flopped back against the wall and looked across at Ex. He was also on the ground, staring back at him cross-eyed — out of it. Chez had already collapsed in Derg's lap — he'd nodded off and was snoring loudly — while Karn was trying to lick the green paint off the breasts of one of the waitresses. Djard was on the floor, out cold.

The mushrooms were not psilocybin as Alice had thought, or they'd all have been climbing the walls, hallucinating. Instead, they were a species of Oyster mushroom, which cause drowsiness, brewed with pituri grass, a narcotic weed. Nodding to himself, smiling happily, Alice passed out.

Alice woke in bed, naked. He sat up with a start, wondering where the hell he was, only to discover a shapely naked blonde beside him. It all came back in a rush — a wild night of sex with Zule, who'd never had sex with a man before. He vaguely recalled being led into her bedroom and stripped of his clothes. The fascination she'd had for his body was noteworthy, since she hadn't experienced an adult male before ... the rest was a blur.

"All right!" he growled. Then there was movement on the other side of him. He rolled over quickly and found Kinks. More flashes flooded into his mind, being womanhandled by both of them in a hazy stupor. He wasn't about to complain, it had been fantastic. Both of them had delighted in having a grown man naked and at their mercy. There had been such passion between the three of them. It was the first ménage à trois he'd had in a long while, and it was one that wouldn't be forgotten.

"Happening!" He mumbled to Kinks, facing him.

Her eyes opened with a contented smile and she whispered: "Are you ready for a morning glory?"

"Is the Pope a Catholic?" Alice growled. "Bring it on!" He dragged her on top of him, which woke Zule, who immediately joined in.

When Alice eventually emerged into daylight he was travelling on extremely wobbly legs. The first person he found in the temple was Djard, and it didn't take him long to find out why she was wearing such a sour face: all of the guys had been in an orgy during the night and she'd been left out.

There were naked bodies entangled with each other all around the floor.

Alice felt sorry for Djard, and put a comforting hand on her shoulder. But he got an unexpected reaction — she hissed at him like a viper, pulled away shirtily and belligerently strode off outside.

Alice shrugged his shoulders. "Women!"

After they'd got themselves together and had brunch, it was time to work out the next move. Alice could see the barbarians were pretty keen to stay where they were, except for Djard, and he was also partial to spending time as the meat in this very tasty sandwich. But at the same time, he felt a sense of urgency to determine what had happened to Sydney, to his world. He knew he wouldn't be able to rest until he found out.

Kinks gathered the girls together to select a hunting party. Now that they had visitors they needed more supplies. When the two green-painted girls Karn had made his own were selected, he immediately volunteered to go along too.

Alice, Zule, Ex, Derg and Chez stood on temple steps to watch Kinks lead the party into the jungle.

"What do you do with your time, Zule?" Alice asked.

"I read books or sometimes listen to music."

"No hunting parties?"

"No. I leave the hunting to Kinks these days. When I was younger I went."

"It must have been tough, losing the older folk when you were only twelve."

"It was. Some were lost to disease, some died in childbirth … but it was when the men died that we really felt vulnerable. I remember as a kid, standing right here with my mother watching my father and six other men leaving in a hunting party, then waiting all day until only two of them returned, all ragged and torn. My father wasn't one of them.

"I waited hours for him, until the dark came. I could hear the wail of Roogas bellowing triumphantly in the jungle, and I could do nothing but wait and weep. And then he walked out of the dark like the hero of a Greek tragedy — my Hercules, my dad.

"But he was never the same again. He collapsed on the stairs, his body laid threadbare by the claws and teeth of the Roogas. They had been attacked by a whole pack. They stood no chance. The tendons in his shoulder had been severed, and there was a terrible chunk of flesh missing from his hip. We had only limited medical supplies, mostly homemade recipes from a book of herbal medicine. But none of it could help my father.

"He was the leader of the hunting party, and he'd lost his men. The guilt had taken his will. He died a few weeks later from his wounds. My mother never recovered. She was pregnant with my sister at the time. The trauma caused her to lose the baby, and that killed her."

"I'm sorry," Alice said, compassionately. "It must have been terrible."

The emotion of those dark memories was clearly getting to her. She changed the subject.

"Hey, I wonder if I have one of your albums is in the collection," she said, excitedly. "Let's take a look."

She led Alice inside. On the way to her study, she asked: "What are your plans now that you have found us, Alice?"

Alice knew he had to be diplomatic. He couldn't stay with them. He needed to go on to answer his questions. But at the same time, he didn't want to let Zule down. As competent as they were, he knew it was valuable for them to have men around.

"The guys need to find a way back to the surface," he said, and added gently: "And I need to find out what happened to Sydney."

She stopped, took his hand and said, with lost puppy-dog eyes: "Don't you want to stay with us? Does it not please you here?"

"Hey, I didn't say I was bailing out on you," he said. "I just need to find some answers. I can't rest until I know what happened. You must understand that?"

"Yes, I do," she replied. "But we can take that journey together."

"Yes," agreed Alice. "I suppose we can."

When they reached Zule's study, she went to the wall of vinyl. "What was the name of your record album?" she asked.

"There's been a few," said Alice. "The first was Endangered Species..."

The collection was categorised alphabetically, so Zule quickly found the album. She brought it over to him. "This one?"

He took it with a big grin. "Yes. Brings back plenty of memories, looking at this." He sat in an armchair, studying the cover, while Zule went over to a cabinet, opened the door, took a wooden box from inside and then sat in the lounge opposite, the box perched on her knee.

"In here is the most valuable object we have," she said, emotionally. "My grandfather Declan's diary."

Alice sensed the significance of the relic — it was probably the only direct connection Zule had with her family. At the same time, the thought of what it might contain lifted his spirits. He watched as, with reverence, Zule lifted the old, crumpled book out of the box.

"Sadly, the first sixty pages were destroyed," she said. "The book was found on his body after a Rooga had ravaged him. He was floating in the swamp near the Gash, and the water had obliterated the writing. But the rest of the book survived. I think you might find your answers — or at least leads to your answers — in it."

"The Gash?" said Alice. "What's that?"

"A great chasm at the far end of the forest. It stops us from exploring any further," she answered. Alice remembered seeing the great rift from the cliff when they first sighted the park.

He took the badly-decayed book from her. "I see what you mean by the water damage," he said, gently opening the first dog-eared page, yellowed with age. The first chunk of the book was so affected by water damage that they had virtually rotted into mouldy flakes. The first page he was able to read was numbered sixty-two. Even then, it was difficult for him to read the handwriting, it had faded so much.

Seeing the problem, Zule hopped up and retrieved a magnifying glass from inside the cabinet.

"Here," she said. "This should help. We use it to make a beam to light our fire."

She had told him it had been difficult for them to learn to read, so it was likely Zule had never read the diary. Alice held the glass over the text and read out loud:

"From then on it was decided we had no alternative but to find a way back to the surface. Living here isn't sustainable. But the question is: what lies between us and there? If the Rooga is any example of the menace we have to contend with, we won't stand a chance.

"Aaron is positive there's a way to cross the Gash. He was on a hunting party a week ago that went out further than anyone had so far. They sighted a narrow section that looked possible to cross. We all know that the other side of the Gash holds the key to the surface, and that it's the Gash that keeps us trapped here, at the mercy of the Roogas. Killing them off just isn't an option — they are too cunning and too strong.

"I've lost any comprehension of what day it might be, or what year. But today Aaron will lead myself, Jacob, Billy, Sam, Johnny and Ahmed on an expedition to the surface. My wife, Lizzie, and the other woman do not agree with our quest. But we, that is the men, realise that, following six recent deaths from Rooga attacks, it won't be long before they kill us all. If only we can find a way out ... or at least find some better weapons to deal with these frightful monsters. God, what we would give for a gun.

"Day one," Alice read on.

"We left at dawn. It was an emotional parting. My wife and three young daughters stood on the steps of the Memorial in tears, waving goodbye. It left a hollow feeling in my gut.

"We headed for the Elizabeth Street side, because there seemed to be fewer predators there. I'm not sure why that is so.

"The first attack came tonight. We had camped near the Museum Subway Station, what's left of it. Johnny and Ahmed went to survey the subway entrance. Even though the building itself has gone, the staircase down is intact.

"They came back after an hour with things they'd found, none of it of any value now, but at least we know there may be things down there for a later expedition to find. It had been so dark they'd only made it down to the first level, and found what remained of a shop, a newsagent, ticket vending machines and a kiosk.

"We were looking at a couple of books when we heard them moving in the bush. There were four of them. We hadn't lit a fire, so we didn't have a torch to frighten them off.

"A big, ugly, albino Rooga, with piercing red eyes and arms like a bodybuilder, charged out of the dark bush. It grabbed Johnny and dragged him off — he was screaming and kicking. There was nothing we could do.

"Three more of them came at us out of the darkness. Desperate, unable to put up any resistance, our spears were useless in the dark. Ahmed led us into the Subway entrance. Johnny's screams of terror and agony filled the darkness and will remain in my memory for as long as I survive in this world of horror.

"But out of the terror of this night I have discovered something important: the Roogas are reluctant to follow us into the subway. For some reason it frightens them."

"Day 2: morning. We have just returned from searching for Johnny. I found his head and some bones not far from us, in a small clearing saturated with blood. They had eaten him alive. Ahmed said a prayer, but the rest of us couldn't believe in a benevolent God who would allow such a detestable creature to exist, or to let such devastation befall the world."

Alice put down the book. "He said the world. Not just Sydney. Something happened that destroyed the world."

CHAPTER 16
UNDERWORLD

A LICE TURNED THE page of Declan's diary and continued to read out loud. "After the attack we were too afraid to continue in same direction. Once the Roogas have your scent, they stalk you until they can lay an ambush at their convenience. We won't last a day travelling in the direction of the Gash. We have no alternative but to try and find a way through the subway.

"There was a light beam, so I used a glass to light a fire while the guys scavenged for components to make torches. We expected to need them to navigate the dark subway tunnels. Two of us carried burning torches, while the rest carried spares.

"We found the shops on the first level. I knew there were three levels: the original station had northbound and southbound platforms on the city circle line, and two newer levels: the airport line and the western line. Fortunately, being the eldest, I remembered the Sydney subway system well — I had been a train commuter in my younger days. If the train line is intact, we should be able to get close to the Gash and bypass further Rooga ambushes.

"We entered the subway and started up the line. Initially all seemed well. But by the time I reckoned we had to be near the Gash, which lay near what was formerly Park Street, we were down to our last torches. So the question is: is there a way back to the surface from down here? As the last torch sputtered out we were surprised that we could still see. Either our eyes had become accustomed to the dark or light was seeping in from somewhere.

"We arrived at the end of the line, at least for us: the tunnel is cut off by a huge chasm that must be the Gash. We need to find a way up to cross it. Half of Hyde Park and then St. James Subway Station must be on the other side.

"I found a service exit that would have been used by railway linesmen. It was a narrow winding staircase that I guessed would lead up to a manhole. I was right, but getting it open was a problem. After rummaging around for a battering ram, we found a broken sleeper and used it with much exertion to knock the manhole open.

"We have come out right on the edge of the Gash. I'm looking down into it now, even as I write. At a guess, it's more than a hundred metres deep. Jacob just dropped a rock into it and we counted fifteen seconds before it landed. At nine point seven metres per second, say ten, it must have fallen around one hundred and fifteen metres. I can see a massive hole about half way down, among all the broken pipes and cables, that must be the continuation of the northbound subway tunnel. I must stop. Aaron has recognised something...

"I've just returned from Aaron showing us the crossing he found last time he was here. The width of the Gash is consistently thirty metres across, but at the most westerly end, where it butts against the cliff face to the canopy, it's only five or six metres across ... too far to jump, but not too far if we could find something to bridge it. We saw just the thing in the subway.

"We've been back down below and retrieved a six-metre length of planking that was shoring up a wall. It was a struggle getting it up the manhole, but we managed it with nothing more than a few splinters.

"We've got the plank to span the Gash, but it's only five centimetres thick. I think it will bow in the middle under our body weight when we're trying to cross. A fall into that abyss is too much even to contemplate. But we have no choice. We're giving it a go. Being the lightest, skinny Sam has volunteered to cross first. We've found a coil of rope below and tied it round his waist. We'll anchor it to the trunk of the nearest tree as a safety harness.

"I write with sadness ... poor Sam only made it half way across. The bridge snapped under his weight as I'd feared, and down he went. The rope held, but when we were hauling him up it rubbed against the jagged edge of the cliff face and frayed through. Sam screamed and screamed as he disappeared into the void.

"I sat at the edge of the Gash for an hour with my head in my hands, punishing myself for trying the impossible against my better judgement. In retrospect, it was never going to work, the plank was just too springy. Two of us dead now, and we haven't even made it past the Gash. While I'm sitting here writing and regretting my bad decisions, Aaron, Billy and Ahmed have gone below to search for another way to solve our problem.

"They've just come back with another plank, this one way shorter than the last one and even springier. I can't believe it!

"Billy completely blew me away when he told me what he planned to do. He would fix one end of the plank under the exposed root of the big old Morton Bay Fig tree nearest the Gash, the one we'd fastened the rope around before, and point it out into the Gash. The he'd bounce on it, using it like a diving board to spring across. It's madness. I'm not prepared to lose another man. I want no part of it.

"Youth is impulsive. The three of them have outvoted me. Billy, the most athletic of us and the originator of the idea, volunteered to make the jump. We have fastened a new, thicker rope around his waist, and the plank is firmly jammed under the tree. He's about to give it a try.

"Once again, I have to say: I can't believe it! Billy stepped out onto the plank to test its springiness. We all held our breaths. Looking back, he said: 'I better make the first jump the best one, there'll be no room for seconds.' Always the joker.

"Billy walked back to the anchored end of the plank. Then, with a hop, skip, bounce and a huge leap of faith, he flew through the air and landed safely on the other side. Boy, we let out a cheer. We figured it was so loud you probably could hear us back at the Memorial!

"Billy tied off the rope, so that if one of us failed in our jump, we could at least be hauled up the other side. Aaron went first, followed by Jacob, then Ahmed, then it was my turn. It wasn't as difficult as I'd thought. Once I got out to the end of the plank, it didn't seem such a huge distance to the other side. Pity we hadn't thought of it before we lost Sam. We had to leave the plank in place, but it's unlikely a Rooga would be smart enough to use it as we did. But we took the rope with us, in case we need it.

"This is the first rest we've taken since a long, hard trek through rugged terrain: concrete blocks, twisted iron and wreckage everywhere, all of it tangled with thick vegetation. There are a lot more rusted, smashed and partly-melted vehicles on this side of the Gash — cars, buses, even a couple of trucks. When we reached the end of the cavern, there wasn't as much left of the park as we'd expected. My aim was to reach the entrance of St. James Subway Station, but we found it was blocked with rubble.

"I remembered that in Market Street, opposite the station, there was an entrance to a massive series of subterranean shopping malls, connected up all the way to the Town Hall. But when we looked it wasn't there ... all we could find was a massive cliff face. It was frustrating. Then I remembered the entrance to the Domain Underground Moving Footway wasn't far from the Archibald Fountain, which is up this end of the park somewhere. So we headed in that direction. Because it was underground, I expected the footway might have survived and would continue through the wall of the eastern side of the cavern. If it did survive, then the underground parking facility it linked with could be a way to the surface.

"We have found what remains of the Archibald Fountain with its classic depiction of Theseus and the Minotaur, with Apollo watching them from above. The wonderful bronze figures have melted into an amorphous blob. But at least I know where I am ... it's not too far from here to the moving footway. Even though the cliff face on the eastern side of the cavern is near, I have a gut feeling the entrance to the footway might still exist.

"We had to remove a lot of bush and debris, but we eventually found the entrance to the footway. It's getting dark, so we've set up camp just inside the entrance. I'm writing this in the hope that tomorrow we will find a route to the surface.

"Day 3. We started today full of hope, but only got a little way before finding an obstruction. Part of the ceiling of the moving footway has collapsed, totally blocking us. We had to make a choice: clear it or go back. We voted to go on, and set to work making a hole big enough to squeeze through. It took most of the day but eventually we succeeded. Now we're hoping there aren't any more collapsed ceilings.

"We entered the footway. It was full of cobwebs — huge cobwebs. We're worried about where the spiders that made them are. We found a human skeleton, then a little further along we got the shock of our lives as a disembodied voice spoke to us from a speaker on the wall, giving us directions. I figured it was a recorded message from someone living nearby. We moved quickly along the footway in case the voice was from an enemy, and came to a crossroads at the end. We had to make a decision: left or right, up or down. We chose to go right and up. I was against taking directions from the recorded voice. We agreed to ignore it and follow our instincts — that's what had got us this far.

"I've stopped to write this note. I think we are near the surface. Since we entered the footway yesterday, we've found two staircases that took us up, then an elevator shaft we had to scale. By the time we broke through another huge obstruction, we figured we were only one level down. We're pushing for the surface soon.

"I'm back where I made the last entry, a level below the surface. We lost Ahmed and Billy up there. It was terrible. All we want now is to go home. The surface is no place for us now — there is nothing there for us, only desolation, heat and predatory monsters far, far worse than Roogas.

"My hand shakes as I write, but I need to record what happened in case only this dairy survives. When we broke through onto the surface, something the size of a small dog, with stumpy legs and a dragging tail, waddled around the base of a tangle of metal and sat on its rump, staring at me. Its pale-furred body rather resembled that of a squat rodent, and it had similar chisel teeth.

"It makes sense that radiation might, over time, have caused mutations in the sort of creatures that would have survived, like rodents, snakes and cockroaches. This one also had a round tail, overlong for its body, and only holes where its ears should have been. Its eyes were small, buried deep in its head, like a platypus. Billy, curious, went for a closer look.

"The creature began gnawing on a strange-looking plant, its teeth grinding. It was only an arms length from Billy when there was a loud crunch as its broad skull cracked, and its body slumped, barely twitching. A tendril from the plant had whipped around the creature's head and cracked it open like a nut. We recoiled with shock, but Billy, ever curious, leaned closer.

"The tendril had penetrated the creature's earhole, and appeared to be gorging itself on the brain. Suddenly, another tendril emerged from the body and wrapped about Billy's wrist, pulling him along the ground. We couldn't believe its strength.

"Billy didn't panic. He pulled a knife from his belt and quickly severed the tendril to cut himself free of its grip. But as soon as he made the cut, a dark green liquid squirted out. The tendril whipped around on the ground like a snake with its head cut off, spraying the stuff everywhere. Some of it got in Billy's eyes. He fell to the ground, rolling around and screaming in agony. We were struck, frozen, not knowing what to do to help. When he looked our way his eyes were gone.

"Ahmed was nearest him and rushed to help. But yet more tendrils sprouted out of the ground and wrapped around Billy, as though the owner had sensed its next meal. Ahmed suddenly let out a scream — more and more of those terrible tendrils were shooting out of the ground all around him. It was like a field of octopus tentacles. We were trapped. Every exit was blocked.

"Next thing, the ground shook. A great, bulbous head broke through ... it was like nothing I've ever seen or could imagine. Like the head of an octopus, except a metre and half high and a metre round. It was a ruddy brown colour, with two deadpan eyes ... all of the tendrils were attached to it. When it lifted them to attack, we could see a monstrous, ugly beak underneath. It was a carnivorous predator, clearly lurking under the surface away from the searing heat of the day, while its tentacles searched for food.

"A tendril stabbed into Billy's stomach and lifted him off the ground, waving him about like a rag doll then emerging from his mouth. I knew it was over for him. I screamed at the others to go back, and we ran for the elevator shaft. When we got there we were only three, Ahmed was nowhere to be seen. I told Aaron and Jacob to wait while I went back to check for him.

"I crept out from the landing to the elevator shaft and immediately saw Ahmed being lifted in the air by half a dozen tendrils, which had punctured all parts of his body. The giant beast was gorging itself on his bodily fluids. There was nothing I could do.

"After serious deliberation we have agreed to return home.

"DAY 4. Today we blocked the footway entrance we'd opened. Unlikely as it is that we'll ever come back this way, at least this diary explains the route in case someone else is brave enough to try again in the future.

"We reached the Gash and were faced with the same problem as before. We'd seen so many horrors that we'd become almost immune to fear. Aaron tied the rope around his waist and jumped. He landed on the plank and somehow kept his balance long enough to bounce onto the other side. We didn't cheer — there was nothing to celebrate. Aaron tied off the rope and we all rappelled across.

"We are not far from home. We have set up what should be our last camp. It will only be a few hours before we're reunited with our families. I dread the thought of having to account for our losses. We can hear Roogas moving in the dark…"

Alice put down the book. There was nothing more to read.

"Those were my grandfather's last words before he was attacked," said Zule, so softly that Alice barely heard her. "Only Aaron made it back home. He took the journal from Declan's partially-eaten body. I remember vividly his story of how Declan and Jacob had been torn apart by three Roogas."

Alice and Zule sat in silence for a moment, thinking of the enormities Declan and the others had endured.

"How terrible it would have been for the families when Aaron returned with the story," Alice said, sorrowfully.

"He died from his wounds only a few days later," Zule said. "Over time the Roogas got all the men."

"But you say now there's only one Rooga left?"

"We think so. He's red, so he's easy to remember. Did you learn anything from the diary?"

"Yes, I did," said Alice. "Declan talks about radiation and what's left of Sydney. That tells me it was some sort of nuclear attack. But the main thing is that there's someone else out there that might have the answers to my questions."

"Who?"

"Whoever spoke to Declan in the moving footway."

"But he said it was a recorded message, didn't he?"

"Yes, but it still needed power for the message to play, didn't it?"

Just then, a Vixen head poked around the corner of the doorway and said with urgency: "You better come quick!"

They rushed outside and found Vixens crowded around someone on the ground. The mob opened to let Zule and Alice through.

CHAPTER 17
HUNTER BECOMES THE HUNTED

I T WAS KINKS, sprawled out on the ground, bleeding badly from numerous lacerations.

"Alice, help me get her inside," said Zule.

Ex arrived and helped Alice pick up Kinks and carry her into the temple. She was conscious, but losing a lot of blood.

"Zule, we'll need a tourniquet for her right arm, that's where she losing the most blood," said Alice. "And a needle. She'll need stitches."

Zule rushed off to her study while Alice and Ex laid Kinks on her back on the dining table.

"What happened, kid?" Alice asked, compassionately.

"The Rooga..." she groaned. "I think we were hunting the same rodent. It must have grabbed Madonna, it dragged her off into the bush. All we heard was a scream. Karn found tracks and went after her ... I followed with Thin Lizzy. By the time Karn found them the Rooga had eaten half of her. She was dead.

"Karn went berserk and attacked the Rooga with his knife. But he underestimated its strength, it ripped his arm off at the shoulder and beat him to death with it. I tried to stop it ... but..."

She was becoming hysterical.

"It's all right ... shush, calm down," said Alice, gently. She stood the chance of bleeding out from the deep wound in her shoulder.

"I tried to stab it with my spear," she sobbed, "But it snatched it from me and stabbed me with it. Then it came clawing at me … and … and … I'd be dead if it wasn't for Lizzy. She crept up behind it and smacked it across the back of the head with her spear. That rocked the bastard and it let me go … gave Lizzy a chance to help me up and get me back here … she did good. But it was too late for Karn. I'm so sorry!" She passed out, exhausted.

Ex glared at Alice with hatred in his eyes. "Karn dead?"

"Yes, killed by Rooga."

Ex bared his teeth, "Kill Rooga!"

"Wait!" Alice said holding him back from running off impetuously.

Zule arrived with an old leather belt and a darning needle. Alice slipped the belt around Kinks' upper arm and tightened it. The bleeding slowed, then stopped.

"She'll be all right," said Alice, testily. He plucked a thick black hair out of Ex's mop and used it to thread the needle and put in sutures.

"Did she speak?" asked Zule. "Was it the Rooga?"

"Sure was," said Alice, with a snarl. "And you know what? We're going to hunt the fucker down and kill it!"

Kinks' injuries were far worse than Alice had first diagnosed. After she regained consciousness, they found the spear had struck a nerve in her shoulder, paralysing the fingers on her right hand. She'd be without the use of it for at least the next six months, maybe longer. Her hunting days were over for the time being. She agreed, however, that it was better than having bled to death. For preventing that, she had Alice to thank.

But Alice didn't need any thanks. Like Ex and the others, he was riled up, ready for revenge over Karn's death. He and the others wouldn't be satisfied until they had slain the Rooga.

He wanted a plan that would flush the creature into a space where they could surround it. But it was difficult to convey the idea to Ex. Zule came up with the answer, and sketched a diagram on a piece of paper. Ex, Derg and Chez got it right away — it was obviously a tactic they'd used themselves. Four hunters ... find an open space ... fan out to flush the quarry, encircle it, and then close the ring.

"Describe this thing to me Zule," Alice asked. "I need to picture it so I can work out how to kill it."

"It's taller than you, Alice, and wider," said Zule. "It stands on two large hind legs, and has muscular arms and razor-sharp claws ... It's incredibly strong."

"Sounds like a big buck kangaroo," he said.

"Yes, but only because it stands on hind legs," replied Zule. "It has no tail, and its foul ugly head is like a demon's. There's a long muzzle filled with pointed teeth, piercing red eyes set up high, and sharp, pointed ears.

"It's covered in reddish-brown fur that camouflages it in the bush, and — well, it's not difficult to tell it's male. Despite its size, it can stalk quiet as a mouse ... sometimes you might hear a guttural purr. But if you've heard it and lived to tell of it, you've been very lucky indeed — because most don't.

"It is cunning, and it knows how to hunt ... it has had to survive by catching small animals, and that means it has developed skills of slyness and stealth. The Rooga is a formidable enemy."

Alice knew it was going to take more than a simple attack plan to ice this thing. The key rested on the weapons available to them, and they didn't have much to choose from. Spears were okay, but what had happened to Kinks was an example of that weapon's limitations. Swords meant having to get too close to be effective ... They needed something more deadly, more accurate. Suddenly, he had answer: bow and arrows.

Zule gave Alice access to the storeroom — an old, corrugated iron shed out the back of the temple — so he could rummage through items the Vixen had scavenged over the years and stored for later use.

After a couple of hours, he'd found a Shimano carbon fibre deep-sea Ugly-Stick fishing rod with a busted tip. Attached to it was a smashed Accurate ATD-130 fishing reel. To his surprise, it still had three metres or so of two hundred pound breaking strain monofilament fishing line wound on. He'd also unearthed an old rusted toolbox containing a pair of pliers, a hammer, screwdrivers and a heap of other useful tools. Now all he needed was something he could fashion into arrows.

Stacked at the back of the shed was a random selection of timber. Underneath it all he found two lengths of three-eighth inch dowel, enough to make half a dozen arrows. Now he needed arrowheads.

He returned to where he'd found the fishing rod, and after a considerable search uncovered a fishing box. In it were a few more useful items — a paring knife, a packet of feathers for flies, binding thread and hooks for trout fishing. Something triggered a childhood memory of a visit to the museum, where he had seen a display of the weapons indigenous Australians had used for hunting. They'd used bone fragments and animal teeth to tip their spears.

A few hours later, Alice had fashioned a carbon fibre bow from the fishing rod, with a two hundred pound breaking strain bowstring and half a dozen fletched arrows with lethal, rodent tooth arrowheads. Everyone gathered near the hot spring to watch Alice test his creation.

Zule had suspended a pumpkin from the branch of a tree, and Alice stood six metres away, taking aim. The first shot missed and Ex and his barbarian mates grumbled gloomily — they were so keen to see it work. The next shot was a through-and-through, and the congregation cheered wildly.

"You don't have many arrows," Kinks pointed out, nursing her arm in a sling.

"I was lucky to make this many," said Alice. "I'll just have to make each one count. If I can get up high in a tree and we can lure the Rooga into a clearing, I might just be able to get a shot. Might not kill him, but could do some serious damage."

They drew straws for the right to play bait for the Rooga, and Derg won. He relished the thought — he loved a physical challenge.

The hunting party set off just after noon. It was a sad departure, with all the girls worried for the safety of the guys, especially Djard, who was seriously pissed at being excluded.

With Kinks out of action, Zule had offered to join them, and when refused she suggested Thin Lizzy, who knew where Karn had met his fate. They also declined this offer, as they didn't want to risk any more of the Vixen. Instinct would have to be their guide.

A dim memory sparked deep in Zule's mind — she had seen men, full of bravado, behaving the same manner and saying the same things. Those men never returned from the hunt.

"It was tough leaving them behind."

"You make light of the situation Alice. What was tough was taking on such a formidable beast."

Alice knew En-Ki was right. "We needed to revenge Karn's sacrifice. It was payback time."

"You got a long way before you realized you were the ones being hunted."

A lightning bolt flashed in his mind.

Alice had chosen to find the western wall and follow it towards the Gash. At least that route would give him vital knowledge of the topography for the other expedition he knew he would ultimately undertake. His plan was to make it to the western wall via the Museum Subway Station within three hours. After a brutal forced march, they made it with an hour to spare.

Alice studied the wreckage of the Museum Station building, trying to glean an inkling of what might have caused such a cataclysm. Declan's diary had enlightened him to his environment, but the missing pages had robbed him of the certain knowledge of the cause of the catastrophe.

It made sense, though, that the park had been sliced like a piece of cake from its surroundings and sunk into the earth. The cross-city freeway tunnels were deep down under the streets that bordered the park, and were probably responsible for the subsidence. But what could have caused the canopy to seal over the park? It would have had to be the result of massive heat. The more he thought about it, the more troubled he became.

Instead of going down into the subway to follow the route Declan had taken, they continued to follow the western wall – they'd be more likely to encounter the Rooga that way. Alice had already determined from Kinks that it was known to be nocturnal and afraid of fire. So they'd come prepared, with bone handle torches primed with oily rag wicks.

As twilight began to fall they set up camp in a small clearing around the base of a massive Port Jackson Fig Tree, so old it would have to have been planted, in 1850, as one of the original park trees.

Their trek so far had been mostly uneventful. They'd heard no suspicious sounds, seen nothing of a worrisome nature, and were beginning to wonder if they'd done the right thing heading towards the Gash.

They decided to set up for an ambush anyway. Chez found a hiding place on the edge of the clearing. Ex crouched opposite, leaving a clear space for the Rooga to find Derg, who was sitting on one of the huge tree roots as bait. Alice climbed the tree and out onto a bough, where he perched six metres up with a clear three-hundred-degree view of the clearing. Ex covered the rest from his spot on the ground.

They waited … and they waited. And nothing happened. Eventually, at the first sign of light, Alice made a bird call that alerted the others the stakeout was over.

When he got down from the tree he found Derg sound asleep. Ex and Chez had stayed awake and on guard. They joined Alice. Ex kicked Derg's boot to wake him. "Wake up!" he growled. Derg woke with a start and shot them a big grin. "Sorry, Derg snore."

Alice laughed. The more time they spent together, the more he liked these strange barbarians. Derg and Chez were a welcome source of amusement. At first he'd thought Derg was the serious one, but lately his sense of humour was shining through. There was nothing dumb about any of them — on the contrary, they were all very clever. Their ability to grasp language showed that, and impressed Alice no end.

Munching some strips of smoked jerky the Vixen had packed, they headed off in the direction of the Gash ... unaware that they were being followed.

The jungle was getting thicker and more difficult to penetrate. Ex was forced to hack down thick vines with his Katana so they could get through. Eventually, he struck something solid hidden in the bush, letting out a loud clang. Alice came to check. He pulled away vegetation to reveal a huge obelisk. They looked up at it. Alice had seen it plenty of times before — only it had been snapped in half, no longer over twenty metres high, perhaps now only ten.

"This is Cleopatra's Needle," he said, moving around to the other side of its sandstone base. He cleared away more vegetation and found what remained of a commemorative brass plaque. Even though the guys would have no idea what he was saying, he decided to read it to them anyway.

"The Hyde Park Obelisk was unveiled in 1857 by Lord Mayor George Thornton," he started, then stopped. "Bugger!" he said. "The rest is missing."

"Bugger!" mimicked Ex. The others two nodded in agreement.

"Ha!" said Alice, laughing. "I remember the story that in 2014 it was covered with a giant pink condom to raise awareness about HIV. Brilliant." He turned round to face the guys, and the laugh was immediately wiped off his face. Standing only three metres behind them was a creature that defied the imagination. Well over six feet tall, with the barrel chest of a bodybuilder and matching biceps, its head was a weird cross between human and kangaroo. The whole shebang stood, covered with reddish-brown fur, on almost-human hind legs. The Rooga.

Staring at them with burning red eyes, it opened its mouth to display a huge array of long, pointed fangs, then let out a deafening wail. Alice hurried to nock an arrow. Ex, Derg and Chez swivelled and stared at it, thunderstruck. It stood there, pumped up with defiance, like a silverback gorilla exuding intimidation — daring, provoking them, confident it was safe from whatever puny retaliation they could offer. Before Alice could get off a shot, it slipped silently into the shadows and disappeared. Its stealthy appearance troubled them.

"What the stuff was that thing?" Alice questioned.

"What the stuff?" Ex mimicked, along with Derg and Chez. "Rooga?"

"Yes, had to be," said Alice. "A lot scarier than I expected."

He'd realised this was more than a hunt for some dumb animal. On the contrary, their adversary was arrogant, heavy-duty and, worst of all, extremely cunning. The four of them knew the tables had been turned: the hunters had become the hunted.

They needed a fresh plan. It was obvious the Rooga had been following them for God knew how long, so the ambush hadn't worked. Ex and his mates were more adept at hunting, so Alice yielded to them.

Marking out his strategy with sticks on the ground, Ex decided they would head for the Gash, travelling out in the open as much as possible to provoke an attack. It would mean staying vigilant, walking in single file, listening for a sign. Ex planned how they would have to react in the event of an attack. On his signal they would break, Ex and Derg to the right and Alice and Chez to the left — then they would circle round and converge on it.

A little while later they set off, travelled as planned in single file, with Ex leading and Chez bringing up the rear. They followed a route with the least amount of jungle and undergrowth to deal with, which left them feeling exposed and vulnerable, even while it provided the minimum of cover for their stalker.

Ex stopped after an hour or so because the jungle ahead had thickened again. They would, once more, have to slash their way through. Alice had a gut feeling that the Rooga had been stalking them all the way. He wasn't sure if it was his imagination, but he did wonder if the Rooga was corralling them towards the dense jungle, where it could easily set an ambush. He remembered a documentary on how a lion works its prey into its preferred battle zone. He surmised that the Rooga might be doing the same. He also recalled that lions attack in a team, and wondered if that's how the Rooga had worked when there were more of them. Now, with no partners, it had probably developed its own stalking style.

They were losing light fast, and needed to decide whether to continue or set up camp. They agreed it would be safer to camp outside the heavy jungle, to avoid playing into the Rooga's claws. They were, after all, in its territory.

They gathered a good supply of kindling and lit a fire. Keeping a full fire was critical; they could get close to it and be assured that the Rooga, with its fear of fire, would keep its distance. They had another meal of jerky, then set four-hour sentry shifts, so they could all get some rest. Ex took the first watch. Chez was next, then Alice followed by Derg.

It was uneventful for Ex, tough to keep his eyes open, but he managed. At the end of his watch, he tagged Chez to take over.

Chez noticed Alice was still awake and said: "Chez naughty, wants bone." Alice chuckled, saying: "You mean hungry mate. Sorry, can't help." He curled up, trying to get some kip. All of them were struggling, trying to sleep with one eye open. It wasn't that they didn't trust each other; it was the fear of being savaged while asleep.

Close the end of his watch, Chez was leaning back against the trunk of a tree, struggling to stay awake. It was so quiet, and the warmth of the fire was making him sleepy. He started getting the nods and forgot to stoke the fire. Slowly, it went out. The crack of a twig nearby jolted Chez wide awake. He clenched his sword and listened intently, but heard nothing more.

A little while later, Chez thought he heard Derg snoring. He kicked Derg's boot to snap him out of it. But it hadn't been Derg at all. It had been the guttural purring of the Rooga stalking its prey.

Suddenly, from behind the tree, a pair of clawed hands reached at lightning speed around the trunk and sank into his eyes, blinding him instantly. Before he could get a word out to the others the powerful, taloned hands ripped Chez's head clean off his shoulders.

CHAPTER 18
THE GASH

A LOUD THUMP woke Alice. It was the sound of Chez's head hitting the ground — the Rooga had hurled it at them. It rolled to stop at Alice's feet. He dived for his bow and arrows. Ex and Derg were on their feet in a flash. They scanned the surroundings but could see no sign of the monster, only the mark of its depravity: Chez's headless body, propped against the tree, a fountain of blood spraying from the torn neck.

Derg was livid. He howled mournfully, like a lone wolf over a dead mate. Ex tried to console him — they needed him to keep it together. Alice poked furiously at the fire to get it going again.

With Derg settled down, they set to digging a grave to bury their friend. They didn't want to leave the body for the killer to devour. Alice was worried the Rooga had killed, not for food, but because it was threatened. It felt like it was aiming to pick them off one at a time. Now more than ever they were intent on ridding the world of the horrible thing — but how?

As they were digging, Alice got an idea. Maybe the Rooga was killing for food, and planned to return to its prey once they'd moved on. Miming, he convinced Ex and Derg to leave Chez's body propped up against the tree and take up positions to wait for the beast. At least that way Chez's grisly death would amount to something.

Alice climbed a tree three metres from Chez's body. He crawled out onto a limb, about six metres up and within good range to hit the target if — or when — it appeared near Chez. Then settled into position to wait.

Ex was holed up in a hide with an unobstructed view of the target, sword at the ready. Derg was more audacious. He was lurking behind the trunk of the tree Alice had climbed. So he would get closer without being detected, he coated his face, forearms and upper torso with a mix of ash from the campfire and some animal lard the Vixen had given them, to mask his scent.

Thin beams of light were descending through fissures in the canopy. From his vantage point in the tree, Alice could clearly see the Gash. It was obvious from up here that Hyde Park had collapsed into the cross-Sydney subterranean tunnel system. Without warning, everything around him shimmered like a mirage. He lost his balance, and almost fell out of the tree. When he looked at the ground it was spinning — vertigo? No, this was something else, something worse.

He blinked his eyes, and tried to focus on his hands. Battling to regain his composure, he threw up a horrible, bitter green liquid. He had to grip the tree to steady himself. Suddenly, he was shaken by a tumultuous thunderclap, reverberating through the cavern. As the dizziness subsided, he looked up to see an electric flash of fluorescent green lightning, that reflected through the fissures from the surface. It was followed by another enormous thunderclap that shook everything around them.

The strange thunder lightning was nothing new to Ex and Derg. Being from the surface they were used to it, and knew exactly what to expect. They took cover.

Drizzle descended through the fissures, but it was not ordinary rain. When droplets struck Alice's exposed flesh, his hands, forearms and face, it felt like bees stinging. He quickly realised what it was and climbed out of the tree to seek cover.

Each droplet of the caustic, acid rain was more like a miniature hailstone than a raindrop. The fizzing globules travelled through the humid cavern air like tiny meteors, leaving smoky chemtrails. After fifteen minutes, the trails coalesced into a mist that hung suspended in the forest with oily tenacity, a noxious gas that forced them to cover their faces to avoid taking it into their lungs.

Now Alice understood why there were no birds and few insects inside the cavern. This deadly miasma would kill any creature that wasn't able to avoid it.

The atomic storm eventually ceased, but without a breeze the toxic mist would hang for some time. However, as the surface was being lashed by a cyclonic gale, wafts entered the fissures in the canopy, generating a refreshing, swirling breeze that gradually began to diffuse the mist.

Alice sighed. He was glad both his giddiness and the atomic storm had passed, though his mouth still tasted like the floor of a parrot's cage. He figured the giddiness and the green vomit were residual effects of Secta's vaccine, and quietly cursed the mad scientist again and again.

He was about to climb back up, when he saw a flash of red moving through the bush about six metres away. It was the Rooga, and it was within range. He quickly nocked an arrow, took aim and fired. He missed.

The Rooga saw the arrow strike a tree, and immediately whipped around to face his attacker, a wicked look in its red eyes. Letting out an earthshattering shriek, it charged through the bush towards Alice.

Aware he had only one more shot before it got to him, Alice steadied his aim and fired. The arrow sank deep into the Rooga's left shoulder, and stopped it dead in its tracks. Gripping the arrow, it snapped it off. Blood spurted from the wound: an artery had been hit. The Rooga glared at Alice, and snarled.

Because it had stopped its charge, Alice had time for another shot. Moving quickly, he nocked another arrow. Before he could fire, Ex and Derg came charging from their hiding places, wielding their swords, and unknowingly shielded the target from Alice's aim.

As soon as the hideous creature saw them it pumped itself up, and fended off their blows with its powerful arms. Though Alice could see its strength was being sapped by loss of blood, even in its weakened state it easily held its attackers at bay with vicious swipes of its razor-sharp claws.

Screaming like a banshee, Derg rushed up close, trying to get inside the Rooga's defence. Easily pushing his blade aside, it snapped at him viciously. Powerful jaws fastened around the sword blade, and with a jerk of its head, it easily wrenched the weapon from Derg's grip. It was rearing back to snap at Derg's face when Ex barged in to save the day. A perfectly placed blow from his Katana severed the Rooga's right forearm. It let Derg go, held up its bloody stump and let out an almighty howl.

Ex seized the moment. Pushing Derg out of the way, he proceeded to hack again, this time severing the Rooga's left arm at the wrist. He was dismembering the Rooga piece by piece, limb by limb. The grisly sight caused Alice, still queasy from his previous attack, to turn away. Ex continued attacking, a man possessed ... it was death by a thousand cuts. The squealing and shrieking, the crunching of flesh and bone while the creature was slashed to pieces, was horrifying. Eventually, blood gurgling in its throat and spewing it from its mouth, the Rooga collapsed to the ground. Panting, drenched in blood, Ex stood over the Rooga, raised his sword in the air and let out a loud triumphant roar. Slashing down, he finished it, lopping off the hideous head. The battle was over ... the enemy had been defeated. It had cost another life, but they had gained their revenge.

Arm in arm, the three men stood over the body, remembering their fallen friends. Ex picked up the amputated left paw as a trophy. Then they turned to the task of burying Chez.

With the Rooga dead and their duty to the dead complete, they could proceed with more confidence on mission number two: surveying the Gash and planning their next move. It took twenty minutes to find the edge of the enormous chasm. The three of them stood, staring into the abyss.

"Shit, it's a long way down there," said Alice.

"Shit down there," Ex and Derg repeated, in unison.

As cheerless as they were after losing Chez, Alice still found the way the guys instinctively repeated his swear words amusing. He managed a smile.

They followed the Gash towards the western wall to find the place Zule's grandfather Declan had described making the crossing. After battling through thick scrub for some time, they came to the massive Port Jackson Fig Tree he'd described. Part of the plank his team had used was still wedged under a huge root. It brought another smile to Alice's face as he recalled how they'd used it all those years ago, a springboard across the four-metre gap to the other side.

Ex pointed up at the big Fig Tree. Over time, it had grown branches that jutted over the Gash. Ex held his hands together and rocked back and forth. Alice got the idea — if they could fasten a rope to the big branch leaning into the middle of the Gash, they could swing across. It was a great idea, and it would work — all they needed was ten metres of strong rope. But that would have to wait until they could search the storeroom back at the Vixen stronghold. For now, they needed to concern themselves with the task of getting back. But at least they didn't have to worry about predators — although Alice would remain vigilant, not yet convinced that the Rooga was the last of its kind.

Taking the opportunity to explore more, the team decided to follow a different route back to the Temple. They set off, following the Gash east. The gap widened as they proceeded. By the time they reached the eastern cliff face, Alice estimated it was twelve metres across. Even though he couldn't see them, he knew the Archibald Fountain and the entrance to the Moving Footway were not far, just on the other side of the Gash. The footway was his ultimate objective, but not right now.

Skirting along the eastern cliff face, they found nothing unusual, other than a lot of small mammals: brushtail and ringtail possums, bush rats, brown rats and water rats, grey-headed flying foxes and a few other creatures Alice couldn't identify. An echidna-like creature the size of a small dog, but with flat brown scales similar to those on an armadillo instead of spines, scurried into a burrow. He was tempted to use his last few arrows hunting it, but chose to keep them in reserve, just in case.

When they reached the southeast corner of the park Alice found what he was looking for; the four-inch naval cannon from the German warship SMS Emden. The old gun had spent the years since 1917 facing Whitlam Square, and was now lying on its side, rusted, neglected and derelict.

Ex and Derg were impressed. Alice, in a mixture of charades and simple words, showed them that if it was loaded at one end, it would shoot a shell out of the other and explode. He was starting to enjoy this means of communication.

They turned west, and soon arrived at the Temple.

A loud, excited squeal erupted from the first couple of Vixen lookouts to see them emerging from the forest. Zule arrived quickly and stood at the top of the stairs to greet them. Her happy expression faded quickly when she realized only three had returned.

Alice led them up the stairs, backslapped all the way by elated Vixen. When he reached Zule she held out her arms, and they embraced. Djard looked on, stony-faced. Alice turned to her and caressed her cheek. That cheered her up a little.

"Chez?" she asked, looking into his eyes.

Alice slowly shook his head.

Overhearing the news, the buxom Vixen with whom Chez had been bonding let out a wail, and ran off in tears.

Ex handed the Rooga's paw to Kinks. She held it aloft, and let out a triumphant roar. There was general jubilation. Their main predator was dead. They could finally live in peace.

Festivities went on into the night. Alice was asked to tell the story of the battle with the Rooga over and over, and each time he embellished it a little more. The three of them were heroes, and they relished the adulation.

That night, Alice retired with Zule. Kinks didn't join them this time: it was too serious. At dawn they were lying in together in a state of bliss. Alice hadn't felt so fulfilled for a very long time. But deep down inside he knew he would soon have to leave, to continue his search for answers. He wasn't sure how to tell Zule, especially now. But she was one step ahead of him.

She looked him in the eyes and said simply: "You're finding it difficult to tell me you have to leave, aren't you?"

"I've no choice," he said, gently. "I need to find out what happened. Your grandfather's diary opened the door just enough to give me hope. But it also created more questions."

"I knew once you saw the eastern end of the Gash you'd figure a way of crossing it."

"It would be possible to swing across, but I need a length of rope."

"There might be rope in the storeroom."

"Then that's today's job: a search."

They kissed. Locking eyes with him, she said solemnly: "I'm coming with you."

"What to search for a rope?"

"No, on your expedition."

"No way! It's too dangerous ... I—"

"Alice," she said sternly, "You killed the enemy. We are safe now. I need to know what happened just as much as you. Our future depends on it. Do you understand that?"

"Yes, but it sounds more like an excuse for wanting to keep an eye on me," he said, with a cheeky chuckle.

She playfully punched him on the shoulder. "You!" she accused. "I'm not about to give you up, Black Alice."

Later, Alice emerged from his love crib, ready to search for the rope he needed. He found Ex, Derg and Kinks waiting for him. "Hey folks, let's go search for some rope," he said. Ex and Derg copied. "Rope."

"Is it to cross the Gash?" Kinks asked.

"Yes," said Alice. "D'you think there's one that might work?"

"I think I've seen one," she said, and led them to the storeroom.

Ex and Derg were impressed by all the junk. Unlike Alice, they hadn't been there before. Ex picked up a pair of chrome handlebars and studied them.

"They're from a chopper mate … a Harley," Alice explained.

"Harley chopper," Ex repeated.

Derg took a look but wasn't as interested. He was far more attracted to a naked female mannequin.

In the far corner of the room, Kinks was foraging with one arm; the other was still in a sling. She found what she was looking for under an old tarpaulin.

"Alice, over here," she called. "I think this is it."

Together, they opened the big aluminium tea chest she had uncovered. Inside it was packed with what Alice quickly recognised as Declan's belongings. On top was a framed wedding photo, faded with age. It was Declan and Lizzy outside St. Michael's Anglican Church in Surry Hills, Sydney, with other members of the family. They were both young, maybe only twenty.

"Look at these guys," said Alice. Mr and Mrs Declan Murphy, just married. What a stunning couple." He handed the photo to Kinks. "Hold onto this for me," he said. "Zule should have it."

He dug deeper, eventually unearthing a coiled rope. "This must be the rope they used on the expedition," he said. "It's probably just long enough, but I'm not sure it's in the best shape — it's pretty old."

"I don't think you'll find another," said Kinks.

"Yeah, I guess it'll have to do."

On the way back to the temple, Alice thought about who should accompany him. Ex and Derg were naturally on board, and he'd already agreed to Zule coming, but what about Djard? He wanted to limit the numbers to reduce the risk.

He found Djard moping about in front of the temple and approached her. "Djard, you come with me or stay here?" he asked. She looked surprised by the question, then snapped: "Djard no stay!"

Alice could see she was distressed. He knew she didn't like it with the Vixen. It was either the competition, or her inability to communicate with them — she was finding it too difficult to make friends. Whatever the case, he couldn't leave her behind.

"Okay," he said, with an understanding smile.

CHAPTER 19
VALEDICTORY

EX AND DERG stretched the coil of rope on the ground outside the temple. After Alice had trimmed the rotted sections off each end, they were left with only ten metres, and even that was suspect. Alice wasn't confident it would take their weight under stress, but they had little choice but to try it. They flung it over the branch of a tree outside the storehouse and Alice swung on it dubiously. It held. Being heavier, Ex gave it a try. Again, it passed the test.

Kinks watched despondently while they stocked up with food and prepared their weapons. She wanted to join them, but her injury wouldn't allow it.

Zule took her aside.

"I'm going with them," she said. "You must take my place. Are you okay with that?"

Kinks nodded. "I would have gone myself except for this," she said, motioning to her arm in its sling. She sighed. "At least now we don't have to worry about the Rooga. I will come with you to the Gash, though, in case I can be of help."

"Good," agreed Zule.

"Who is going with you and Alice?" asked Kinks

"Ex, Derg and Djard."

"Can't you just leave one guy here?" she complained, with a wicked little smile.

This time there was no need to follow the boundary to the Gash. Without the threat of the Rooga, Kinks and Thin Lizzy would take them the most direct route. After only a few hours they arrived at the big Port Jackson Fig tree.

Alice stopped them at the tree root and said: "Look, Zule, you can still see part of the plank Declan used so bravely as a springboard. The tree root has even grown over it."

Zule and Kinks looked at it then down into the great chasm of the Gash.

"Unbelievably brave," Zule said.

"You're not kidding," Kinks agreed.

Ex handed Derg the rope and pointed at a big branch, five metres up the tree, that reached out over the Gash like a withered arm.

"That branch wouldn't have been there for Declan," Alice said. "Up you go, mate."

Derg scaled the tree and crawled out onto the branch. It lurched, creaked and bowed under his weight. He stopped halfway out and looked worriedly down at Ex, who motioned for him to tie the rope off.

Derg wrapped the rope around the girth of the branch, tied it, and dropped the end down to Ex. While Derg was climbing down, Ex tested the rope with his weight. The branch dipped, but held.

"Okay boys, time to give the Gash a lash," said Alice, light-heartedly. He went over to Kinks and gave her a hug. "See you, mate," he said. "Don't worry, I'll get your Queen back safe and sound."

"Just be careful Alice," she replied. "There's no telling what awaits you."

Never fond of goodbyes, Alice nodded, went over to Ex and took the rope, sizing up his jump. He walked back about ten paces, rope in hand, tested the tension and took off like a bat outta hell. When he reached the cliff edge he leapt, swinging out over the Gash and across to the other side. Letting go, he dropped to the ground, landing on his feet. He punched his fists in the air and cheered like an Olympian.

The others copied his elation — so far, so good!

Ex caught the rope and handed it to Djard. Being lighter than the guys would make it easier for her, but still dangerous. Like Alice, she walked back then took a deep breath and shot towards the cliff edge. When she hit it she jumped, and swung across the chasm like Tarzan — well, Jane — and dropped neatly into Alice's waiting arms. Again, they all cheered. The plan was going great.

Ex caught the rope again, and walked back towards the tree. When he reached the rope's full extent he stopped, secured the scabbard holding his sword, and raced towards the cliff like a raging bull. Reaching the edge, he jumped. The rope took his weight, but the tree branch bent a long way down, groaning in protest at his bulk. He had to lift his legs up sharply to clear the cliff edge on the other side. He let go of the rope, hit the deck and skidded along the ground on his backside.

Alice went over and helped him to his feet. There was no cheering. Ex's near miss has brought back to them just how dangerous the jump was.

Derg caught the rope when it swung back, and offered it to Zule. "You go Derg," she said, her arm around Kinks' shoulders. "I'll go last."

Derg understood. Quickly racing back to the tree for a run up, he took off like scalded cat. Alice looked up from helping Ex and yelled: "No, Derg! Stop!"

Derg was carrying extra weapons and supplies, and Alice didn't think the branch would take two heavy bodies in a row. It was too late. Derg was committed, already airborne. The branch bent ominously. He was halfway across when there was a loud crack. The branch snapped, and crashed into the Gash. The rope, jammed between two rocks jutting out from the cliff-face on Alice's side, held Derg precariously by one arm, a loop of it around his wrist.

Ex dived for the cliff edge. Hanging perilously far over it, he reached a hand down to Derg, dangling only a metre below him.

Alice rushed over and took hold of Ex's legs to keep him from slipping off the cliff.

Zule and Kinks watched helplessly from the other side.

No matter how far he stretched, Ex couldn't quite reach Derg's hand. Only 30 centimetres away. He yelled at Alice: "More! More ... give me reach!"

Alice was battling to hold him. Ex was heavy, and he was already overbalanced. Realising the problem, Djard threw her arms around Alice's waist, trying to provide more leverage.

Derg was struggling, trying desperately, but unable to reach his other hand up to grab the rope or Ex's extended arm. His weight was causing the rope to cut through his wrist, and his struggling was causing him to swing. With each swing, the rope broke away the rock jamming it. It crumbled, the rubble dropped onto Derg face. Ex could see that one swing too many would cause the rope to break through the snag.

"Still!" Ex growled through gritted teeth, his fingers now only 20 centimetres from Derg's hand. "Stay still!"

A sweat had broken out on Alice now, his arms were aching. But he held on to Ex's legs for grim death, desperately trying to lower him enough to reach Derg's hand. He couldn't hold on much longer.

Ex's and Derg's fingers touched ... Ex grinned in triumph and then, to his horror, he saw the rope slip out of the snag. His friend fell backwards into the void.

Alice, horrified, watched him disappear into the darkness. Derg didn't scream. A true warrior, he went to his death in silence. The only sound was the soft crying from Zule and Kinks coming from the other side of the Gash.

Djard and Alice pulled Ex back from the cliff, and the three of them lay on the ground, exhausted and stunned. A minute earlier Alice's warning would have saved Derg's life. Djard looked sadly at Ex and asked, "Derg gone?"

"Gone," Ex replied, sorrowfully.

After a pause of utter silence, the gravity of what had just happened registered. The rope and the branch were gone. Derg was dead. Zule was stranded on the other side of the Gash. Alice rose slowly to his feet, walked forlornly to the edge and called out to her.

"Looks like you won't be coming with us after all, love."

"It seems fate has played a hand in our plan," Zule called back teary eyed.

"Where was your Star Lord when we needed him?" Alice asked, half-joking.

"Choosing for me to stay here, I guess," she said. A tear slid down her cheek. She had a feeling in the pit of her stomach that she'd never see Alice again.

"I'll come back," he called. "I promise. It'll take more than the Gash to keep us apart!" His words echoed in the huge chasm. Zule was crying. "I'll keep you to that promise, Black Alice." There was nothing Alice could do or say. He turned away, muttering to himself: "I hate goodbyes."

With one last look back at Zule, standing with a sorrowful expression on her pretty face, and a sombre wave of his hand, Alice led Ex and Djard morosely into the jungle.

It had been an expensive effort crossing the Gash. They'd lost Derg, their weapons, their supplies, and been forced to leave a friend behind. But they had no choice they had to keep going.

The jungle closed in very quickly, consuming as much as the loss they were feeling. The mood was mournful. The trek back to the Temple for Zule and Kinks was equally gloomy. They could only live in the hope of seeing their friends again, just as, when they were kids, they'd waited for the men to return from their hunting trip. Which, more often than not, they failed to do.

It took an hour of hard going before they reached what Alice assumed were the remains of Archibald Fountain. It was pretty much as Declan had described it in his diary, perhaps more overgrown with vegetation, but it was still easy enough to discern what was left of the bronze Apollo, Theseus and the Minotaur. The heat needed to melt them would have to have been seriously intense. An alloy of copper, aluminium, manganese and nickel, bronze melts at around a thousand degrees Celsius. Alice knew that from his days in the mines. He wondered what on Earth could have caused such a high temperature, and why had it melted some metals and not others? Why was the Anzac Memorial virtually untouched? None of it made any sense. He looked around for clues, but found none.

They moved on, in search of the entrance to the moving footway. It took a lot of slashing to strip back enough foliage in the area Alice thought they would find the entrance. When eventually they uncovered it, he realized how good a job Declan, Aaron and Jacob had done to block it. The effort required to undo all their good work was daunting.

Declan had made sure that no predator would be able to find a way from the footway to his Hyde Park settlement. Even with the Gash as an obstacle, he was still made paranoid by the horrors beyond the footway.

When darkness fell they still hadn't made much of an impression on the obstruction, so they called it a day and set up camp for the night.

Alice was awakened at dawn by the sound of demolition. The source of the racket became clear when he found Ex, with Djard helping, well into removing more rubble from the entrance. Alice joined in, and within a few hours they'd broken through. Alice peered into the hole they'd created, but couldn't see if it was clear inside. Convinced the gap was big enough, Djard squeezed through. Seconds later her hand emerged from the hole and waved them on. It took removing a couple more large hunks of concrete, but eventually they were all on the other side.

The entrance tunnel was dark, and they could have done with the torches that had plunged into the Gash with Derg. Alice ran his hand along the tiled wall, knowing that if he traced it he would eventually arrive at the footway. He started to feel dizzy, steadied himself on a handrail, then looked down at it incredulously.

"A handrail?" he said. It dawned on him where they were. "The moving footway!" They had made it. Through squinted eyes, he could make out a long, double lane of cobwebbed footway stretching out before them. There was the faintest glimmer of ambient light radiating from the ceiling, providing just enough illumination to make out a small obstacle blocking the way. It was a human skeleton, on its back on the footway, skeletal legs hanging over the railing. Djard flicked the wheel of a rusted roller skate attached to the foot.

Ex shoved the skeleton aside, and started along the footway. Before he could get far there was a roar, and it sprang into life and moved. Totally freaked out, Ex almost instantaneously hurdled the railing onto the centre aisle.

Suddenly, the ambient light increased a few notches. An all-encompassing voice boomed: "How lucky you are, my guests, to have found me."

Alice figured this was the same recorded voice that Declan had heard all those years ago.

"It seems I've saved you from the beasts," it went on. "I'd say you owe me one at least. Just step back onto the footway, and at its end keep going left. You'll find me."

The fact that the footway was moving, and that the voice seemed to be speaking in real time, had Alice perplexed. He looked up, and in the still, dim light saw a surveillance camera. That helped make a little more sense of it. They must have triggered a sensor that had activated the camera and walkway.

Alice remembered that Declan had turned right at the end of the footway, which led him to the surface and the horrifying octopus beast. He knew that route would take Ex and Djard home, admittedly past an enormous predatory monster, but for now his priority was to meet whoever had spoken. They turned left, as the voice had instructed.

They went through a doorway entering a descending staircase, which looked to Alice like a fire exit. He led them down the staircase until they eventually came to metal fire door, closed, with a rusted lever suggesting the way through.

"The voice didn't say anything about this little obstacle," said Alice.

Ex tried to raise the rusted metal lever, with no luck. Alice reckoned he could do better. Taking a grip, he flexed his muscular biceps and applied all his strength. The lever creaked and groaned, but wouldn't budge. Alice's muscles trembled under the strain. Just as he was about to quit, it moved a fraction. Applying his last reserves of his strength, Alice pushed the lever home, and pulled open the half-metre thick door. Djard looked on, evidently impressed.

As Alice stepped through the doorway Ex grabbed his shoulder and wrenched him backwards. Before he could react, a fierce, hot wind hit him square in the back, so hard it nearly knocked him base over apex. He regained his footing, turned to look for the source of the wind, and discovered why Ex had grabbed him. On the other side of the doorway, the floor had collapsed into what looked like the remains of a lift-well. The wind was coming from the shaft. That step he'd been going to take would have been his last. He turned to Ex and gave him thumbs up, signalling his fervent thanks. Ex seemed to understand the gesture, and nodded in acknowledgment. Alice signalled for Ex to lead the way.

It was going to be very dangerous, getting around the shaft. Ex waited for the wind to die down before stepping onto the narrow concrete lip around the edge of the lift-well. Then, with nothing to hang on to, he hugged the wall, edging his way around to the other side. Alice waited for the next gust to pass, then sent Djard after Ex. Her smaller feet and petite frame made it easier for her. Then it was Alice's turn. Trying not to look down, he delicately inched his way along a ledge no wider than his boot. It only fitted one foot at a time, side on. The shaft seemed bottomless. Alice stopped, shut his eyes and convinced himself he wasn't going to fall to his death. His mettle revived, and after a few well-placed steps, he made it safely to the other side.

Emerging from the lift well, they found themselves at the entrance to a dark, damp tunnel, with water seeping through the fissures of its sandstone walls. Alice figured they must be somewhere near the subway system.

CHAPTER 20
FISSION CHIPS

AT THE END of the tunnel, they were confronted by a high pile of construction debris that was going be difficult to negotiate. Ex held up his hand to stop. Alice started to speak, but Ex shushed him with a sharp wave; he'd heard something. After what had happened previously, Alice wasn't about to ignore Ex's instincts.

Ex was standing between two huge, mangled air conditioning ducts that had long ago fallen to the floor. He peered into the gaping duct on his left, and could see nothing but stagnant, slimy water. He checked the duct on his right, but saw only darkness. Up ahead, beyond the mound of debris, he could see a dim glow, indicating the entrance to another tunnel.

"What is it?" Alice whispered. Ex put his finger to his lips and squinted, listening intently. In a sharp movement he turned back towards the left-hand pipe. The attacker came suddenly, rearing a gruesome head and gnashing at Ex with yellow fangs dripping with saliva. Hysteria welled up in Alice's chest as fear formed a knot in his stomach. He lurched backwards in horror.

Ex instinctively drew his sword from its scabbard and tried to stab the thing, but couldn't get a decent swing in the confined space. The snarling, squealing and hissing from the creature was ear-splitting. When it lunged at Ex, viciously gnashing its teeth, he was lucky that it sank its teeth into the tyre over his shoulder and missed his flesh.

Its jaw was locked, its teeth fastened into the tyre. It was not about to let go. Ex managed to drag the growling thing partially out of the duct, enough to take a swipe with his sword. He slashed, and decapitated it in a single blow.

Alice let out a relieved sigh and looked grimly at the severed head, lying a puddle of blood at Ex's feet. It was the size of a fully-grown Rottweiler's but hairless, grotesque.

"It's some sort of mutated giant rat, by the look of the ugly thing," said Alice. "This is madness. A bloody giant mutant rat … this place is getting weirder by the minute."

His polemical outburst was suddenly interrupted by a loud rumbling from deep inside the ducts.

Ex glared at Alice wide-eyed, then grunted loudly: "Shit!"

Alice got the message. There were more Rottweiler Rats on the way, and they were coming fast.

"They're probably pissed coz you killed their leader," he yelled. "Let's get the stuff out of here!" He whipped past the ducts, half expecting a giant rat to jump out and snap at him.

Ex bulldozed through the mountain of debris blocking their path. They worked as fast as they could to move the junk, mindful that the rats were getting closer. When they finally broke through the barrier and scrambled to the other side, Ex and Alice moved like greased lightning to seal it back off. Alice was filling the last gap when a rat's foul head pushed through a hole and gnashed at him. Ex drew his sword, but Alice beat him to it and belted the thing with a powerful punch that smashed its eye socket. It let out a hideous squeal and backed off. Ex gave Alice the thumbs up.

While Alice and Ex were blocking the tunnel, Djard had shot ahead to scout. The two men were in a hurry to get away from, by the sound of it, the hundreds of giant, angry rat-things gnashing at the barricade, and sprinted to catch up. She motioned for them to halt, and pointed to a hole in the wall to the left, saying they should go there, rather than proceeding toward the dim light. The voice had said to keep going left, so Alice agreed it was the right move.

They stepped through the hole and struggled over a pile of fallen bricks, to find a long dark cavern with a curved roof on the other side.

"Looks like we've made it into a subway tunnel," said Alice. "We won't be too far from a station ... Wait!" He'd noticed a high voltage insignia on the floor. Squatting down on his haunches, he started fishing around in the dark.

"It's a long shot, but it's worth a try," he said, reaching into a cavity in the wall and grasping at something. "Got it..." He pulled hard at whatever he'd found. It came loose with a jolt, and catapulted him backward onto his butt.

Djard giggled. Ex grunted.

Unperturbed, Alice bounced back up and fiddled with the two thick cables he'd uncovered. He held them up and touched them together so they sparked.

Ex and Djard immediately recoiled.

"Power! Don't ask me how," he said. "Now, there must be something down here..." He groped industriously around and came up with a stick. "Cool," he said. "This'll do..." After another few minutes of groping, he uncovered some matting. "Perfect," he announced, and wound the matting around the stick. Then, using the sparking wires, he set the matting alight. He proudly held up a burning torch to show his friends. "See, not just a pretty face, eh?"

Alice stood and held up the torch so he could see better. "Now we can see where we're going," he said, happily. Suddenly he recognised what he was holding. "Shit!" he yelled. "This is bone ... and hair ... human hair!"

The torchlight lit up the walls around them. When Alice saw the detail in them he was mortified. Bodies had been melted into the very fabric of the walls. With their mouths gaping open in silent dying screams, hundreds of people had been frozen in situ. It reminded him of the devastating mass petrification of the citizens of Pompeii following the catastrophic eruption of Mt Vesuvius.

"Bodies," he gasped. "Melted bodies ... this is a graveyard!"

He stood there stunned, unnerved. His mind was doing somersaults, trying to rationalise it. Why did it all look so old? What on Earth could have vaporised people and fused them into the concrete?

Ex didn't care. He snatched the torch out of Alice's hand and walked off. Alice was too mind-blown to even notice. He stood transfixed while Djard and Ex blithely navigated their way over a mountain of human remains, searching for an exit.

Left alone in the darkness Alice felt the strange world closing in on him. Suddenly, a rustle from behind reminded him of the rats, and he yelled after Ex and Djard: "Hey, wait!" He took off after them, running over a veritable carpet of brittle human bones. They crunched under his feet: skulls, shinbones, rib cages and skeletal hands rose from the eerie, foggy, earthen quagmire, seeming to claw at his legs like a nightmare from the pages of Dante's Inferno.

At the end of the tunnel Alice climbed through a hole in the wall. Djard and Ex were on the other side, waiting for him. With the panic attack subsiding, he was beginning to think more rationally. He looked about, and spotted an alcove leading off to the left. He pointed at it.

Holding the torch, Ex led them into the alcove, which revealed a narrow staircase leading up into darkness. Climbing the stairs, they emerged into a claustrophobic, low-ceilinged tunnel. Alice could see the torch in Ex's hand was just about spent, and feared they'd be lost in pitch blackness if it went out.

As though he'd read Alice's mind and got it dead wrong, Ex tossed the torch on the ground, where it promptly went out. Alice was just about to go off at him when he discovered his fear amounted to zero. Instead of being pitch black, the tunnel was glowing in bright blue phosphorescence.

Djard looked about in awe, like a kid on her first visit to a theme park.

"Probably some sort of firefly," Alice concluded, knowingly.

Whatever it was, it gave enough illumination for Alice to negotiate their way. It forked just ahead of them. Sticking to the plan, he led the way into the left fork. As he entered, he was engulfed in vertical banded rays of arcing blue lasers. Then he disappeared. Djard and Ex were forced to shield their eyes from the intense light. When they opened them again they were left dumbfounded ... their friend had disappeared.

Alice was alone in a strange dimly lit room that appeared to be a mix of living room and museum exhibit. Confused by his apparent transportation through a solid wall, he scanned his surroundings, noticing display cases containing all sorts of unusual artefacts: fossils, skulls, shrunken heads, antique Victorian curios and old rusted toys. Stacks of mouldering books lined the walls in bookcases, others were piled up in corners. It was elaborately furnished, but not tastefully. There were a couple of marble busts on pedestals. All in all, a weird collection of the most bizarre curios.

"Hello? Someone here?" Alice growled, suspecting he wasn't alone in the room.

A single spotlight lit up over a tall, high-backed Victorian chair in the middle of the room, its back facing him. "Welcome, Alice," a voice declared from the chair.

He recognised the voice from the footway and moving around to the front of the chair he growled, "How do you know my name?" He stopped suddenly, stupefied at the sight of the person sitting in the chair.

Dressed in a pair of modified black coveralls, with long white hair receding from a widow-peaked high forehead, and facial skin that had an unhealthy transparency, the alien-looking man looked up and said with an ironic chuckle, "Because you were my experiment."

Alice's jaw dropped. "You? What the...?" he exclaimed. "No, it couldn't be!"

"Indeed, Secta," he expounded arrogantly, "the very person who reduced you to zeroes and one's."

Alice was reminded of the stingray and felt his neck. "I don't get it. What is this? Where the stuff are we?" Alice eyeballed the skinny man mean as a cut snake and hissed, "You better start talking Secta or this'll get real ugly ... and believe me, you don't want that to happen."

He got the desired reaction. Secta was intimidated and acquiesced. "Okay, okay, keep your hair on, happy to accommodate." He got up gingerly and motioned to Alice, "Please, take a seat."

Alice reluctantly obliged, reminded of the last time he took one of Secta's seats.

The name Secta had struck Alice's forehead like a fist — his brain was ready to explode.

"This is impossible! You brainwashed me!"

"No Alice, it has been one hundred and thirteen years since we last met. I de-molecularized you, transformed you into energy, safe for aeons, never to be freed — those were my orders. But somehow you transmute to life, though I suspect because your atomic structure is unstable you will soon disintegrate."

"What? Get to the point!"

Secta began to pace like a thespian on the stage. "You see while you were entombed your little demonstration went wrong. Your ferry full of peace mongers collided with the submarine and then zap, Sydney was gone. A nuclear explosion enveloped them all and you my dear experiment, you were the cause. What irony, what pathos."

Alice was horrified. "Hang on, are you saying the ferry hit the sub and it exploded?"

Secta stopped pacing and fronted Alice. "That's exactly what I'm saying."

Alice folded him arms defiantly. "Crap. How could you have survived all those years?"

"More irony, it just so happened I had injected myself with a longevity serum I'd formulated, so the explosion you triggered also condemned me to an eternity in this underground prison."

"Right, now I get the irony. You condemned me to a holographic prison and wound up in one of your own."

"Precisely."

Alice had got the picture, it all added up. With what he'd experienced with the Vixen, the devastation, the mutations. "So, was only Sydney destroyed?" He muttered sorrowfully.

"Hardly, it set off a catastrophic chain reaction. All of the warring nations with missiles aimed at one another launched them — retaliatory— you my dear Alice surpass Robert Oppenheimer as death the destroyer of worlds." Secta grinned macabrely, letting the horrific thought sink in.

Alice buried his face in his hands. After a moment of contemplation, he looked up at Secta. "But how, how'd you live down here?"

"This was my office at Oceana headquarters." Secta said motioning to his habitat. "It's an old, World War II fallout shelter. I was here when it happened."

Alice get out of the chair and prowled about like an angry tiger. "So what, only you survived?"

The statement rattled Secta. "I locked my sister Hope in her lab and she died ... there were a few others trapped down here but over time they died. The feed from the old CCTV camera has revealed others over the years, you know, out there. You obviously came across some of them."

Alice froze, he'd had an epiphany and turned to face Secta. "There's only one thing to do, I have to go back."

"What do you mean, back?"

Alice shirt-fronted Secta and bellowed, "You got me here buddy now you're going to send me back!"

Secta shook his head. "Impossible. Can't be done."

Alice let go of him, "Why not?"

Secta took over pacing the floor. "Because everything I would need to do that is in my old lab and between it and where we stand are mutated creatures that would kill you the moment you set foot there."

Alice prowled closer to him, "Don't give me that!" His aggression made the skinny man flinch. "You've had to survive all these years, you have to get food and power from somewhere."

"The power comes from tapping into Oceana's nuclear grid that remains active ... food, well there's a way to an underground shopping mall ... but."

"No buts Secta. How come these creatures haven't killed you on your shopping sprees?"

"Because I stocked up when I was younger, fitter ... I haven't needed to go back for years. The things there would have proliferated by now, creatures grown bigger, more dangerous."

Alice was on a roll. "So, if I can get us to your old lab can you send me back?"

"That's a massive if Alice, but yes, then maybe I could try."

"I tell you what, if we don't try then I'm going to throw you to those mutants for what you did to me. If I had been on that ferry history might not have turned out the way it did. You got that? Now, release my friends, we've got work to do."

CHAPTER 21
THE SURFACE

O NCE DJARD AND EX had joined Alice in Secta's quarters, Alice continued with his questions, still confused. "Tell me in more detail how it happened?"

"Well," said Secta, indifferently, "The last short-wave radio broadcast we received came from America. It was the week after the Sydney nuclear explosion, and it spoke of a catastrophic chain reaction worldwide.

"Within days of the explosion, nuclear missiles were launched by Russia, the United States, China, the UK, France, Israel, Iran, Pakistan, India, North Korea and others, all targeting their enemies. It was mayhem. The entire world erupted into an apocalyptic nuclear war."

"So I assume they had nuclear weapons aboard the sub that collided with the ferry, and that's why Sydney was blown away," said Alice. "What about the people down here? How did they survive?"

"Are you talking about surface dwellers like these two Ex and...?" asked Secta.

"Djard." Alice answered.

Secta Continued. "Hmm, Djard, they're more than likely descendants of the biker gangs who had built fallout shelters in western Sydney. The diminishing resources after the holocaust would explain why they devolved over time into illiterate, primitive barbarians."

Alice glanced at Ex, "We need to get them back to the surface."

The mention of his friends reminded Alice of Zule, her pretty face looking back at him over the chasm of the Gash. But getting back, stopping that ferry, took precedence over returning to her. Alice knew he had to take the high moral ground. He had to save the world.

"After the first year or so down here, we were running out of food. We dispatched scouts to the upper levels to search for supplies. When they failed to return, we assumed they were dead, victims of predators or other perils.

"At that stage we were only twenty: twelve women and eight men. Two of the men had become reasonable hunters, so we were making do with eating rodents ... beggars can't be choosers," he added, at Alice's look of disgust.

"The ladies foraged for insects as a secondary source of protein. In searching for a reliable source of pure water, we discovered a continuous seepage of groundwater through the bedrock, and a growth of green algae. We cultivated the algae — once harvested, it was a good source of additional vitamins.

"But being deprived of sunlight for so long caused a breakout of serious skin conditions that we found difficult to heal. We were forced to rely on those medicines I could synthesize with the limited resources in my laboratory. By the third year, only six women and four men, including myself, had survived. It was then we decided to send another expedition to find a safe passage to the surface.

"I set off with Doctor Carlisle Fox and Major Ann Church. We were armed but in reality, only Ann had any real experience with weapons. She was the former officer in charge of the Oceana arsenal. A tough cookie. Carl was a biologist — handy for our hunting and cultivation ventures, but not so for a high-risk adventure. Mind you, I'm no fearless explorer myself.

"We knew our journey would be riddled with pitfalls. It started with having to break through the blast-resistant doors on our level and Level Eight. Ann came up with a little shaped charge of plastic explosive. The next challenge was getting past the rubble and debris beyond those doors.

"After six hours we were about to give up, when Carl spotted the entrance to an elevator. Once we'd managed to prise open the elevator doors, Carl climbed the steel cable inside, and dropped us down a rope. In this fashion we scaled up a floor at a time, until we eventually made it to ground level. That was when things got really scary.

"It was so bright it was difficult for us to adjust our eyes — we hadn't seen sunlight for three years. I'll never forget what we saw when our vision finally adjusted ... There were no buildings left to speak of, all that remained was the mangled, twisted, half-melted steel frames, masses of blackened concrete and areas the size of football fields transmuted into a black sea of obsidian molten glass. Scattered here and there were liquefied lumps of metal that we assumed were melted cars.

"In the distance, north, we could see the huge chasm that was once Sydney Harbour, and a twisted ornament of impressionist sculpture that was formerly the magnificent Bridge. There was no sign of the Opera House. In fact, it was impossible to discern anything that resembled the former. The city and the population had been totally obliterated. All the water in the harbour had been evaporated, leaving a huge crater. Debris and rubble had mounted up at the harbour entrance, preventing the ocean from refilling it. There was nothing but ruin as far as the eye could see, and not a single sign of life.

"We didn't know until later that there were pockets of survivors out west, mainly biker gangs like your friends here. I only found out because, much later, I captured one of them on Level Seven ... but that's another story.

"The heat was so oppressive, the ground so hot that our feet were burning through the soles of our shoes. The sky had a strange, greenish hue. I suspect that was due to fallout, radioactive dust, a highly dangerous contamination. I was carrying a Geiger counter, and it immediately began to click at the max. I realized we had to get back down below or the radiation would kill us … little did we know that Ann and Carl had already been fatally contaminated. It turned out I was immune due to the serum.

"As we started back down below, Carl noticed a plant growing from the base of a lump of twisted metal, and went to investigate. While he was doing that, I tried to interpret the atomic blast pattern. It was obvious that the Harbour was the epicentre, but what interested me was why some areas were harder hit than others. The question that most nagged me was why the great fields of obsidian? Then I realised — the blast had liquefied the roads and sandstone bedrock, which spread with the atomic wind before solidifying into obsidian — black glass.

"That's what would have caused the huge canopy that encloses the Hyde Park cavern!" Alice exclaimed — another question answered.

"Exactly," nodded Secta, like a pleased schoolteacher. "Anyhow," he went on, apparently unstoppable now he had someone to share his story with. "I heard a scream from Ann. A long tentacle, like an octopus arm, had grasped Carl around the waist and was dragging him along the ground. Ann aimed her gun but couldn't fire without hitting Carl."

Alice nodded glumly, recalling the similar story from Declan's diary.

"The more Carl struggled with it, the tighter its grip," Secta continued. "His face was red, he was struggling to breathe. Suddenly, a patch of sand ahead of him started to swirl, and a giant head appeared — like an octopus, but huge: the size of a small car. We could see now it had a lot more tentacles under the surface. Carl managed to draw a knife, hacking at the tentacle holding him. It squirted green blood and retracted, but as Carl hightailed over to us we noticed the ground moving all around us. Tentacles! More tentacles!

"As the head sank back down, more tendrils emerged, as though they had sensed our movement. I yelled to run, and we shot off like rockets, heading for the way back down. There were tentacles everywhere, jutting out of the ground like a field of snake tails."

Alice couldn't speak. He was dealing with the reality of the hazards he'd have to face to save the world.

Secta continued his story. "We headed back down, totally disheartened and very shaky," he said. "It was obvious that it would be generations before any of us could again walk on the surface in the sunlight. I have no idea how your friends here have been able survive."

"Maybe the radiation isn't as bad now," Alice suggested.

"That must be it," Secta agreed.

"Ann died a terrible death from radiation poisoning six months later. Even in the horrible state of decay she was in, she managed to give birth before we lost her. She had twins. It was difficult to tell whether they were girl or boy, they were so seriously mutated by radiation. We managed to keep them alive for three years but they were far too mutated to live. Eventually, we left them in one of the tunnels to die."

Secta's account had left Alice speechless.

A few hours later, Alice was sitting alone in a room annexed to the armoury. From there they would launch their sortie to Secta's lab. Secta had doled out some food. Alice hadn't bothered to question what it was — he was far too hungry to ask.

He was taking a moment to ponder his predicament, searching for a reason, an explanation for the bizarre, life-threatening situations he'd been whirling through. For his own sanity, he needed to determine some pattern. Had he just hit a run of bad luck? No, he thought. Bad luck comes when you stop trying.

The world as he had known it had fallen apart. Was it because the city, the planet, the entire human race was winding down, ceasing to function in preparation for death? Was he experiencing the aftermath: an insignificant time of fragmentation and decay? What was he? The carrier of some kind of psychic plague? A courier, who had only to materialize for his world to be torn apart by violence? He felt like a cork in a stormy ocean of insanity. But he knew he had to ride the waves and damn the consequences ... he had no choice. His only option was to return and correct his mistakes.

He recalled that JFK had once said: an error does not become a mistake until you refuse to correct it. The correction would require him to change the timeline, to stop the ferry. He almost laughed at his train of thought: the possibility of the existence of multiple dimensions of time. He theorized: when you wake up in the morning, your brain organizes your accepted reality. It allows you to recognize your reality — everything you see, hear, smell, touch and taste is the result of your brain's familiarization map. What if that map was changed or replaced? Would that alter your perception into something you wouldn't know or couldn't recognize? Was that what had happened to him? Was he, in fact, unconscious and locked away in an asylum, living a dream induced into his reality by Secta's drug? "How can I find out?" he thought. "Was it real? Did I meet a tribe of barbarians and go adventuring with them? Did I find a relationship with Zule in the ruins of my world? Did I hunt and kill monsters? Did any of it really happen?" All of a sudden, he felt dizzy ... the room was spinning. He braced himself ... he'd been through this before ... he just needed to survive the rollercoaster ride.

"Are you ready?" Secta's voice broke into his thoughts, snapping him out of his spinning, dizzying reverie.

Alice looked up at him through narrowed eyes, and said, simply: "Prove to me all this is real."

Secta held his chin and regarded Alice thoughtfully. "That's a valid request, Alice, given the circumstances," he said. "I guess by now you must be questioning everything. That's quite understandable. The trouble is, our grasp of reality is subjective. What I perceive as reality may not be the same as you."

"I get that," said Alice. "But how do I know this is real, and not the result of what you injected me with?"

"Oh, but it is both, Alice," said Secta, almost gleefully. "It is the result of what I injected you with, and to that end we are in the same predicament — because what I injected myself with led me to wind up at the same place in space and time as you."

Alice pulled a face. "That still doesn't answer my question, Secta."

"Your proof will come when you arrive back ... if you make it back."

The answer was no answer at all. But in the face of what he could only accept as reality, and the alternative of staying here and self-destructing in a matter of hours, Alice knew what he had to do. He had only one more question.

"What happens to you, and everyone else in this reality, if I make back it and change time?" he said

"Another good question Alice," said Secta, the pleased schoolteacher again. "I can only surmise that once the timeline is broken, we'd all cease to exist — it would be futures end."

"You'll die?" said Alice. "By helping me get back, you're condemning yourself to death."

"Well, there's not much to live for down here is there?" answered Secta. "But before we do any more morbid waffling, you've got a job to do. Can't do anything about sending you back otherwise. That's our reality for now."

Alice's mind struggled to take in the fact that his friends — Ex, Djard, Zule, Kinks, the Vixen — would cease to exist if he changed time as Secta said it would be futures end. Secta, apparently understanding his struggle, sat down beside him.

"One day," he said, "Time travellers will use my process to venture into different dimensions — different realities, if you like—"

"That'll never happen," Alice interrupted.

"Oh? Why not?"

"Because we're over a hundred years in the future, and it hasn't happened yet."

"Yes, it has."

"When?"

"Now, Alice. You're here. That proves it."

"Don't confuse me, Secta," groaned Alice. "I'm already spun out by the whole concept."

Secta smiled. "That's because you're the first Alice," he said. "The first time-traveller of many."

"You know," said Alice, leaning back. "I met someone like you in a bar once. A seedy little joint somewhere in Victoria, a town on the edge of nowhere, just this side of the black stump. It was a town where a bloke like me could walk into a pub and get a drink without being recognised and hassled. But somehow, this bloke did. He sat next to me at the bar and started talking. I normally don't mind, I'm a good listener. But this guy talked shit. He kept repeating himself. I hate it when someone gets rhetorical about drivel … it's an insult to intelligence. I told him so. He had a go at me for being half-cast and wanted to fight."

"What did you do?" Secta asked, intrigued.

"I broke his damn nose," Alice said. "Now, I guess you're wondering about the moral to this story?"

"The thought did cross my mind."

"Don't talk shit to Alice. I hope that makes sense to you, Secta. It's a safe way of steering clear of a broken nose."

CHAPTER 22
TRIAL OF COURAGE

A WHILE LATER Alice, Djard and Ex were being led by Secta along a dimly lit hallway, while walking Secta explained, "I'll be truthful with you Alice. The last time I visited the mall three of the people with me were killed by beasts. It was terrible, two of them were women, the only remaining women."

"Were they lab workers?"

"No, security guards. I'm taking you now to the armoury, they were in there when the explosion happened. It's on this level."

"What killed them?"

"Crocodiles or alligators or both. There was a zoo not far from here, you might remember it, at Darling Harbor? Well, the explosion set the surviving animals free ... Many of the most dangerous of them escaped into the sewers."

The expression on Alice's face was priceless. It made absolute sense.

"That probably explains the Rooga."

Ex growled, "Rooga."

"What on earth is the Rooga?" Secta asked.

"Near here is what remains of Hyde Park enclosed inside an enormous cavern. A tribe of women that call themselves the Vixen live in the Anzac War Memorial. In the thick tropical jungle surrounding them was a seven-foot, part wolf, part kangaroo, part human, man-eating monster thing the Vixen called the Rooga. It terrorized them until Djard killed it, the last one."

Secta glanced at Djard. She shot him back a macabre grin.

Secta cleared his throat, "Well done girl. Yes, the Rooga would have been an escapee from the zoo that had over time mutated from radiation."

They arrived at the security arsenal steel door. Secta pulled it open, a light flicked on and they entered. Al looked about at all the weaponry like a kid in a candy store. He selected a Glock 19 pistol and checked the magazine.

"Only four bullets, we'll need more. What about these sub-machine guns?"

Secta shook his head lamentably, "No ammunition. There are some explosives and a flare gun."

Alice helped himself to three packs of C-4 plastic explosive and detonators. He took the two flare guns, then discovered a torch. Flicked it on —it worked.

Secta smiled knowingly. "It's a fusion torch. I invented it."

"You'll need a gun."

Secta raise a hand in defiance. "No, guns are not my speed. I'll leave all that to you. Follow me."

Secta led them along an adjoining corridor. After a brief walk they came to a caved-in section and stopped.

"This was the way to the Mall," Secta explained. "I blocked it with C-4 to keep myself safe."

Motioning with his arm for them to take cover Alice planted a charge of C-4 and a detonator in a cavity in the collapsed wall, and then got clear. A few seconds later it exploded. Once the dust had settled, Alice shined the torch at the cleared way through. Amazed by the power of the explosion Ex and Djard followed Alice into the darkness on the other side of the cleared obstruction. Secta lagged behind, nervous about what may lay ahead.

Ex had his sword unsheathed, Djard her spear, Alice the Glock 19. Alice stopped, his flashlight had illuminated the entrance to the decayed mall. They would need to pass through a mass of cobwebs, dusty, scary, roots from trees above that had broken through the concrete ceiling and hung like octopus tentacles. Water was dripping from the hanging roots and seeping through cracks in the concrete — the smell was pungent, dank and musty, the air humid, thick and difficult to breath. Alice's torch-beam fell on a mannequin. They all stopped dead with a shock before realising it wasn't a living person. Ex grunted and pointed at an animal tracks in the dust on the floor. Al trained the beam along them and stopped at a large pair of red eyes glaring at them from the darkness.

Alice mumbled anxiously, "Don't like the look of that."

A low guttural growl came from the darkness on the right side of them. Al flashed his torch at it and found more red eyes.

Secta was getting panicky and spluttered, "We're surrounded. I warned you Alice."

Keeping the torch on the eyes to the right of him Alice said, "Low to the ground they must be reptiles." He flashed the torchlight and highlighted the body of massive crocodile.

"Oh hell!" He exclaimed.

"Oh hell!" Ex copied as the three on them behind Alice backpedalled at the sight of the monstrous creature.

Al flashed the torch about looking for an escape route and it fell upon an escalator leading up to the next level. There seemed to be a clear path to it.

"Quick," he commanded. "Follow me."

With the light off the beady red eyes a scurrying sound snapped Ex, Djard and Secta into action and they hurriedly followed Alice towards the escalator. The terrifying sound of something bustling after them motivated them up the escalator quick smart. Once at the top Al turned and shined the torch back down below. It flashed on half a dozen snarling crocs.

Alice confessed with a gasp, "That was lucky. Now, which way?" He looked at Secta's pale face in the dim light.

"Don't ask me," Secta shrugged, "I've not been up here before."

Al let out an exasperated sigh frustrated by Secta's lack of guidance and then led them on to a descending escalator to the lower level they'd come from, where they needed to be. He shined the torchlight down and about checking for red eyes.

"Clear. Come on," he ordered and then started down.

Back on the correct level he waited at the base of the escalator for the others. When he shined the torch about he found a fresh set of obstacles: collapsed ceiling and walls.

"We need to find a way down my lab on level seven," Secta said.

Alice asked, "So what level are we on now?"

"Four … we need three down. The only way is via an Oceana security elevator, there would be one on this level."

"Where?" Alice asked.

"I'm not sure," Secta said hesitantly.

Alice rolled his eyes and growled wryly, "Great." After a moment to collect his thoughts, he led the way into the carnage of a former time. After a struggle they came upon an alcove.

Alice stopped turned to Secta. "Looks like an elevator, this the place?"

"Yes, I'd say so."

"Give me a hand Ex," Al asked needing help to open the closed elevator door. They forced it open then Alice shined the torch into the shaft. The elevator was one floor up. He faced the others. "We'll need to descend the cable."

"Don't be ridiculous, I'm a scientist not Tarzan!" Secta whined.

Al ignored him, reached into the shaft, grabbed the steel cable and slid down it. Djard followed, then Ex irreverently pushed Secta aside to follow her. Secta had no choice, he needed to comply or be left behind to face the crocodiles.

On the level three floors down Alice forced open the door and found a dark corridor on the other side. He waited for the others then for directions from Secta. He pointed left but just as they were about to move off Ex raised his hand to stop them — he'd heard something.

Al aimed the torchlight in the direction Ex was pointing.

Ex snarled, "There!"

About twenty metres along the dark corridor amid huge chunks of collapsed ceiling the beam flashed on a pair of red eyes. It was too difficult to discern what species of creature it was but a low rumbling growl that erupted from it being blinded by the torch, suggested it was big and hostile.

"Don't like this ... the eyes are too high off the deck to be a croc. Whatever it is, it's big."

Secta was petrified and stuttered, "We have to run ... it, it could be anything!"

Trying to placate him Al said, "Take it easy Secta ... it's not..." He had been stopped mid-sentence by the rumble of the creature charging towards them. Alice caught it in the beam. Powering towards them on all fours, teeth bared in a snarling muzzle was a creature more frightening than a Rooga.

Secta squawked, "It's a black bear!"

With eyes the size of dinner plates Alice roared, "Run!"

They took off with Al leading the way along the narrow corridor the horrific sound of the rampaging bear trailing them, closing on them. The torch flashed on an elevator door at the end of the corridor.

"It's a dead end!" Alice growled, puffing.

"We need to go down a level," Secta frantically explained.

They stopped at the elevator door and turned to face the marauder. Djard held her spear ready, Ex drew his sword. Alice flashed the torch beam to try and blind it. The massive beast stopped just short of them and rose up erect on its hind legs, needing to crouch to avoid hitting the ceiling. It was a massive bear with scroungy fur.

A loud whoosh! — a flare trailed through the air, and struck the monstrous creature in the chest. It lit up in a blast of burning red hot phosphorus. The bear let out a deafening roar. Al turned and forced open the elevator door. Wasting no time, he stepped into the shaft and slid down the cable. The others didn't wait round and quickly followed suit.

The glow from the orb shimmered whenever En-Ki spoke — a living thing. "While you were busy fighting for your survival," En-Ki's voice resonated, "back in your time, the ferry you needed to prevent from colliding with the nuclear submarine, was boarding."

A bolt of lightning flashed in Alice's mind to somehow transport him mentally to visualise Jones Bay Wharf at night extending like a withered finger into Sydney Harbour. The two old single storey former maritime warehouses extended the length of the pier with narrow Bayview Street intersecting them. There was a ferry moored at end of the wharf, with a line of activists all clad in black, waiting to board.

Inside the pier reception office area, dressed in black jeans and a white T, Mal Function was anxiously pacing the floor. He stopped abruptly when a guy garbed in a Captain's uniform fronted him.

"I don't know how close I'll be permitted to get to the sub you know. I'll do my best, to be sure," the Captain said, with a strong Irish accent. "The weather's not looking hospitable ... there's a fierce storm forecast that could well affect where we can safely go."

Mal nodded with a concerned look on his face. "Yeah well, judging by the lightning and thunder it could get a bit rough. Might claim a few seasick passengers. Anyhow, when it comes to getting close to the sub, we'll trust your judgement, skipper."

The Captain tugged on his Peterson Irish Harp Fishtail pipe, it so suited his long white hair, full beard and accent, looked at Mal with one eye squinting. "Where's the young feller who organized it all? Black ... um...?"

Mal grinned, "Oh, Al, he's running a bit late," he half lied.

"Well lad, he better get a shuffle-on or we'll be leavin' without him. In half an hour, no sooner, no later."

That got Mal looking anxious again. "I've tried his mobile, he's not answering. He'll turn up. Stuff always goes down to the wire with Al," he said dismissively.

The Captain started towards the exit door. "We've got 55 on board now, that's nearly capacity." It wasn't a question it was a statement. The entrance door rattled as it opened and a blast of wind blew in Ratsso. Wearing a red beret and a black denim outfit — always cheeky — he saluted the Captain in passing. Once the Captain was gone Mal's entire attitude changed to deadly serious.

"Mate, where have you been?"

Ratsso looked about to make sure the coast was clear, then whispered deviously, "Okay to bring it in now?"

"Yeah, he won't be back. Need a hand?"

"Nope, back in a sec," he said, and then quickly made for the door.

While waiting Mal went to the wall-mounted flat-screen and waved his hand.

A middle-aged female Newsreader come on and said, "Back home, the Oceana Government has refuted claims it will be in breach of the Pacific anti-nuclear treaty by permitting a nuclear submarine to enter Sydney Harbour tonight. Protests are expected during the next 24 hours as the Octagon plan demonstrations against the visiting sub. The SSD have issued a warning that protests without a permit will not be tolerated."

Ratsso returns carrying a guitar case in one hand and a suitcase in the other. He stopped beside Mal and looked up at what Mal was watching.

The Newsreader continued: "The Oceana Government today signed off on a twenty-year heads-of-agreement with Zen Corporation to subcontract national law enforcement. Spokesperson Gorrick Khan, CEO of Zen, announced..."

"What a crock of crap ... where do I put..."

Mal sharply held up a hand to shut Ratsso up, "Shush mate, this might be about Al." They both watched intently.

The Newsreader went on: "Oceana Government reported today they had come to an agreement with the management of rockstar and peace activist Black Alice for them to create an experimental holographic clone of him. Wilson Stanley, Black Alice's manager, confirmed the hologram will be premiered globally in the next few days. Watch this space."

Mal waved his hand angrily in the air switching the TV off, then growled, "Yeah, right, Al fired Wilson. So, how could he?"

"Yeah, the bastard rang me bitchin' about it," Ratsso barked.

"It's just government spin."

"There's a rumour there'll be a grass on board, mate."

Mal face tightened. "Where'd you hear that?"

"At a party, from someone who knows someone at the SSD."

Mal looked annoyed. "You didn't mention the paint cannon, did you?"

Ratsso pulled a solemn face and almost sung, "No-way-man." He bent down and opened the aluminum guitar case. Inside was the chrome paint cannon.

Mal crouched down and looking it over said. "She's a beauty mate, he looked up at Ratsso. "What's the range?"

"Twenty meters. We'll paint that sub red man! It's even got a night-scope!"

Mal stood up. "Now all we've gotta do is smuggle it past the Captain on board."

Ratsso closed the case. "Why did Alice go meet the filth for stuff's sake?"

Mal ran his fingers through his spikey blonde hair, "Something about wanting to get closure on Stain's death, reckons she was whacked."

"You think he'll make it here in time?"

"Your guess is as good as mine mate, but somehow I feel his presence. Yeah, yeah, I get the feeling he'll make it."

211

Ratsso nodded in agreement, "Okay, let's go."

Mal placed a hand gently on his friend's shoulder, "You go, I'll catch ya on board … I'll just hang a bit longer for Al."

CHAPTER 23
ON THE LEVEL

O**N HIGH ALERT,** every noise they heard caused Alice and the other three to flinch. Vortices of dust generated by their footsteps whirled through the light beam, revealing zillions of suspended particles.

"Hope this dust isn't toxic or something," coughed Alice. "Phew! There's plenty of it!"

The gloomy cavern was filled with rusting machinery and decaying building materials. The gargantuan, shadowy shapes of the old machines were enough to unnerve anyone. Whenever the beam flashed across the massive hulks, it was easy to imagine a mutant monster on the attack leaping out from behind them. Alice was reminded of the mutant rats, the land octopus and the crocodiles, evil red eyes shining out of the darkness. Ex and Djard were less anxious, having had plenty of experience with dangerous creatures on the surface.

Alice stopped next to a massive iron wheel with large, interlocking cogs, like the teeth of some fossilized dinosaur.

Suddenly, Alice started shuddering, his body wracked by an attack. He would have collapsed had it not been for Ex, who sensed Alice's plight and grabbed him by the arm.

"I'm all right," Alice gasped, struggling to keep his composure. "Thanks mate." Djard came to him, her face showing concern. He wasn't looking good. He was pale his eyes dull, his spirits low. But he steadied himself and stood upright.

Secta gave him the once over. "Hmm, you're beginning to destabilise — the very molecules holding you together are pulling apart," he explained half scientist, half doctor. "We must get you to my lab and quick." In a move unlike Secta, he snatched the torch out of Alice's hand and with Ex and Djard helping Alice, led the way along the narrow corridor.

At its end Secta recognised a door, stopped and struggling, managed to pull it open. They followed him inside. On the other side was a small room. A mental picture immediately stuck Alice's mind — the burial chamber of an Egyptian Pharaoh. In the middle of the room was a large casket or sarcophagus on a plinth. On top of that, a statue of a reclining naked woman. It was all veiled in the dust of ages. Everything in the room seemed well preserved. Alice could see by the lack of footprints on the dusty floor that they were most likely the first people to enter since the holocaust. Looking around, he thought the room seemed to be some kind of promotional exhibit.

Alice, Djard and Secta watched Ex who, in a trance-like state, as if driven by some kind of magnetism, slowly but deliberately removed the Shine from around his neck. He walked mechanically to the female statue on top of the sarcophagus. Then he slotted the metal talisman into her mouth.

For a moment, Alice and Djard thought nothing would happen. Then there came the sound of power being engaged. The statue's eyes opened, and lit up like a pair of burning lasers. The yellow beams flashed through the dark, illuminating the ceiling. The burst of light brought Ex back to his senses. Instinctively, he recoiled from the sarcophagus.

A loud servomotor hummed, and the four of them watched in awe as the legs of the naked woman parted. Once spread wide, a purple light illuminated in her crotch. It was then Alice realised what was happening: the woman was giving birth.

Another servomotor buzzed, and from within the sarcophagus, between the woman's legs, two chrome horns emerged through the mass of cobwebs.

Awestruck, Ex groaned: "The Shine..."

To Alice, desperately fighting against passing out, Ex's words sounded slowed down, deep and mysterious. Then it all came together in his mind. The smoky grey room, the chrome horns, the cobwebs — the slurred words from Ex: it was his vision ... the one he'd had at the hospital after Stain's death, backstage at the Units' gig and during the interview at Oceana SSD headquarters. It had come to fruition.

Within a billow of smoke, an immaculate, brand-new Harley-Davidson Softail with beefy forks and skirted fenders miraculously emerged. Djard, who had walked over to the side wall and was pointing at a poster, called out: "Alice?"

Alice and Ex joined her. The poster was of the very bike birthed by the woman.

Alice read the poster out loud: "It says 'sons of steel ride the Shine!' Ex, you ... son of steel!"

"Ex, son of steel!" he proudly proclaimed.

Alice grimaced, his whole body was aching. His nightmarish premonition had been realised. Without him, the Shine would not have opened the sarcophagus. Without him, Ex could not have found the bike and discovered his biker heritage.

Secta was bemused. "What does all this mean Alice, what on Earth is the shine?"

"The Shine is a bike: a Harley. I can't explain right now ... Ugh!" The pain caused him to drop to one knee. Djard held him.

"We need to move on or he'll die," Secta said urgently. "Follow me."

After negotiating a few obstacles, they arrived at the St. James station subway platform. As Ex gave Alice a hand up Alice dropped to his knees and threw up. Secta looked down at Alice shaking his head.

Djard crouched down beside her suffering friend and warmly said, "Alice, no die."

He grabbed her hand and pulled himself back to his feet. Stoic as always, he growled, "How far Secta?"

Unsure as to whether Alice could make it Secta said tenuously, "A little further. Hyde Park collapsed because of the subway tunnels bordering it. There still could be serious obstacles."

Djard assisted Alice to follow Secta along the platform then up a staircase. They emerged in hallway of dilapidated shops, rubble everywhere. Their progress appeared to be blocked when Secta slipped into an alcove.

He called back to them urgently, "Come on, it's this way."

When they entered, he was standing at a blast door that showed signs of scorching. Mumbling to himself Secta entered a code into to the security panel by the door. "We're fortunate there's still power ... hopefully this thing survived the heat." A sharp click sounded, and with a relieved grimace Secta pulled open the door. "If it hadn't opened we were sunk."

Failing fast, hanging onto Djard for grim death, Alice glared at Secta and snarled, "Ah! So, that was your little secret was it?"

Secta didn't offer a reply, he just flashed the torch on a sign on the wall that read LEVEL 7-LABS 6-12, SECURITY ZONE RED. Alice knew the sign well because on the floor nearby were the eroded remains of Secta's android.

"You should've made it to last Secta," Alice scoffed. "Might've kept you company."

Secta again ignored Alice's snide remark, entered lab 7 and began removing plastic dust covers from his scientific equipment. He wasn't wasting any time, he knew Alice was deteriorating fast, and so needed to boot up the technological accoutrements required to facilitate the procedure.

Ex and Djard helped Alice into the terrifying chair responsible for causing all the grief in the first place.

Alice handed Ex his pistol muttering hoarsely, "If you can't make back to the surface, go to Zule, you know the way." The through gritted teeth he added, "They will need you ... understand me?"

Ex nodded. Djard was almost hysterical. Somehow she knew that, whatever happened, she would never see Alice again. There was something special between them. She took his hand and gently kissed it.

Alice could feel her warm tears splashing onto his forearm. He wanted to say something, but had lost the power of speech. He smiled at her, sadly. She stepped away, and Ex placed a comforting arm around her shoulders.

Secta got up and came close to Alice. He leaned down so Alice could hear him above the noise.

"Only sixty seconds now Alice," he said. "I've set the coordinates and the time margin ... you understand, this might not work. But if it does, you will appear at exactly the same moment you left. By my estimate, you will only have one hour before the accident. You hear me Alice? One hour. Only you will know what's going to happen. Everyone, including me, will try to stop you. No one will believe where you've been. So don't tell them. Hear me, Alice?"

Alice used up the little strength he had left to nod affirmatively.

"Whatever you do Alice, save Hope," said Secta. "I do appreciate it!"

Those last, plaintive words — 'I do appreciate it' — resonated in Alice's mind.

Secta flicked a switch above Alice's head, and the fishbowl apparatus lowered to just above his nose. The main lights dimmed with the power surge. The sound increased to a roar and Alice felt himself shooting backwards, tumbling through time.

The shimmer in time hardly distracted Secta and Honor from their face off in the corridor of level 7.

Secta, laughing at Honor's sexual advance, strolled back to his lab, throwing up Alice's 8-ball and catching it. "Don't even think about it Honor," he said, maliciously. "I'd rather make it with a corpse."

Humiliated by the rejection, Honor raised her foot to vent her fury by stamping on a cockroach. Suddenly, she changed her mind and let it go. The timeline had altered.

"Don't knock it till you've tried it," she sneered, venomously.

Secta reached the door of his lab, chuckling, still tossing the 8-ball. The door slid open and a hand snatched the ball out of the air.

Secta was taken unawares. Staggering backwards in shock, he shrieked: "You?"

Honor rushed up behind him and stared, dumbfounded, at Alice, like she'd seen a ghost.

He wasn't dressed as they'd seen him before. He was battered and bruised, filthy, his white dress shirt torn, tattered and grubby. His black slacks were ripped and crusted in mud.

Honor let out a stupefied squawk. "Black Alice! But how?"

Alice scowled at her with a look designed to kill. Tension crackled though the air. Honor backed away, anticipating Alice's next move. Too late. He let go a powerful right jab and smacked her right on the chin. She crumpled and hit the floor. Hard.

Secta's eyebrows shot up. "What are you doing out of the hologram?"

Alice shook his head sorrowfully and delivered a blow to the chin that knocked Secta out cold. Alice caught him before hit the deck, threw him over his shoulder and carried him into the lab.

"You'll appreciate this one day," he said.

As he laid him in the chair, he was reminded of the future Secta's last words: I do appreciate it.

"He knew I made it?" he said, perplexed.

Had Secta been toying with him all along? Had all the talk of not being able to change time been a game? Did he know all along he could do it? A heavy thought struck him. What if he knew I made it because this is the way it happens? What if I can't stop the ferry, if it collides with the sub and the world goes up in smoke anyway? Was he just remembering it? Is destiny unstoppable?

Then he looked at the 8-ball in his hand and smiled. He was no longer in the future, and dying. The question he had asked Secta had been answered: it had all been real. He hadn't been dreaming, or in an asylum, off his head. On the contrary, he was feeling strong and vital. The old, agile Alice had returned.

He tossed the 8-ball up and snatched it out of the air, shoved it in his pocket, and growled at Secta as though he was conscious: "Gotta get to that ferry."

He shot out of the lab, raced up the corridor and stopped at the elevator door. Punching the call button and prowling like an angry tiger while he waited for it to arrive, he chanted to himself: "Hurry, hurry, hurry... come on, damn it, I'm running out of time ... Hope I can still make it!" Suddenly, he froze, remembering. "Hope! Damn!"

He turned and backtracked at express speed, hurdling Honor's prostrate body on the way. There were only seven labs in the corridor. One of them was Secta's — that only left six to pick from.

Frustrated, he growled: "Which lab, Secta! Damn it! You didn't tell me which bloody lab!"

He stopped outside Lab 6, looked at the security lock and thumped the wall angrily with his fist. "The combination! Damn it!"

Suddenly, a hand grabbed his shoulder. He froze, then whipped around and let go an almighty punch to the solar plexus of the seven-foot android guard he'd met before.

It didn't budge, but said in monotone: "Did-not-compute."

Alice straightened up, a look of futility in his eyes. Honor appeared behind the android, a handkerchief up to her mouth, dabbing blood from a split lip.

"Get out of my way," said Alice. She glared at him, eyes tight little slits, and sniggered. It was a cold, brittle, sound devoid of humour. "Kill him!" she barked at the android.

Alice lunged, grabbing Honor, an arm around her neck. He slipped behind her, using her as a shield against the android.

He growled menacingly in her ear: "Which lab is Hope in? Tell me!"

"Why should I tell you?" she snarled through gritted teeth.

The android advanced. Alice snapped, "Stop that friggin' thing or I'm gonna snap your fucking neck!"

In a panic, Honor raised a hand. "All right, all right!" she gasped. "Guard! Stop!" The android ground to a halt.

"Which lab?" screamed Alice, pulling his arm tighter around her throat, almost choking her.

Through clenched teeth she choked out: "Number zix! She is in Lab Zix!"

Fortunately, they were right outside Lab Six. Keeping a tight grip on Honor, Alice backed to the door. The android swivelled its head, tracking their movements, while its body remained stock-still.

"Pump the code in!" Alice rasped. She hesitated. Again, he tightened his stranglehold. "Put it in now!" he growled.

"I haff to get zer card from my pocket," she squeezed out.

"Do it!" He knew he was risking her pulling out a weapon. But she drew a metal card and held it up for him to see.

"Swipe it!" he ordered.

With his back hard against the door, Alice glared at the android's sweeping red eye while Honor twisted in his grip to swipe the card in the security module.

A servomotor sounded, and the stuttering door jerked open. It stopped half way. "Hope, you there?" he called. "It's Black Alice."

"Black Alice?" Hope answered, as she peeped around the door. "But ... you..."

He cut her off with urgency: "Now listen, I haven't got time to go into the details. This will sound insane — but I've been to the future and now I'm back, thanks to your brother. He told me to let you out of your lab and to tell you he's sorry."

She shook her head disbelievingly. "Yeah, sure," she snarled.

"In less than an hour a ferry will collide with a nuclear submarine in Sydney Harbour, and trigger an apocalypse that will blow mankind away. You and I have got to stop that collision, you get me?"

Honor was listening intently. Unable to contain herself, she burst out: "Ha! It couldn't happen to a better bunch of...."

"Shut up bitch!" hissed Alice, shaking her

"Fill me in on the rest later," said Hope, trying to muscle past. "Let's move."

He held her back with a strong free arm, the other keeping a firm grip on Honor. "Wait!" he said. "Go guard the fire stairs while I take care of this lot — and don't take the elevator."

He let her past and she took off along the corridor.

"You von't get avay vith this!" Honor croaked, and fastened her teeth into his forearm.

He released her, growling savagely.

She stepped back and barked to the android: "Kill him!"

Alice realized he was in mortal danger. The only way out was to take on the metallic behemoth. He shaped up in a defensive stance, and said: "Okay, let's do this!"

CHAPTER 24
SHINE

AS THE ANDROID lumbered forward, Alice jinked around, then scrambled onto the giant android's back, his hand searching its skull. Gripping the 8-ball in the palm of his hand, he punched his fist into the top of the android's head. It broke the seal covering its central processing unit. As the creature swung around like a mechanical bull, furiously trying to throw Alice off its back, he threw a second punch. This time his fist disappeared inside the android's head. Sparks flew as the dome exploded and Alice was catapulted off its back, bouncing off the wall and onto the floor.

The android staggered around in confused circles, what remained of it head sparking and crackling, then collapsed against the wall and slid down until it was sitting on the floor, systems blown and short circuiting. The elbow of its left arm was jammed in its crotch, and its forearm was jerking up and down, one finger extended like it was giving Alice the bird.

"Alice! Hurry!" Hope's voice echoed down the corridor.

Honor's face had paled. She knew she was a sitting duck and was eyeing off an emergency Stingray in a glass box mounted on the wall.

Before she could make a move, Alice grabbed her arm. Holding her tightly, he smashed the glass box with his elbow, seized the Stingray, took the ball out of the wristlet and stabbed it into her cheek. He turned the dial to full.

"No ... Argh!" she screamed and erupted into convulsions.

This was his chance for retribution. He turned down the juice. "A bit of your own medicine," he snarled. "This is for my girl Stain?" He turned up the juice. She contorted.

"Who killed my girl, who killed Stain? Was it Drago? Was he acting for you?" He turned it down.

"I … I have no idea who you are talking about! Who is zis Stain?"

He cranked up the juice, and she screamed in agony.

"I … I … know no one by zat name!"

He wound it down, then cranked it again. Her body contorted violently, her knees buckled.

She held up a hand in surrender. "Alright, alright," she sobbed. "I tell you!"

Alice turned the Stingray down. A look of abject relief broke across her face. "It vos an executive order," she moaned. "I personally had nothing to do vith it."

"You think I'd believe that?" Alice growled, turning up the juice again. She screamed as he manoeuvred her backwards, just as she'd done to him back in Secta's lab. She couldn't resist the Stingray: it had a grip on her nervous system.

He allowed her to flop down, straddling the android's lap.

Its hand, still rising up and down between her legs, delivered a shock to her lower body with every thrust.

He flung the Stingray wristlet at her feet.

She squealed as the android's forearm rose and seared the inside of her thighs.

"Chaa!" he said sarcastically, with a quick wave of his hand.

When he reached the base of the staircase, Hope asked, "When's the collision?"

"Midnight," he said. "I reckon we've got about forty-five minutes."

"We should go up to the lobby, the moving footway would be a death-trap."

"Lead the way."

Alice followed her up the winding fire stairs. It was six floors to the top.

The art deco Bent Street entrance to Oceana was grandiose by any standards. Four blue marble columns extending two storeys, an expansive yellow marble floor, and a wide, palatial central staircase with a bright red carpet and gold balustrades. Carefully concealed around the entrance and all its 1930s grandeur, armed SSD agents waited in silent ambush.

Hope led Alice into the lobby on the lower mezzanine level. They both stopped when they spotted the first agent blocking their path. Madder than if he'd come off the back fence like a wrecking ball, Alice whipped up a hand to stop Hope.

"Leave this to me!" he growled, shaped up to the agent. With no time for Alice's theatrics, Hope pushed past him up to the agent, and whacked the unsuspecting man with a powerful right hook that dropped him to the deck like a rock.

Alice spread his hands, shrugged, and conceded: "All right!"

Immediately, another agent appeared from behind the columns ten metres away. This one Alice would take on. As the agent went to draw his pistol, quick as a flash, Alice threw the 8-ball with all his might. It sank into the agent's forehead and he dropped, dead as a doornail.

Sitting in a grand chair at the head of the palatial staircase, watching the melee below, Karzoff was reading a newspaper by the light of an art deco lamp on a table at his side. Alice and Hope had walked right into a trap. Two agents stepped out from behind columns at the foot of the stairs, blocking the exit, weapons trained on them.

Karzoff had set up the ambush in case Alice managed to escape and attempt to leave the building, having been alerted by Honor via their mastoid implants that Alice had returned. On such short notice, he had only managed to rustle up four agents. He figured they would be more than adequate to apprehend a woman and a rock singer on the run.

Karzoff lowered his newspaper and casually yelled orders to the two agents: "Take them…"

Alice and Hope raised their hands in surrender.

Karzoff slowly made his way down the long staircase, a smug look on his craggy dial. He was visualising being presented with a medal for bravery for apprehending the dangerous escaped dissident.

With hands still raised, Alice shot Hope a sly wink. She got it. Like greased lightning, they each simultaneously brushed away the gun hand of their opponent. Both guns fired and missed. With precision timing and brute force, Alice and Hope each landed knockout punches on their opponents … both went down, out cold.

Alice turned to Karzoff who was stuck, frozen in time, halfway down the staircase, his face now wearing a look of incredulity. He figured Alice might have packed such a punch, but he had no idea Hope would be so handy with her fists.

"Check the exit," Alice growled at Hope. "I need to take care of this."

"Leave him, Alice, there's no time…"

But Alice wasn't listening. He had an all-important score to settle with the red-haired man. Mad as a cut snake, he stalked to Karzoff. The man panicked.

"What have you got to say for yourself?" Alice growled, slowly climbing the stairs, forcing Karzoff back on visibly shaky legs. "You're a miserable bloody liar, aren't you?"

"What are you talking about?" wheedled the cowardly officer. "You're not into violence, remember? You're a peace activist!"

"Is that right?" Alice was having none of it. Loping up the staircase like a panther closing in on a kill, he forced Karzoff to all the way back up to the top landing. "You'll be able to tour as a hologram, you said," he snarled. "You bloody liar! a feeble excuse for a human!"

Terrified, Karzoff bleated: "But, but … they made me do it…" He flopped into the chair on the landing and pleaded: "I was only following orders!"

Alice stood over him, swinging a boot onto the arm of the chair, pinning Karzoff into it. "Orders?" he hissed. "This is for the order to kill my girl!" Alice grabbed the lamp from the table beside the chair, inverted it and jammed it on top of Karzoff's head. The globe shattered on contact with the red scalp, and sparks flew. Karzoff's legs kicked wildly, his body convulsed uncontrollably. He screamed as two hundred and forty volts blasted into his skull. Even Alice got a shock. He let go of the lamp, stepped backwards, and left Karzoff to fry.

Watching the scene from the glass exit doors, Hope stood with arms folded, impatiently tapping her foot as Alice ran across the marble floor.

"Was that really necessary?" she rebuked.

Alice spread his hands in resignation and said, insolently: "Yeah."

Shrugging aside her annoyance at his cavalier attitude, Hope asked: "So, where do we go from here?"

"I dunno. I just gotta follow my instincts."

"Fine, what do we do? Commandeer a car, catch a taxi, what?"

"We'll have to hoof it."

He pushed open the doors, and they raced out into the street, only to be greeted by the sound of approaching sirens. Alice led the way.

The street was wet. A cold wind was blowing in their faces as they ran. Thunder rumbled, warning the approach of another storm. Seeing lightning crack in the distance, Alice felt like the storm was a metaphor for impending doom. They were lucky that at this time of night, mid-week, there were few cars on the road, and even fewer pedestrians. Alice guessed the troopers would try to encircle them. His instincts told him to head for the nearest subway entrance and go underground. Then he remembered a back alley that would get them close to the subway and avoid the main streets, which the troopers would certainly be patrolling.

When he finally found the alleyway, Alice and Hope shot up it, emerging beside a major hotel onto a main street. They found heavy traffic from cars exiting the underground car parks at the Opera

House — a show had just finished. This was good and bad; the traffic would impede the patrol cars, but the pedestrians would obstruct their progress. Alice stopped.

"If we run we'll be more noticeable," he said, panting breathlessly. "Let's just walk along to St James subway station. Act like nothing's happened, okay?"

Hope nodded, gassed.

Slowing to a walk restored some energy, but as they rounded a corner they came upon troopers random-checking ID's. They recognised Alice immediately. A trooper pointed, and all four quickly brushed aside the people they were checking and headed towards Alice and Hope.

"Cross the road and head for St James Station, I'll distract them," he said. "See you there."

Hope got across the road without attracting the attention of the troopers: they were more interested in Alice anyway.

Alice checked his surroundings. Cars were jammed a long way back from the traffic lights, and he could see the strobing blue lights of patrol cars trapped in the gridlock. The troopers on the footpath ahead were coming towards him, Tasers drawn. He scanned the scene for a way out, found one, and took it. Running up the back of the nearest gridlocked car, he followed a route over the tops of the stationary vehicles, jumping from one to the next. As his feet banged on the roofs, irate occupants popped their heads out of windows to yell abuse after him.

The heavily-armed troopers were doing their best to run after him between the cars, but the vehicles were jammed so close together that their progress was slow.

Up ahead of Alice, a single-deck tourist bus offered an obstacle. The driver stared at him, wide-eyed, as he gave a thumbs up and, to the driver's shock and wild cheers from the busload of Japanese tourists, scrambled up the front of the bus, onto the roof and along it towards the rear.

From this vantage point, Alice could see Hope closing in on the St James subway station entrance, only a short distance away.

Next to the bus, a shelter provided Alice the means to leap back down to street level. He jumped to its flat roof and slid down an adjacent light pole. The troopers following him were left dumbfounded — and with no chance of catching him. After a short jog, Alice arrived at the entrance of St James station, where Hope was waiting.

"That was amazing," she conceded, shaking her head, half laughing. "I don't believe you."

"Comes from riding missiles on stage and fighting angry androids," he said, puffing.

Just then, a siren sounded — a small patrol car had made its way through the traffic by mounting the footpath and scattering pedestrians, and was charging towards them.

"Quick, let's move," he said.

CHAPTER 25
LOCKED IN LATITUDE

ALICE CLUTCHED HOPE'S hand and led her at speed down the staircase of the entrance tunnel. Half way along, and running like the clappers, he stole a quick glance over his shoulder. The patrol car was bumping its way down the steep staircase into the tunnel. There was no way he had expected that to happen.

"Faster!" he yelled, lifting the pace.

With a loud bang, sparks flying from its chassis and exhaust as it bottomed out on the last few steps, the patrol car landed on the tunnel floor. Somehow it had made it in one piece, just as Alice and Hope reached the end of the tunnel.

A quick scan of their predicament presented Alice his escape options: the train platform or a small group of shops.

Following his gut, he headed directly to the front door of one of the shops — to Hope's shock and horror he barged right through it, leaving the shattered remains of the door hanging on its hinges.

Hope was left speechless, wondering to herself: what is this guy?

The interior of the shop was decked out with an elaborate promotional display. In the centre of the room was a plinth supporting a sarcophagus. On top of that was a statue of a reclining, naked woman. Alice recognized it, and the realization shook him right to his boots. He looked around and saw a massive banner on the wall, featuring a Harley Davidson motorbike.

Absolutely astonished, he read the caption out loud: "Sons of steel ride the shine."

As Hope joined him he said: "What a trip ... I was right here, on this very spot, one hundred and thirteen years from now. Djard was there," he pointed at the floor. "And Ex was there, Secta over there..." He turned back to Hope, took her by the shoulders and said excitedly: "I'm not spun out ... it really did happen!"

"I never doubted you for a minute, Alice," said Hope, almost laughing.

He swivelled to the sarcophagus. "The bike came out of this thing..."

"I see," she said, trying to piece together what he was talking about. "Extraordinary."

She figured he was reliving the experience of being in this place in a different time, perhaps even a different dimension.

It was a ghostly experience for Alice, and difficult for him to grasp. He racked his brain, trying to determine what weird magic had drawn him to this very place, when he could have gone anywhere trying to escape the cops. Was it destiny?

"If there's a bike inside it we could take it," Hope said hurriedly.

"No, we have to leave it for Ex?"

Hope pulled a quizzical face, then realised Alice was trying to make sure of the future.

He walked towards an advertising display on the wall, as if drawn by some supernatural force.

He stopped at the display and read the sign out loud, "The key to the future. The shine!" He reached out a tentative hand to take the chrome pendant hanging by a loop of thin leather in the elaborate display. He stared at it with great reverence. This was the key. Alice knew it would open the sarcophagus to give birth to a bike — a bike that would somehow alter the destiny of mankind.

He slipped the leather thonging over his head so the talisman hung around his neck.

Hope heard a noise outside and said urgently: "Troopers! What are we going to do?"

Alice wasn't listening. He was still tripping on the future. Hope shook him and shrieked: "Alice! listen up!"

The jolt worked. Alice switched back to reality. Desperate to find an escape route, he spotted a Honda XR600R off-road bike on display in a dark corner of the room. He raced over, hopped on and kick started it. The big thumper 600cc 4-stroke engine growled like an angry beast.

"Come on," he yelled.

Hope darted over, jumped behind him and together they rode through the smashed door.

The two cops who had made it down the stairs were standing beside their car, barring the exit. They drew Tasers and took aim.

"Hold on!" Alice warned Hope.

He revved the engine and fanged the bike right at them, knocking the first trooper out of the way. His partner had no hope of getting off a Taser shot, so he scrambled back into the patrol car and tried to execute a quick U-turn to chase the bike up the tunnel.

Alice pulled the bike up twenty metres short of the fifty or so sandstone stairs leading out of the subway and up to freedom. He revved it like a bull getting set to make a charge.

Hope figured out what he was thinking, and shouted: "You're not going to do that, are you? You're not going to—"

He was ... Alice gunned the bike, dropped the clutch and popped a wheelie over the bottom steps so the power of the rear wheel would take them up. He gunned it hard, and roared towards the top of the staircase and into the night.

The bike soared out of the subway station and broadsided to a stop in a screech of smoking rubber. Blockading their escape route were patrol cars with dozens of troopers taking cover behind them and aiming their weapons. One was aiming what appeared to be a remote control. It wasn't looking good for Alice and Hope: the odds were stacked against them.

Alice turned to his passenger and said: "I don't think they'll shoot if you're with me ... You sweet to have a crack?"

"I've come this far, haven't I?" said Hope, bravely. "By the way, that trooper with the remote is identifying us to a drone ... It's now or never Alice. Give it your best shot my friend."

Alice revved the throttle and dropped the clutch. Once more, the bike reared up in a wheelie, heading directly for the closest patrol car. With impeccable timing, Alice gunned it and the powerful bike scrambled up and over the bonnet of the car.

Behind it were the other two cars, and the sheltering troopers were heading for cover. As the bike landed, the trooper with the remote was running for cover behind the open driver's door of his car. Just as he made it, Alice ploughed into the door, knocking the trooper over back-breakingly hard and jamming him between the door and the car. This opened a narrow corridor of escape — not down the road the troopers were expecting him to take, but cross-country, through Hyde Park.

The bike was perfect for the terrain, and Alice enjoyed fanging it through the lush green spaces, hurdling paths and other obstacles.

Hanging on white knuckled, Hope was keeping one eye on the sky, knowing that a drone was tracking them.

Alice rode down a flight of stairs to the footpath over Park Street. Surprisingly, there was no traffic jam and they crossed the intersection easily. He zoomed up more stairs to the Liverpool Street side, and headed for the Anzac War Memorial. As they reached, it he could see blue flashing lights speeding along Elizabeth Street, running parallel with them on the right. Looking at the Memorial, Alice couldn't help thinking of Kinks and Zule, wondering if Ex and Djard had made it back to them safely. It seemed another world away. It was more than that — it was another dimension.

He slowed down as he passed the Emden Gun, and descended the stairs to the footpath on Liverpool Street. This time, traffic had backed up in front of him. That let him wend his way across Liverpool Street without the troopers on the ground seeing him. But they were seeing him through different eyes.

Hope gave Alice a prod: "The drone is at three o'clock."

Alice looked up to his right. She was correct — the drone was hovering about two hundred feet in the air, directly over Liverpool Street. He could almost feel it staring at him.

"I'll fix the little bugger," he snarled, and slipped into a quiet little lane away from the main streets. He stopped the bike.

"Hop off," he told Hope. They both climbed off and stretched their tense muscles. "We'll hang here to see if we've lost the drone. The filth will arrive any minute."

He was banking on being covered by the narrow lane, which ran like a gully between twenty storey buildings. And in truth, both of them needed a break from the chase, if only for a chance to catch their breath.

"I've got to ask," said Hope. "And I guess this is as good a time as any, especially considering we might not get through the night alive ... You said you went to the future and found Secta there."

"Yes, he'd survived the holocaust in the bombproof section of Oceana headquarters. Oh, and he'd shot up some sort of longevity serum."

"Yes I know, we'd been developing it together. How long had he been trapped there?" Hope asked.

"Get this ... a hundred and thirteen years!"

"Unbelievable! The serum worked then? Did he look the same?"

"Not much different," said Alice. "Aged some, if that's what you mean. A little insane. A lot insane, in fact."

Hope paused for a moment, thinking. "So you turned up one hundred and thirteen years into the future," she said. "How did you escape from the hologram unit?"

"A barbarian babe called Djard apparently triggered it to play," said Alice. "Then a big dude called Ex got dirty with it and whacked it with his sword. Next minute, I was there."

"So ... how did you get back to now?"

"Secta used his scientific voodoo shit to send me back. He wanted me to stop the accident ... oh, and to release you."

"But how? How did he do that?"

"I dunno. We went to his lab, the one with the chair and all on Level Seven. He fired up all his equipment — I guess he just reversed the process."

"Brilliant," she breathed, awestruck.

"I guess so," said Alice. "Lucky too, because I was dying. Now that was rough."

"Dying?"

"Yeah, he said I was demolecularising, whatever that means."

"Means your cells were breaking down ... But Alice, you realise what you've become? By succeeding, my friend, you are the world's first time traveller."

"Right. The weird thing is," said Alice, lost in his own story, "Even though Secta is such an arsehole, he knew that sending me back to save you and change time meant his own death."

"Because once you succeed, his timeline would become invalid," she said, nodding.

"Yeah, future's end."

"I didn't think he had any humanity left in him," she said. "Well I guess there's a first time for anything."

"There was a tribe of female warriors called the Vixen living in the Anzac Memorial that we just rode past ... they had a Queen called Zule, and a warrior chief called Kinks."

"All female?"

"Yeah, no men. All killed off by these horrible mutant monster things — Roogas. We killed the last one so the Vixen would be safe."

"God," said Hope, shuddering. "But hey, if we're successful, none of it will never happen," she added.

"That's pretty difficult to get my head around," said Alice. "Sad, too ... these folk became my friends."

"Time travel has its quirks."

"You got that part right," said Alice, with a grimace. "And I gotta tell you, I still don't feel so great."

"What do you mean?"

"Maybe it's like mega jet-lag, but all this junk Secta pumped into me, all the demolecularizing crap, has me feeling pretty crook."

"Well, once we're done, we'll go back to the lab and fix you up," said Hope, not sounding entirely convinced.

A dizzy spell passed over him. He staggered a little, and had to grip Hope's shoulder to stop himself falling.

"Whoa!" he cried. "See what I mean? I feel punch drunk. Everything sort of shimmers and I spin out … makes me want to chunder."

She took his hand, "It's not surprising, after all you've been through," she said.

"Yeah, well," he said. "There's too much to do to be crook right now. Can't waste any more time chinwagging."

"There's so much more I want to know," said Hope.

"It'll keep for another time," Alice replied. "Can you ride a bike?" She raised an eyebrow. "Course I can," she said.

"Okay, to make sure this happens it's smarter for us to split up," said Alice. "It'll double our chances of getting to the ferry on time. You take the bike and head for Jones Bay Wharf. I'll find another way and meet you there. If I don't make it, get to the bridge of the ferry and make the captain stop the cruise. Got it?"

"Got it," she said, then suddenly kissed his cheek. "Just couldn't resist kissing the great Black Alice," she grinned. "I expect to see you at the ferry, so don't do anything foolish, you hear?"

"Watch out for that drone," he said. "It'll be up there, lurking."

She hopped onto the bike and kicked it to life.

Alice gave her a playful slap on the butt. "Ride like there's no tomorrow," he yelled. "Coz if you don't, there won't be one. Chaa!"

With a cocky wink, she tore off up the alley.

Blue lights flashed on Alice's face. He jogged off in the same direction Hope had driven. A cop car pulled into alley and blocked his path. Two troopers got out with guns up. A screech came from behind Al, he swivelled round to see a black van taking up the alleyway, troopers pouring out of the back hatch. He was surrounded. The ranks of troopers from the van parted to allow a black uniformed SSD official with bright red hair to step through. Karzoff stopped ten metres from Alice and glared at him. "There is no way out of this for you Alice."

"Thought I zapped you Karzoff ... let me go, I've gotta stop the ferry ... it's going to..."

Karzoff cut him off. "I have my orders," he paused for effect, then announced sharply, "open fire."

Everything shimmered supernaturally for Alice — a hail of bullets was travelling towards him in super slow motion. He easily dodged them like a prize-fighter weaving from side to side.

To Karzoff watching with the troopers firing, Alice appeared to be moving like greased lightning.

Several of the bullets Alice had dodged took out the two troopers at his rear, who had also fired. One of their bullets, Alice had avoided, hit Karzoff. The red-haired officer dropped to his knee and screamed, "Kill him!"

Alice watched the second volley coming towards him. This time he crouched and then sprang into the air like a big cat, high enough to get over them. He landed on the bonnet of a cop car parked behind the van.

Amazed by his own supernatural abilities he mumbled to himself, "Far-out, what a trip." He jumped down, got into the car behind the wheel and burnt rubber reversing out of the alley. Another cop car blocked his exit. He stepped on the gas, rear-end rammed it, and then with the tires screaming, pushed it out of the alley.

"So, I guess that shimmering of time was your doing?"

"Some assistance perhaps but only to energize you enough to help yourself. You have great powers of imagination Alice your path is set out before you."

Alice walked closer the glowing orb, it's light reflecting in his eyes. "So it seems," he mumbled, deep in thought.

"You know nothing of it, as it is yet to come."

"You're speaking in riddles again. Look," he snapped irately, "I lived it — I'm alive to tell it all aren't I? Why do I need to relive it?"

"You re-walk the path of consciousness because there is much more for you to learn from the experience."

He accepted there were things he had missed, important things. "Okay, okay, I get that ... but why me?"

"To understand that we must continue, only you can answer your own question."

A light flashed in Alice's mind.

There was a motorbike tailing him. He figured it for a trooper or agent despatched to beat the traffic, and guided after them by the drone. The positive side was they were onto him, which left Hope free to complete the mission.

Hope had decided to continue through alleyways until she was clear of troopers, but the next one she turned into was blocked by a patrol car. She was hemmed in. The alleyway was so narrow that the patrol car's doors were only a foot from the walls, preventing the bike from getting past. Hope had no option but to go over the top in the same way Alice had done earlier.

She hit the gas, raised the front wheel and climbed the bike onto the bonnet of the car. When the front tyre hit the windscreen it skidded sideways, and she came off, plummeting down behind the car. The troopers opened their doors and scrambled out. Ignoring them and her fall, Hope leapt to her feet, climbed back on the bike and roared off.

The driver rammed the patrol car into reverse without closing the doors, and promptly wedged the car firmly between the alley walls, much to the dismay of his partner.

The traffic ahead had prevented Alice outrunning the bike. He pulled over and got out of the car. The bike stopped, the rider took off his helmet, drew a pistol and started Alice's way.

Alice needed a weapon. He spotted an old-fashioned, metal rubbish bin in the gutter, overflowing with junk. When he lifted the lid he found a half-metre rusted iron bar and pulled out ... it would have to do. The bin lid would also be handy. Holding it in his other hand like a shield, he stepped out to confront his adversary.

The clouds in the stormy sky parted for a moment, allowing the full moon to shine on the face of his opponent. He recognised him immediately. Drago ... the very dude he suspected of killing Stain — a suspicion Honor had all but confirmed.

Garbed in black leathers, Drago stopped a few metres from Alice.

"Didn't get enough when I belted you at the Bourbon and Beef?" Alice growled.

The big man said nothing — just glared at Alice.

"Your boss Honor told me you murdered my girl," he said, stretching the truth to get a reaction. "Get off on killing defenceless women, do you? Weak bastard!"

Drago simply raised his silenced 9 mm pistol and fired.

Alice anticipated the move, and used his shield to deflect the shot. There was a zing as the bullet passed through the lid, missing him.

Alice wasted no time. In a flash, he lowered the lid and flung at Drago like a Frisbee. It was a terrific shot ... it hit Drago's gun hand, giving Alice the opening to rush him with the iron bar.

The first blow came down hard on Drago's wrist, knocking the gun from his hand and breaking his arm with a loud snap. Alice brought the bar back up on an angle at speed, and with an almighty blow sliced it across Drago's cheek, opening him up big time. Drago staggered backwards, blood pouring from the deep cut, but he wasn't done yet. He let fly with a huge punch to Alice's solar plexus.

Alice was only just hanging on after his last dizzy spell, so the punch in the guts had him in bad shape. With the breath knocked out of him, he pulled Drago into a clinch to give himself time to recover.

Suddenly, the flashing blue light of a patrol car lighted up the street. It pulled up next to Drago's bike and two troopers got out.

With an almighty heave, Drago freed himself from Alice's clinch. He looked at the gun on the ground. Alice anticipated he'd go for it … but he'd have to bend down to pick it up.

Drago knew Alice was on to him. It was a Mexican stand-off.

The two troopers had exited their vehicle and were aiming their guns, but couldn't make out who was who in the dark.

After a moment's hesitation, Drago went for his gun. Alice brought the iron bar down on the back of Drago's head. Drago collapsed onto the roadway, skull split open. Alice had done it. He'd fought through and beaten the bastard who'd killed his girl. He dropped the iron bar irreverently on Drago's sprawled body, and staggered to the cop car.

Inside he looked in the rear-view mirror. A shape appeared: Drago, rising to his feet with his gun in his hand.

Alice didn't give it a second thought, just jammed the car into reverse and trod on the gas. The car roared and ploughed back into Drago just as he was aiming the gun. There was a bump as the rear wheels went over him, then another as the front wheels followed suit. Alice hit the skids once he'd cleared his enemy, and could see him in the headlights, still trying, torn and bleeding, to get up from the ground.

"Stuff you!" Alice snarled. "Chaa!" He floored it, hitting Drago in the midsection. Draped over the bonnet of the car, staring at Alice through the windscreen with a horrified expression on his bloody face, Drago could do nothing. Another cop car pulled up as a blockade.

With Drago draped over the bonnet Alice drove at the cop car and T-boned it. He then whipped it around, flinging the remains of Drago off the bonnet, and gunned it up onto the pavement around the crippled cop car.

Mal made his way forlornly up the gangplank onto the ferry. Blue was waiting for him at the midships doorway at the top of the gangplank.

"Where's Al?" Blue bellowed to get over the music playing on board.

Mal stopped and shook his head, "Don't know mate. It's too late for him now."

Hope had struck a main street with heavy traffic. Expecting to see troopers at any moment, she decided to cut through an adjacent park. It was tougher than she'd expected — she was forced to dodge between trees, flowerbeds, dog walkers, evening joggers and park benches.

She bounced across the uneven ground, and when the rear wheel fishtailed as it skidded in the soggy soil, she nearly lost the bike again. Regaining control, she could see the harbour up ahead. In the distance was the wharf, and hopefully the ferry. It was time for a dash through the city, racing time, the cops, and the coruscating purple flashes of sheet lightning, which emblazoned the canvas of the rolling storm clouds above. Loud crashes of thunder boomed along the chasms of the city streets as she raced, like the mighty metallic blows of Thor's hammer.

Again, in the rear-view mirror, Alice could see his pursuers closing on him. He saw a narrow, cobblestoned alleyway up ahead, constructed during the early nineteenth century and intended for nothing bigger than two horses passing. He got an idea, and slowed down to let the troopers catch up.

When he came to the alleyway, he turned sharp into it and floored it. At a blistering pace, he roared through the seriously tight alley, scraping both sides of the car against the brick walls, but with enough precision to make it through. The patrol car in pursuit wasn't so fortunate and jammed tight in the middle of the laneway.

Unable to open the doors, the troopers would be stuck there until they could be towed free.

Alice glanced at the dashboard clock. It was 23:40. He was running out of time. "Damn!" he cursed, stomping on the gas. Harris Street was a long line of cars, stuck at a series of traffic lights. Each time the lights changed only a couple of cars edged through. No time! "Stuff it!" he growled, and pulled the car onto the median strip. He drove along it, wheels straddling the low barrier, clearing the strip by a whisker.

As he approached the traffic lights he could go no further — their poles were set into the middle of the strip. He wrenched the steering wheel. Sparks flew as the car bottomed out on the wrong side of the road. Oncoming cars swerved sharply to avoid colliding head-on.

One car swerved the wrong way and smashed into a parked vehicle. The car behind rear-ended it, then a truck trying to avoid the pile-up drove onto the pavement and slammed into a shop window. The truck, unfortunately, was carrying a load of pigs bound for the abattoir, and the impact shattered the wooden cages on the back. Huge honkers were galloping helter-skelter, running for their lives among the carnage of piled-up and gridlocked cars. Alice had spawned unmitigated chaos. Alice hadn't even checked the rear-vision mirror. Completely unaware of the pandemonium, content that he'd pulled off a coup, he simply turned onto the right side of the road, now free of traffic, and continued his merry way toward Jones Bay Wharf.

CHAPTER 26
THERE'S HOPE

MAL WAS STANDING at the rear of the packed ferry, watching a deck hand getting set to unhitch the stern hawser.

Alice had failed to turn up. Mal feared the worst. Ratsso cruised over with a beer in hand. The music on the ferry's sound system was so loud he had to yell to be heard.

"'Sup Mal?" he roared. "You look worried."

"Al's late," Mal yelled back, ruefully. "I reckon those mongrels at Oceana HQ have nailed him. I bloody-well warned him!"

"Alice is too tough for them, ain't he?" Ratsso thundered. "What if he's just running late like he normally does?"

"Too late now," replied Mal. "We're about to get underway. He's got less than five minutes."

"You reckon they've nailed him coz of that sheila jumpin' off the building onto that
Official?"

"Dunno. I reckon they've been planning on getting him for a while. He just wouldn't listen to reason … got pig-headed after Stain died."

Blue had pushed his way through the throng to overhear the conversation. "I dunno, Mal, he seemed all right when we saw him at the club," Blue said, taking a swig of beer.

"Not to me mate," said Mal. "He was somewhere else in his head, somewhere real friggin' weird."

Lightning flashed and thunder cracked ominously.

"Speakin' of Ratsso," said Blue, "I saw you carrying a guitar case and amp on board, what the stuff for, going to have a blow?"

"That was the paint cannon yer dill," Ratsso barked.

"Might be hard to get a clear shot, with it being such a stinker of a night," said Blue, with cackle. "Be wrong if a big swell blows up out on the harbour with the storm and all. There'll be dudes chucking their guts up all over the boat."

Mal wasn't listening. He was watching the road leading to the wharf. He wasn't giving up on Al. After all, the peace rally was his gig.

Alice had real concerns he was going to miss the ferry. The road ahead blurred and shimmered. A patina of sweat beaded on his forehead. He began to drift in and out of consciousness, fragments of thoughts swirled in his head, accompanied by strange visions. His hands, grasping the steering wheel, were beginning to shift in and out of phase, like something was interfering with his very existence. Somehow, he managed to keep steering while fresh images intruded on his sentient self. The visions were quite unintelligible ... a desert, tracer bullets streaking through the inky sky, oppressive heat, a battle, ordinance exploding all around him, making the ground tremble under foot. Then, just as quickly as changing a TV channel, a bathroom, shaving in a mirror, but it wasn't his face ... Then a flickering montage of stills, coming in fast: a Cyborg monster, half man, half machine coming at him menacingly. A pretty girl with blonde hair, speaking with Secta's voice, repeating her name 'Morrigan Hud' over and over again. More battles: this time he was on a motorbike, powering in loops at breakneck speed around the inside of a giant metal globe. A brutal, one-on-one swordfight with a gladiator in a ring. Four men wearing tunics, carrying a golden chest, struggling with its weight with looks of great reverence on their faces. They were moving through destruction, fire, past white marble buildings with Ancient Greek columns, toppling in last throes of a besieged city's existence. A gigantic UFO, hovering over a building, missiles exploding all around. Death and destruction.

Life and death seemed to be both calling him at once. A disjointed thought went through his mind: These aren't visions. These are real. He could feel them, taste and smell them, hear them but not recognise them. He wondered if they were an indication that he'd succeeded in stopping the collision and a portent of things to come. Were they glimpses into the future? But why did some seem to be in an ancient time? That couldn't be the future — could it?

A shiver shot up his spine, and he was suddenly overcome by a strange calmness, a warm comforting feeling. He could no longer hear the sound of the engine. His grasp of reality had all but vanished. But his mind had found a heavenly place: a place of bright light and positive energy. He realised he was moving, speeding through empyrean light towards a dot on a liquid horizon. Not death — his future. It reminded him of falling back through time. Only now he was shooting forwards.

As the dot increased in size, his sense of anticipation also increased. He felt sure he was heading towards something vitally important. There was a pulsating ball, an orb at the end of a tunnel. It had a consciousness, it was alive — and calling him, controlling him. He closed his eyes, prepared to let it happen. He'd been so close to death of late he feared it no longer.

Then sound began to return. It was difficult for Alice to recognise at first, but as it got louder he started to make sense of it. At first, he thought it was a song in his mind. Then he realized it was his own voice speaking to him. But his mouth wasn't moving, he wasn't speaking. His voice quoted; on wings of leather I take you, to a world beyond the skies, were fantasy becomes reality … life and death wear no disguise. He knew the lyrics — he'd written them, after all, but this was the first time his words had related to his present circumstances. A revelation struck him — perhaps he'd been having premonitions for longer than he thought, manifesting them in his lyrics all along, and he just hadn't realised it.

The dot on the horizon was now much larger now. It was no longer an orb. Suddenly, all sound and vision returned to normal. Tyres on the wet road, the car engine. He noticed he could now make out the dot on the horizon: it was the ferry leaving the dock, and the liquid horizon was the harbour. He could see the wharf and the ferry the distance.

Shrugging off the cloak of uncertainty he growled to himself with a steely smile, "If I'm gonna fade away into oblivion, then so be it! But first I've got a gig to do!"

Hope knew it was going to go right down to the wire. Turning onto Bayview Street, which led between two long warehouses and onto the wharf, she expected to find the ferry moored at the end, figuring she was only moments away. But when she emerged at the end of the wharf, the ferry had just cast off and was pulling away. With no chance of boarding in a conventional manner, she only had one option left: she made some quick mental calculations and executed a fast U-turn, backtracked to give herself a run up and hit the throttle.

The bike raced towards the end of the wharf. There was a six-metre gap between the stern of the ferry and the wharf. Dodging the bollards, going like a rocket, she hurtled into the air, leaping off the bike at its apogee. It plummeted into the water with an almighty splash, but her momentum carried her a lot further.

A loud thump on the canvas canopy above them killed the conversation between Mal, Blue, and their friends Prissy and Meg.

"What the hell was that?" Blue gasped. Very nearly spilling his beer, he looked up at the ceiling.

"Sounds like someone's up there," Prissy slurred, tipsy.

The answer became clear when a pair of sexy legs came dangling down and tried to slip onto the main deck. Blue took hold of the legs and helped Hope inside.

"It's all right, it's all right ... I've got ya," said Blue, reassuringly.

"Who's she Blue?" said Prissy, jealously. "Friend of yours?"

"Don't know her," said Blue.

Hope pulled away from him. She wasn't hanging around to get acquainted, and she pushed her way through the crowded deck, trying to get to the bridge.

Blue yelled after her, "Where are you going?"

Mal shrugged, but thinking she might be a government agent, he made a beeline after her through the crowd.

With a screech that smoked the tyres, Alice hung the back of the car out as he turned into Bayview Street. He jammed his foot down hard and fanged it along the narrow service road between the warehouses. When he reached the end he hit the anchors, skidding to a stop. Leaving the car running, he raced to the edge of wharf. The ferry was two hundred metres from him. He'd missed the boat.

Lightning cracked and thunder rolled, warning that the storm was about to hit. With the ferry beyond reach, Alice was shattered. In frustration, he tore the Shine from around his neck. The ball was firmly in Hope's court. Even though he had no reason to doubt her ability to get the job done, he feared the odds were stacked too heavily against her. He turned away, racking his brain, when a flash of lightning caused him to look up. Through the rain, he saw an apparition under an awning at the end of one of the warehouses. Long curly blonde hair, a knee-length red dress that showed off a very pregnant belly, and a small suitcase parked at her feet. The girl was a dead ringer for Djard.

Alice was blown away. He ran over to her, but before he could say anything she asked: "Hey, aren't you Black Alice?"

"Geez," he said. "You look like ... Nar, couldn't be ... Listen, your ferry ain't gonna arrive. Take the car and wear this." He handed her the Shine. "It's called the Shine. Drive west."

He kissed her cheek. She looked puzzled, and studied the shining chrome object he'd placed in her hand.

If the future was going to be as it had when Alice was there, this was it. Alice didn't know if they'd succeed in stopping the ferry. But if not, then the Shine would ultimately make its way into the world of the bikers, eventually ending up with Ex. Full circle.

Suddenly, two troopers appeared on the upper level of the warehouse. Spotting Alice, they started down a staircase towards him.

Looking about frantic to escape, Alice spotted a guy working on a speedboat further along the wharf. The girl realised what was happening and said, "That's my friend over there."

Alice turned back to her. "Give the Shine to your child," he said. "It's the key to the future."

Taking the amulet, she said hurriedly, "He can help you. Go!" She watched him race off.

The troopers arrived and pushed past her in a desperate bid to catch their prey.

Alice was moving like a rat up a drainpipe, aiming for the guy with the speedboat and away from the troopers. As he reached the end of the wharf, he looked down at the boat. The massive V8 inboard motor was purring like a contented tiger. Alice took his chance. Whipping off his boots and socks, he climbed onto a bollard at the end of the jetty, and jumped the three metres down, landing with a thump on the long, pointed bow of a bright red Camero Nordic.

The jolt frightened the crap out of the guy under the dashboard, and he bumped his head trying to get out quickly. "Hey buddy, follow that ferry!" yelled Alice, pointing in the direction of the ferry.

Then the guy sighted the two troopers, coming towards them with weapons drawn. It wasn't difficult for him to sort out it was Alice they were after. An Octagon sympathizer, he had recognised Alice. Moving quickly, he unhitched the rope securing the boat to the jetty, dived into the bucket seat, fastened himself in and yelled: "Hang onto that bow rope buddy!"

The big block Chevy engine let out a deep-throated roar, and the arrow-shaped clinker ski-boat shot off like a missile, planing across the water almost instantly.

The two troopers stopped at the end of the pier, Alice was well out of firing range.

Hope had spotted the companionway to the bridge, but had to fight through people to reach it. Mal burst out of the crowd behind her and grabbed her by the arm.

"Hey!" he shouted. "Where do you think you're going?"

Hope turned and beamed him a big smile. "Just looking for some company," she said. "Why d'you ask?"

He tried to drag her down the stairs.

The speedboat caught up with the much slower ferry in no time. Alice was on the prow, intending to leap onto the ferry once they were close enough. But they were in a squall. The rain was bucketing down, with flashes of sheet lighting illuminating massive, rolling storm clouds. The wind had whipped the waters into frenzied, one-metre whitecaps, charging across the swell with only seconds in between.

The speedboat driver was forced to steer the boat to the windward side of the ferry, ploughing through the oncoming waves. The boat reared as it broached every wave, which broke over the bow as the boat crashed over the crest. Each one almost swept Alice overboard. The only thing saving his life was the bow rope, which he held in a vice-like grip.

As they closed on the ferry, Alice inched along the slippery foredeck, closer to the low gunwale of the speedboat. To the passengers aboard the ferry, Alice looked for all the world like the figurehead on the prow of a great sailing ship, the wind blowing his ponytail out behind him in a long mane, and his muscular upper body drenched with spray from the waves.

He glanced quickly at his driver, feeling the time had come, and got a nod back — the go signal. This was it. The boats were level.

A huge wave belted over the bow and swamped Alice. The water was way rougher between boats. He needed to time his jump carefully, but even then it was going to be a jump on a wing and a prayer.

As they drew level with the ferry, and were as close as possible without colliding, Alice took a deep breath, let go of the rope and jumped. His life flashed before him. Then a gust of wind lifted him like the hand of God, depositing him into the waiting arms of supporters on the ferry's quarterdeck.

Job done, the speedboat driver pulled a sharp one-eighty and hightailed it back to Jones Bay Wharf.

Alice had to fight his way into the main cabin through the crowd of supporters who had converged on him in welcome. Amid the chaos, he caught sight of Hope and Mal at the companionway stairs to the bridge.

"Hope!" he yelled, his voice carrying over all the chatter, the music, the crashing of waves and the general mayhem of the howling storm.

She turned to see Alice, and in doing so released her grip on Mal. He immediately let fly with a kick, which knocked her backwards and into Alice's waiting arms.

Thundering towards Alice like a madman, Mal screamed: "Watch out for that bitch, Al! She's SSD! Hold her!"

When he got to them, he tore Hope out of Alice's grip.

The crowd cleared space around them, and the DJ cut the music.

Mal raised his hand, threatening to belt Hope. "Who the hell are you?" he screamed. "You're the cop they planted on board, aren't you?"

Alice pulled Hope aside and slipped between her and Mal. He was frustrated, and he lined up a punch.

Mal suddenly twigged. "Al?"

"Let her go mate. We have to get to the bridge ... stop the ferry."

Mal couldn't believe what he was hearing. "No way man, not on your life."

"Get to the bridge Hope," Alice ordered, then turned back to Mal, who was having none of it. Alice had no choice and belted Mal with a powerful right hook. Mal hit the deck and lay there, holding a bleeding lip with an incredulous look on his face. Alice, already moving, shouted back, "I'm sorry mate ... no time to explain! Just stay out of this!"

Agitated by the fight between their leaders, the crowd surged. Hope got caught up in the throng and was carried off, away from Alice.

Blocked from the companionway, Alice made for the starboard exit, trying to find another route to the bridge.

Mal scrambled to his feet and yelled furiously at big Joe the bouncer standing nearby, "Joe, stop Alice!"

CHAPTER 27
A MATTER OF TIME

ALICE EMERGED AT THE prow and looked up at the ferry bridge, barely visible through the rain. He could just make out Hope on the port side, climbing a metal ladder to the upper deck. Just as he was about to climb up and join her, Joe, the six-five bouncer from the Jungle Bar, sent after him by Mal, confronted him. With a loud clap of thunder, a torrential squall inundated them both.

Hope was alone on the open deck. The yawing of the boat was forcing her to grip the rail to maintain her balance, and the wind was so fierce it was just about blowing her backwards. Spray from the waves was picked up by the gale and peppered her hands, legs and face with tiny beads of speeding water, which smarted on contact like stings of myriad insects. The wind-chill factor and the pouring rain were making teeth chatter. Wrenching herself along the rail to the lee of the ferry's superstructure, Hope searched for access to the bridge. The half deck above her had a gunwale leading to the bridge deck. She could see the captain through the windshield, doing his best to pilot the ferry through the treacherous conditions.

On the deck below, Alice's muscular upper torso glistened in the light as he shaped up to the big man, who growled at him over the ferocious tempest.

"Come on, Joe!" Alice yelled, his voice trailing into the teeth of the wind.

With the waves drenching the two of them, and the violent pitching of the ferry, it was almost impossible for either man to maintain his balance.

Alice let go a solid left that caught the big man in the throat. He followed it quickly with a right cross, which sent him staggering backwards. Mal came rushing to the side of the bow in a fury, but stopped when he saw Alice and Joe coming to blows. Ratsso, close behind, grabbed Mal to restrain him.

"Come on Mal, ease up," he yelled, "He's a mate!"

"Sure!" screamed Mal. "He clubbed me in the mouth! He's supposed to be our leader!"

"Come on," insisted Ratsso, "just trust him."

Mal looked up to see Hope climbing onto the gunwale of the bridge deck.

"That bitch!" he shrieked, "she's gotta be the spy we were warned about — they've turned you, Alice!"

By now, Alice had big Joe on the back foot, so he grabbed him, pulled him close and launched his body upward, trying to head-butt the taller man under the jaw. It was a disastrous move. The big bouncer dodged the blow, and belted Alice with an almighty right jab that sat him onto his butt. To Alice, the bouncer's fist felt the size of a basketball.

Hope saw him go down and let out a panicked cry: "Alice! No!"

Big Joe grabbed Alice by the throat, lifting him off the deck with one hand and driving the other fist into his exposed gut. Alice let fly with a wishful uppercut, and somehow landed it. Joe countered with a powerful one-two that dropped Alice again. He struck out with a Taekwondo Dragon's tail throw, and brought the bouncer down. In this case the old cliché was right on: the bigger you are, the heavier you fall. Joe hit the deck like the fall of empires.

Alice took the opportunity to stagger to the ladder leading to the quarterdeck, and scrambled up it to get to Hope. Aching all over, he was almost up when big Joe came at him again. Bleeding profusely from the nose, he grabbed Alice by the leg and tried to drag him off the ladder.

A bolt of lightning struck very close to the ferry, punctuating the fight like a feedback loop. The entire boat vibrated from the thunderclap. Alice lashed out with a hook kick that collected Joe smack in the face. Down he went again, this time long enough for Alice to make it over the gunwale onto the quarterdeck.

Seeing big Joe out cold, Mal ripped free of Ratsso and ran out onto the prow. The ferry was rolling so much he had to grab the handrail to prevent slipping over. He glared up at Alice and screamed: "I'm gonna get you Al! I'm coming for you!"

Hope held out a hand and helped Alice over the final rail onto the bridge deck. Mal bolted back inside the ferry.

As lightning flashed again, Alice caught something out of the corner of his eye. It was the American submarine, moving parallel with them, only fifty metres away. A second flash of lightning highlighted the hull number on the conning tower: 666.

Alice pointed at it and yelled: "Look at that evil-looking thing!" Fear gathered like a knot in his stomach.

Hope was shocked, but yelled: "We're not going to collide! We're running parallel!"

Suddenly, with a deafening crash, two arms thrashed through a smashed side bridge window and seized Alice around the throat. It was Mal.

Being choked by bloodied hands, Alice screamed through clenched teeth: "Get inside Hope! Get inside, now!"

"They've scrambled your brains, man!" Mal howled. "You're working for them now, you bloody traitor!"

Hope took off to the door of the bridge deck. It was locked. Time was running out, so she raised her elbow and smashed the small glass window, reached through and opened the door from the inside.

The captain was desperately trying to maintain course, but there were too many distractions: the storm, a woman had smashed her way onto his bridge, a guy was bleeding all over the place, fighting through a smashed window with someone outside, everyone yelling: it was total mayhem.

Hope shouted, "Stop the ferry Captain!"

"Get off my bridge!" he roared.

Hope spotted a bottle of wine on the console, picked it up and threatened him with it.

"Just steer on course, or so help me..." Hope cautioned.

"Don't you threaten me, young lady!" countered the captain.

"What's the matter with you Al?" Mal raged.

"The ferry..." gasped Alice. "It's going to collide with the sub!"

Mal dragged him in through the smashed window. Broken glass lacerated Alice's upper body as he came through. There was blood everywhere. Alice flopped to the floor, gasping for breath. With his back to Hope, Mal had his fist drawn back, set to smash Alice to oblivion. She swung the bottle at the back of Mal's head, but the boat pitched. She missed, smashed the captain's instead. As he tumbled to the floor, hand still on the helm, the big wheel turned.

Mal looked around at the thud of the captain going down, giving Alice the chance to belt him. It was a good short jab, right on the chin. Mal, finally, went down. Hope reached out a hand and helped Alice up. He was a bloody mess, unsteady on his feet.

"You alright?" she asked.

They both looked through the windshield, but recoiled in terror. The conning tower of the submarine, the huge characters of the devil's number — 666 — were looming right in front of them. They were going to ram it.

"The sub!" screamed Hope.

This was the end of the line. Alice had fought all the odds, conquered the impossible to get here. He stared through windshield, wondering fleetingly whether all he had fought for had amounted to this: was the collision inevitable? Was it possible to change time? His mind flashed through his journey — his friends' faces flicked through his mind: fearless Ex, stunning Djard, mighty Derg, clever Karn and Chez, a big strapping man with a little boy smile. The beautiful face of Zule loomed, and his words to her resounded in his mind: "I'll come back, I promise..." Alice remembered that if he stopped the collision, all those friends would cease to exist, that future would end. The question in his mind was whether he could do it. Could he terminate the lives of his friends to save the rest of humanity? The answer was simple: he had to. It was up to him.

Hope was frozen, awestruck, staring at the sub. Shoving her aside, Alice grabbed the throttle and wrenched it backwards with all his might. The old ferry shuddered and protested loudly as the engine roared in reverse. Through the windshield, the conning tower of the sub was growing larger and larger.

Hope shut her eyes tightly and grabbed Alice's arm, ready to accept oblivion.

Alice spun the big ship's wheel as fast and hard to starboard as he could. A massive wave broke over the bow, and splashed violently against the windshield. It rocked the ferry wildly as it finally began to turn.

The huge, upright stern fin of the sub came into view. Closer, closer ... it was no use. He was too late. Closer still, the fin towered over them. They were all going to die. He'd failed. Numb with horror, he watched the huge metal structure take over the world ... and slip by the bow, avoiding collision by the narrowest of margins.

When nothing happened, Hope tentatively opened her eyes.

Face battered, bloody and torn, Alice's mouth still managed a wide grin of mingled disbelief and success.

Reality struck Hope. She looked up at Alice in awe. "I don't believe you, mate," she gasped, almost in a chuckle. "I really don't believe you."

"That'll teach you to mess with Al!" scoffed Alice, as the sub continued past. He turned and winked at Hope with a bloodshot eye, "You know what?" he said. "Time travel rocks."

Sitting on the floor Al was staring thunderstruck at the glowing orb.

"That was cutting it fine ... nearly didn't ice it."

"But you did and changed the destiny of the world."

Alice got to his feet. "Is was you that gave me the power to jump and slow down time, wasn't it?" En-Ki offered no reply, so Al changed tack, "All this time travel should've ended there but it didn't, did it?"

"It was not my fault the formula Secta had used to alter your molecular structure had serious side-effects."

"That En-Ki is the understatement of a lifetime ... Continue..."

EPILOGUE

SONS OF STEEL
CYBERWARS
BOOK 2

ALICE wiped a dribble of blood from his battle-scarred brow. He glanced at the ferry captain, out cold on the floor beside him, and at the dazed face of Hope, who still clutched the remains of the bottle she had used to knock him out in her hand. His best friend and fellow peace activist, Mal Function, was now conscious, leaning against the cabin wall, gasping for breath. He was battered and bleeding, cut in a dozen places from the window that had shattered during their brawl.

Alice shot him a derisive grin, and with his usual swagger proclaimed: "Glad that's over!"

He grasped Mal's hand and helped him up.

"Sorry for doubting you, Al," said Mal, wiping blood from the corner of his mouth. "Now I get what you were trying to do."

Alice stepped towards him. "Function, you turd ... Argh!" He froze in agony, grabbing at his back. "I've done me back in," he groaned. "Help me onto the floor, mate," he gasped through gritted teeth.

He sprawled out on the deck.

Mal was holding Alice's arm when its solidity began to fade and recover, in and out of phase, right before their eyes.

"Jesus!" Mal exclaimed, dropping Alice's arm like it was a hot potato. He looked down at his friend, bewildered. "What the stuff's happening, Hope?"

"Mal, I feel weird!" Alice spluttered, holding his forehead. "Like I'm about to cash my chips or something. What's the story, Hope?" He groaned, confused. The bridge was shimmering; the walls were bulging. "Not again, not again," he groaned, losing it.

Hope knelt beside him, looking concerned. "I think you're beginning to de-molecularize again," she said. "It seems to happen when you're excited or under stress. The increased neural activity activates the rogue strand of DNA Secta implanted in your genome."

The mention of Secta fired him up.

"Him again!" he yelled. Then his face contorted and he screamed, struck by a pain in his arm, which again began to pulse slowly into transparency and back again.

"Calm down!" Hope warned. "You have to calm down!" Despite her scientific perspective, she was a compassionate woman, and found herself fighting back tears. She had gone out on a limb against her brother, Secta, and her employer, the Oceana State Government, risking charges of treason to support Alice in his quest. Now, even though they had succeeded, things were becoming even more insane. Aware that she couldn't let emotion get the better of her, she took a deep breath.

"The more fired up you get, Al, the more you'll slip out of phase," she said, gently.

"What is this phase crap, Hope? The only phase I know about is three-phase lighting at gigs."

"Yeah, mate, me too," Mal managed a grin, despite his anxiety. But Hope wasn't amused. "This is serious, Al. If the process can't be stopped, you'll slip out of phase completely, probably into another dimension. That's what Secta and I have been perfecting: digital matter transfer."

"Easy for you to say, Hope..." Alice growled. "But I'm no Doctor Who — I'm just a frigging rock singer."

Her eyes fixed on him as she sought a strategy. Her gaze sharpened. "I need to get you back to the lab," she said.

"Stuff that!" he replied, struggling to get up. But the movement only made matters worse. His entire body began to slip in and out of visibility. He flopped back to the deck, defeated.

Mal knelt down beside him, and looked up forlornly at Hope.

"Can't we do something for him, doc?"

"Nothing," she replied, coldly scientific and resigned, all trace of the emotional girl gone. "He'll disappear in a few minutes. I can only give him some educated guesses.

"Al," she went on, "My hunch is that your being is about to slip into a parallel dimension. Could be the future, could be the past, I can't tell which. But you'll have to find your own way. You managed it before, and you'll do it again. Maybe then we'll be able to stabilize you. Alice? Do you hear me, Alice?"

"Yeah, yeah, yeah," he mumbled. "Stabilize me, find my way back..." His entire body was phasing in and out of visibility, pulsing rapidly.

Hope moved closer, touching his cheek. "Listen, Alice, it's important. If you appear in another dimension, it could be in a different body. Try to keep a grip on your own identity."

"Eh?" said Mal, confused. "How's that?"

The weather over Sydney was worsening. Hope had to raise her voice to be heard.

"He might phase-shift into another person in another time dimension," she said. "If that happens, some of his neurons will carry the memory of his own identity. They'll just need to be triggered so he can recall."

Gently placing her hand under the back of Alice's head, she lifted it slightly, and spoke calmly and deliberately, even while tears shone in her eyes. "Alice." she said "Alice. Remember. You. Are. Black. Alice."

Flicking on and off like a blinking fluorescent light, Alice mumbled: "I... I'm Black... Black... Black... I'm..."

Then he was gone.

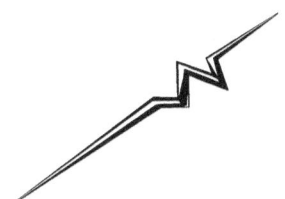

www.ingramcontent.com/pod-product-compliance
Lightning Source LLC
Chambersburg PA
CBHW020400120726
47904CB00002B/650